Hollywood Lies

Also by David Ambrose

the man who turned into himself
mother of god

David Ambrose

Hollywood Lies

MACMILLAN

First published 1996 by Macmillan

an imprint of Macmillan Publishers Ltd
25 Eccleston Place, London SW1W 9NF
and Basingstoke

Associated companies throughout the world

ISBN 0 333 65756 X

Copyright © David Ambrose 1996

The right of David Ambrose to be identified as the
author of this work has been asserted by him in accordance
with the Copyright, Designs and Patents Act 1988.

1 3 5 7 9 8 6 4 2

A CIP catalogue record for this book is available from
the British Library

Typeset by CentraCet Limited, Cambridge
Printed by Mackays of Chatham plc, Chatham, Kent

Acknowledgements

"Everything you've ever heard about Hollywood
is true – including the lies."

Orson Welles

Contents

Living Legend

She lifted her face from the swirl of water in the sink and stared into the mirror. Her eyes stared back, dark and frightened, from a tangle of bleached-blonde hair. She felt her stomach tighten and convulse again and lowered her head, but the feeling passed. The worst was over.

What the hell had gone wrong? One moment she was laughing and joking, putting everybody at their ease, full of confidence and looking forward to the evening; the next she was alone, mascara running down her face, hair all messed up, a great Rorschach stain spreading on the wall where she had flung her glass.

Her hand was shaking as she yanked open the cabinet and knocked half its contents into the sink and on to the floor. Panic welled up in her as she realized that what she needed wasn't there. How could she have let this happen? Christ, she couldn't think of everything herself! There were people who were supposed to look after her. Didn't the self-centred bastards ever think about anything except themselves?

Then she saw across the room the little travelling kit she always had with her, the one she prepared and usually packed herself. She had thought she'd forgotten it. Everything had been so rushed: getting off the lot in that helicopter, knowing that the studio would have stopped her physically if they could; then that long flight from the coast, trying to sleep but with the air-conditioning drying up her sinuses and irritating the infection she'd been fighting for weeks; finally being smuggled across Manhattan and in here through the basement, praying that the people they'd found to replace her usual team would be able to handle the make-up, the hair, the dress.

That dress! One mistake with that dress and the whole thing would be a calamity.

Her fingers struggled with the zipper on the little plastic bag. She definitely didn't remember packing it, but she must have – thank God. But what was in it? She finally got it open, tipped out its contents on the straw-weave stool by the bath tub, and breathed a great, gasping sigh of relief as she found what she was looking for.

It didn't take long for the effect to kick in – two minutes, tops, during which time she did nothing, neither moved nor thought nor heard nor saw, barely even breathed. It was a technique she had long since perfected, an ability to shut down all systems and turn wholly inward until the thing that she was waiting for happened, that tiny click somewhere deep in her psyche that told her she could stop hiding now, that it was safe to come out and connect with the world.

She sat there on the floor, wearing only pants and a bra. She closed her eyes, running a finger slowly up and down an imaginary crease in the middle of her forehead, letting her mind empty. After a while she heard a few faint notes of music in the distance. It took her a moment to realize she was humming, rocking back and forth in time to the simple melody .

What tune was that? And the words? She had to remember the words. It was all starting to come back now. She'd been humming that tune and trying to remember the words, but she couldn't. She had to go out there and perform in a few minutes, and she couldn't remember a single word of what she was supposed to do. It was the ultimate actor's nightmare. Christ, no wonder she'd got upset! Nobody was helping her, nobody had offered to run through it with her, nobody had put a script into her hand. What the fuck did they expect? That she'd stay calm? They weren't the ones who had to go out there in front of thousands of people, all of them just waiting for her to make a fool of herself. None of them understood that fine knife-edge between triumph and disaster which was where you had to operate if you were going to be worth watching. That edge was what being a star was all about. People said they loved you, but they were never on your side.

They'd pay money to see you, but hoping you'd screw up so they could sneer and say you'd robbed them. They'd tell you they wanted to fuck you, but nothing in your life would ever give them as big a hard-on as your death.

Why had she thought of death? She wasn't going to die. Damn it, she could do this. She'd handle it. She just had to do it her own way, in her own time, the way she always did if she was going to get it right.

The tune. If she could remember the words of that damn tune she'd be all right. She hummed a few more bars. The clues were there . . .

She clapped her hands. She'd got it at last. She started to sing in a soft voice, her lips barely moving, her eyes closed.

> Happy birthday to you,
> Happy birthday to you,
> Happy birthday, Mr President,
> Happy birthday to you . . .

★

Waiting in the wings was all the more agonizing because of that perspiring fool out there stumbling over his lines and cracking unfunny gags about her. In truth, she'd never really liked Lawford. They were friends, but in this business being friends didn't amount to a whole lot. You were friends with somebody till they fucked you over, and then you stopped being friends – until you needed them again or until they needed you. Sure, Lawford had introduced her to Jack, but it had been Jack's idea. She knew that because he'd told her how much he'd wanted to meet her. All Lawford had to do was make the call.

Suddenly she'd had enough of standing in the dark listening to that feeble patter on stage. She took a breath, threw back her shoulders under her ermine wrap, and stepped forward into the blinding light. The crowd went crazy the way they always did, though it never helped her sense of nervousness; just raised the stakes. The higher they lift you, the further you fall. If you fall.

'Mr President,' Lawford was saying, 'never in the history of the world has one woman meant so much—' Then he broke off as he turned and saw her shimmering towards him in that long, tight, all but totally transparent dress. She moved with a light, skipping motion through jostling circles of light as the spot operators struggled to focus on and follow her.

Lawford's face was a professionally smiling blur as he stepped back to make room for her at the lectern with its bank of microphones. The set-up looked more like she was going to give a press conference than a performance.

'Ladies and gentlemen,' Lawford continued, his arm creeping around her shoulder, 'the *late* Marilyn Monroe.'

That jolted her, totally threw her for a second – a second in which time stood still. She felt herself freeze up inside, as though somebody had walked over her grave. Why did the son of a bitch have to say that? He'd spooked her. He probably hadn't meant to, but that didn't make it any better. All the pills, that last extra split of champagne, suddenly weren't working for her any more. Everything around her seemed to rush away. For a terrible moment she thought she was going to pass out. She licked her lips, which suddenly felt dry as cardboard.

Then, as abruptly as it had enclosed her, the vacuum popped and the world came back in focus. Out there in the dark they were still cheering and applauding. Nobody had noticed that anything was wrong. Nobody ever did. She shrugged her shoulders, and the ermine dropped from them into Lawford's hands. The crowd's roar doubled as they got the first real look at that dress.

That dress – sequins and beading on a flesh-coloured body-stocking of the sheerest silk mesh in the world. She'd had to be stitched into it, and anyone standing even a few feet from her would swear she was nude except for those artfully arranged little clusters of brilliance which were all she seemed to be wearing. She felt herself trying to suppress a smile as she imagined Jack's reaction. He'd be grinning from ear to ear, probably leaning over to make some crack to Bobby or one of his cronies, loving it. And it was for him, just him. The rest of them out there could watch, but that was all. This was a private thing.

6

She tapped the microphone furthest to her right, the one she had been told to use. There was no reason to check it, except that it gave her an excuse to look down, compose her features, pull that schoolgirl grin back off her face and bury it inside where secrets like that belonged.

Now she was ready. She took a step to her right to get out from behind that damn desk, twisted the microphone to follow her, and gave them her most dazzling smile. The noise went on and flashbulbs were popping everywhere. Then, just as her eyes were adapting and she was beginning to see as well as hear, some fool hit her with a blinding white arc – probably because of the dress, and certainly the public seemed to appreciate the better look that it gave them; but thank God, when she put up her hands to shield her eyes, whoever was on the gantry took the hint and cut the glare a little.

'Time,' something inside her was saying. 'Don't milk it, ride it. Get into the number.'

She began. One word. 'Happy . . .' The notes quavered uncertainly in her ear, but she'd never pretended to be a singer; nobody wanted her to be. 'Birthday to you . . .' She could feel the crowd were behind her, helping her on. In a moment they'd be singing along with her. Somewhere she could hear the band trying to pick up her key and find a tempo, but without success

It didn't matter. It was going to work. It was going to be all right.

It was her night.

★

Later, she wasn't so sure. Yes, it had gone all right; but it was Jack's night, not hers. Somehow, at the end of it all, she had felt diminished by the event. The spotlight had left her with an abruptness she was unaccustomed to, and the brisk way Jack had mounted those steps and effortlessly taken centre stage had made her feel like an amateur in the shadow of his commanding professionalism.

But the thing that had really got to her was that word 'wholesome'. His slightly hesitant delivery had always covered an actor's sense of timing; she'd even told him once that he reminded her of Jimmy Stewart. Now there he was, role-playing to perfection, turning around to acknowledge the band, then back to the audience with that big grin on his face, letting them cheer and stamp and applaud as they hung on to every second of that pause for just as long as he chose to stretch it out. Finally he let them see that he was ready to speak.

'Thank you ... I can now retire from politics after having had "Happy Birthday" sung to me in such a sweet, wholesome way.'

It was the way that he'd turned to the band again between 'sweet' and 'wholesome' that really drove the joke home. It was a nudge in the ribs, a leer between guys: 'We know the score here – right, fellas?' And the audience loved it. It was the biggest laugh of the evening, and at her expense. He had both acknowledged her and trashed her with that one, perfectly timed, ironic 'wholesome'.

By the time she got back to her dressing room she had made up her mind that she wasn't going to the party. Let them snigger if they wanted to behind her back. She felt like shit, she had a picture to finish in LA, and she needed sleep. She had done her patriotic duty; fucking him was optional, and this weekend it was off the menu, birthday or no birthday.

She had just told someone to bring her a fresh glass of champagne, and was mounting a stool so that they could start peeling that dress off her, when the room fell silent. She hadn't been expecting it, but she knew at once what that kind of silence meant. It happened when somebody very famous joined a small group of people. It was the kind of reaction she herself often provoked. But this silence went further than that. These people were used to movie stars. It took more than fame to provoke this kind of response. It took power. She looked over her shoulder, and saw Jack.

Everyone was already leaving as though in response to some order from him, though he didn't look at any of them, didn't even seem to be aware of them. His eyes were fixed on her, and there was an amused half-smile playing around his mouth. He didn't move until his Secret Service detail had shut the door, staying outside in the corridor with everybody else. Then he spoke.

'You were great. Song was great. So's the dress.'

'Wholesome?' she said, lifting one eyebrow a fraction.

He laughed. 'Yeah. Wholesome.' He took a step forward. 'What are you doing up there?' As he said it, he held out a hand to help her down from the stool. She ignored it.

'I was about to get changed,' she said.

'Don't do that. Wear it to the party,' he said.

His hand was still out. She took it and stepped down. It gave her a moment to think about what she was going to say.

'I'm not going to the party,' she said. She was looking up at him now instead of down. She wished that she'd stayed on the stool.

'Oh, come on,' he said, not taking her seriously. 'You can't let me down. Everybody wants to meet you.'

What was he planning, she wondered? To hand her around like a slice of birthday cake? 'I'm not feeling great,' she began, but he wasn't listening.

'We'll ride over there together,' he said. 'Get your wrap and let's go.'

She wasn't expecting that. Ride over there together? It made a big change from the hide-and-seek games they usually played, with her wearing sunglasses and a dark wig, being smuggled in back doors and service elevators to the President's suite. What was going on? Was it possible that he was about to acknowledge their relationship openly? Everything she had dreamed of since their first meeting raced through her mind. She knew that her fantasy of supplanting his wife and becoming First Lady of the United States was just that – a fantasy. But she also knew that fantasies come true. Look at her life: the girl from nowhere who became the biggest female star in Hollywood, married the greatest athlete in America, then its most famous playwright. If that wasn't a fantasy come true, then she didn't know what was. And now?

He kissed her on the lips. At the same time his hand ran down her back and squeezed her left buttock so hard that she gave a little gasp. But she didn't mind. He was looking at her with that

9

softness that made her forget and forgive everything except how much she loved and wanted him.

'How the hell does this thing come off?' he asked, his hands fluttering all over now, pulling and tugging at the dress.

'I thought you wanted me to wear it for the party,' she said.

'I do but . . .'

'If it comes off, it stays off,' she told him with a laugh. She was feeling wonderful now, light as a feather, like a little girl.

'Let's go,' he said, his grin widening as he took her hand and headed for the door. The two Secret Service men snapped to attention as he pulled it open. Everyone else had been cleared away.

She was still laughing as he strode down the corridor, pulling her along so that she had to take awkward little running steps to keep up with him in that tight skirt. Then they were at the limo, its door open, the soft interior beckoning. The door slammed shut with a solid, reassuring sound.

Outside the darkened windows the lights of Manhattan zipped by. She leaned her head against his shoulder and closed her eyes, listening to the sirens as they cleared a way for them through the dense uptown traffic. She was, she realized with that little shiver of surprise that always accompanied the feeling, happy.

The sound penetrated her consciousness only slightly. Its familiarity made it both something to ignore, or, depending on where you were and what you were doing, something to pay very close attention to. Present circumstances favoured close attention: somewhere a zipper had unzipped. It wasn't hers. There was only one – clear plastic down the back of the dress – and that hadn't budged. She opened her eyes a fraction. Jack's pants were undone and his hand was pulling out his penis in a way that left no doubt about what he wanted from her.

It was over in about a minute; Jack was always on a short fuse. It didn't do much for her, though the thought of giving head in the presidential limo with the cops on their motorbikes riding right alongside made it kind of appealing. She lifted her face to look up at him. His head lolled back in ecstasy on the plush upholstery. It always amused and in some ways bewildered her that men were so easy to keep happy, at least on that level. She

10

tidied him away and was about to zip him up, when she felt him move. He was looking down at her.

'Leave it,' he said.

'You can't arrive at the party like this,' she answered with a smile.

'Fuck the party. We aren't going to no fucking party.'

The tone of his voice shocked her. There was a thickness to it that was alien to him, crude almost. Jack was a lot of things, including sometimes crude; but always with a touch of lightness, and usually some wit. There was no lightness in the voice that had just spoken.

'What d'you mean, no party?' she protested. 'You can't not show up at your own party. Think of all those people who are waiting for you.'

'Fuck 'em. I've got other plans for you and me, baby.' He was looking at her now, and there was something in his face she didn't recognize, a coarseness, an almost drooling carnality that alarmed her. It was a look that made her feel cheap, anonymous, disposable: a look that she had never seen in him before.

'What plans?' she enquired, not managing to hide the unsureness in her voice.

'You'll find out. Don't worry about it.'

'Who says I'm worrying?' She drew away from him slightly, making an effort to steady her voice and sound more confident than she felt. 'A while ago you were telling me how everybody wanted to meet me and I had to be there. Now why the change of plan? I don't understand.'

The truth was that she understood only too well, or feared she did. She almost laughed aloud when she thought back to her fantasies of barely half an hour ago. How could she have been naive enough to think that Jack would even dream of walking into a roomful of socialites and political bigwigs with her on his arm, let alone one day acknowledge their relationship to the whole world? The years of psychoanalysis, not to mention countless hours of gruelling self-examination in acting class, had taught her to face things that could not be escaped. Ultimately she always faced the truth; it was what kept her sane.

'Where are we going, Jack? Can you tell me?' She tried to

sound casual, but his arm was around her and his weight against her, and his other hand was trying to find a way under her skirt and up her leg.

'Hey, baby, we can go anywhere we like.' His voice was even rougher than before, breathless, like an animal with the scent of prey in its nostrils and the taste of blood already in its mouth. 'We can drive around a while . . .'

'Drive around? Like this?'

'Why not? Aren't you having fun?'

'Jack, I . . . I really wanted to go to that party with you . . . you know?'

'Will you stop going on about the fucking party? The party's no part of this deal – all right? Will you try to get that through your fucking head? There's no party.'

She didn't respond. She didn't trust herself to speak. So this was where it ended, full circle, where it started: on her knees to some guy – starting in a field behind the orphanage, then a hotel room, then maybe a million hotel rooms. After that it had been studio bungalows, executive suites, private yachts and penthouse apartments. And finally, now, in the back of the presidential limo, in the middle of the presidential fucking motorcade, going up (she looked out of the window) Fifth fucking Avenue.

'Not bad for an old broad of thirty-six,' she had joked earlier in the day when they were getting her into the dress. Everyone had laughed and said she was good for a long time yet. But how much time did she have? Already it was too late for so many things. And what did she have to put in their place? How much longer would she even be a star?

Like a fool she had left her pills in the dressing room. There was nothing between her and the raw panic she could feel coming at her like a tidal wave. She couldn't handle this. She had to get out. Somehow.

She moved so fast that he didn't know what happened. There was a tearing sound and he looked down at the flimsy shred of fabric in his hand. He saw a flash of hair, of flesh, her hands outstretched, reaching for the door. She yanked the handle back, pushed, and launched herself full length into the night.

12

His cry echoed behind her. Echoed, but did not die away as it should have. She hit the ground, and realized that the car wasn't moving. Had they stopped without her noticing?

She became aware that she wasn't hurt, not even grazed. She hadn't fallen far or hard enough. And this was no road surface she was pushing herself up from. It was smooth and firm, yet had absorbed the impact of her fall.

'What the fuck—?' Jack roared behind her.

She turned. He was getting out of the car after her. But it wasn't Jack. He was dressed like Jack, and he was the man she'd just been with. But how in hell had she ever thought this man was Jack? She saw now that he was shorter, heavier, with thinning black hair and a round face flushed with anger.

'What the fuck is going on here?' he yelled over her head at somebody she couldn't see.

She followed his gaze, taking in her surroundings in a single sweep; and she realized that something was terribly wrong. She could still hear the sounds of the street, and she could see people on the sidewalk and lights and traffic and movement of all kinds; but it wasn't real. It was some kind of back-projection, but a kind she hadn't seen before. There was a three-dimensional quality to it, and it didn't seem to be projected on a screen so much as hanging there in the air, a glittering, moving model of reality.

'Somebody fuckin' answer me!'

The man she'd thought was Jack was screaming now in a paroxysm of rage. She turned back – and saw that the thing she'd just jumped out of wasn't a vehicle at all. It didn't even have wheels. It was a section, a mock-up, a studio set for an interior limo scene.

She was almost on her feet now, but her legs buckled under her. She would have blacked out – except that the world blacked out first, which grabbed her attention so hard that she stayed conscious and watching.

Where Fifth Avenue had been just a moment ago there were now only black drapes with a couple of weird tripod-type arrangements in front of them, each one supporting a little metal box with a tiny camera lens on the front. She figured that these

13

must be projectors, but she still couldn't work out what they had used for a screen.

A couple of seconds after the world vanished the sound of it died too. In the silence she heard running feet coming towards her, and voices, men's voices, alarmed and angry.

She looked around for some escape. There was only darkness everywhere, so she ran in the opposite direction from where the men seemed to be coming. She had lost one shoe; now she kicked the other off and ran barefoot. She heard another sharp tearing sound as the tight skirt split up beyond her knees. Holding her breath, she pushed through the heavy black drapes, fighting her mounting sense of panic as the darkness went on and on it seemed for ever.

Then, suddenly, there was light. A single bulb suspended overhead illuminated a bare, black-curtained semicircle in the centre of which a narrow stage had been erected. But it was the thing on the stage that caught her eye. She had to look at it for several moments before she could be sure. Then, still not taking her eyes from it, she mounted the wooden steps that 'Jack' had mounted earlier, and stood before the lectern and the bunch of microphones where she had sung 'Happy Birthday' not so long (but how long?) ago.

Slowly she turned, numbly looking for the vanished vastness filled with twenty thousand cheering people who had laughed and loved and sung along with her in celebration of the birthday of their glamorous president. But all she could see were a couple more of those little camera-like things on their tripod supports. Above them, suspended on the end of filament-thin cable, were half a dozen or so miniature spots which, she found herself thinking, must have far more power than their size suggested to have dazzled her as they had before.

Only as the shock of recognition wore off did the questions rush in: Why? Where? How? What sense did it all make? Was she insane, imagining it all? Was that the only explanation?

She looked down at herself, at the torn and ragged dress, the bare feet dusty from the floor, and thought of Cinderella. She could feel her hair was all mussed up and her make-up smudged and running. She must look a fright. A sound came from her throat, something between a sob and laughter.

'She's over here!' she heard someone shout. 'On the Garden stage.'

Out of the corner of her vision she caught a flash of movement but she didn't wait for more. Leaping from the low stage, she plunged once more into the dense black drapes like some B-movie heroine fighting her way through a studio jungle.

It was more frightening this time. She could hear them all around, closing in on her. She expected any second to be seized roughly in the darkness, and gave an involuntary cry of alarm as one of the invisible drapes wrapped itself around her and clung more tightly than the rest.

Pulling herself free, she stumbled backward against something flat. It wobbled and gave way. As it fell, she found herself standing in the bathroom of her dressing room – minus one wall which was now under her feet. Nothing else had changed. There was the mirrored cabinet, the straw-weave stool by the bath tub, and on the stool her little plastic travelling kit of pills.

She lunged for it like a junkie desperate for a fix, a tormented soul in search of salvation. Her trembling fingers had sorted twice through all the phials and bottles before she realized with a cold sensation down the spine that there was no drug, no upper, downer, tranquillizer, stimulant or vitamin that was capable of making any impact on the surreal nightmare in which she now found herself. There was nothing between her and what was happening. If she was hallucinating, she didn't know how or why, and she sure as hell didn't have the antidote. And if she was insane, if that final, primal terror of hers had at last risen up and come to claim her, then there was nothing she could do.

For a moment she just knelt there by the little straw-weave stool and the bath tub, paralyzed by a sense of emptiness. A second or a year could have passed without her knowing the difference. Then she felt eyes burning, the way they always did, into her back. She spun around. Watching her from the door of her dressing room was a handful of anxious faces: hairdressers, wardrobe, make-up. But what was wrong? They were the same people she'd worked with, talked with, laughed with, screamed at earlier. And yet, like Jack when he got out of that mock-up limo, they were subtly different, not quite the way they'd seemed.

They scattered as she came towards them. By the time she stood in the centre of the dressing room itself the place was empty. She turned around. On an instinct she went up to one of the walls and pushed. It rocked. A goddamn set. Not real.

But the shouts in the distance were real enough. Whoever those men were who were after her, they weren't giving up. She ran to the door that led to the corridor and looked out. It was deserted. Last time, with Jack, they'd gone to the right. Now she turned left. After ten yards or so another corridor crossed it. She remembered vaguely that left had been the direction she had taken earlier for the Garden stage, so now she turned right – and let out a shrill scream of pure terror as she cannoned into somebody's arms.

It was Lawford, without his tuxedo now, tieless and in his shirtsleeves. Their faces were inches apart, and he looked more terrified than she was.

Except it wasn't Lawford. She knew he was the man she'd somehow taken for Lawford, but he wasn't. She didn't even have to break away from him; he pressed his back to the wall and just watched, open-mouthed, as she ran.

This time the darkness lasted only for an instant. As quickly as she was in it she was through it, running across a vast, empty, enclosed space, the smooth, warm floor slapping beneath her bare feet. Ahead was a postage stamp of daylight, growing as she approached.

She knew where she was now: a sound stage in some studio. Why or how were questions without answers, but it was some small comfort to be in surroundings that at least she recognized.

Her breath came raggedly and her lungs were starting to burn. She didn't remember when she'd ever run like this. She kept her eyes on that small patch of light, letting its growth push all else from her mind. In a few moments she would be through it, leaving this madness behind her on the studio floor where it belonged.

16

The warm, bright air hit her like a hammer blow. Blinded, she stumbled, tripped and fell – but never hit the ground. Strong arms caught her, held her, then lifted her lightly, easily upright.

He had dark, thick hair, slicked back. His skin was pale but not unhealthy-looking. His features were chiselled, the nose fine and perfectly symmetrical, the cheekbones high and prominent. He wore sunglasses unlike any she'd ever seen; they seemed moulded to the contours of his face instead of resting on them: part of him, not accessories.

'That's enough. Calm down. You're going to do some damage to yourself.'

His voice was soft, filled with the bland confidence of someone who knew that his authority over her was total. She didn't like that; it was the way the doctors had spoken last time she'd been hospitalized with that so-called 'breakdown'.

'Let me go!' She struggled, but he held on, long fingers curled with effortless strength around her wrists. Something in the way that black-gazing, eyeless face stared down at her, into her, unmoving, made her stop struggling.

'That's better,' he said. 'Nobody's going to hurt you.'

'Who the fuck are you?' she asked, so short of breath that half the words were swallowed as she gasped for air.

'It doesn't matter,' he answered. The way he dismissed the question, and by implication the questioner, as unimportant angered her more. Who the fuck was this flunky to talk to her that way?

'Do you know who I am?' she shouted in his face.

'I know exactly who you are,' he replied. There was a hint of movement somewhere around those hidden eyes, a twitch of the tip of that all-knowing nose.

She bit him. She sank her teeth deep into the heel of the hand that was gripping her right wrist. He gave a howl of pain and let her go. She ran without looking back, careening around corners and down the white-walled avenues between sound stages, finally reaching the long, low, colonial-style executive offices with their venetian-blinded windows and trimmed herbaceous borders.

The strange thing was that nobody was about. It was the first

17

time she had seen a studio lot without people passing and crossing everywhere, either on foot or riding golf carts, talking urgently, delivering messages, hurrying to meetings. Even on a public holiday there was always somebody about. Now it was as though the whole place had been cleared for some mysterious purpose she knew nothing of.

Another corner; then, on her right, she saw steps leading up an outside wall to the second floor of one of the office buildings. She ran up, grasped the handle of the door at the top – and froze.

From where she was she could see a section of the studio main gate. She had glimpsed a couple of things as she ran that had given her a good idea of which studio lot she was on, and that famous gate confirmed it.

She could also see out over the boundary wall and clear across to downtown LA. But something elusive, something she could not put her finger on, was wrong. She ought to have been looking out over cars, freeways, and block after block of ugly buildings to a skyline eternally shrouded in that yellowish haze that always looked the way she thought bad breath would look if you could see it.

Instead, she found herself looking out over a gleaming city of glass and chrome, marble and stone. The air was so crystal clear that she could see, for the first time she could remember, mountains in the distance. And the skyline itself was not only crisply defined against the cloudless sky; it was also different. It rose higher, spread further.

She barely had time to question what she'd seen, let alone wonder what it meant, before the voices of her pursuers bore in on her again, dangerously close. Her fingers still gripped the handle of the door. She pushed, and a moment later was running down a long carpeted corridor, reassuring in its relative familiarity.

On the walls hung portraits of movie stars and stills from pictures that she mostly recognized. She heard a door bang somewhere up ahead, then another one behind. They were checking the building. She didn't think they'd seen her, but she was trapped. She pushed open the nearest door, and found herself in

18

some executive office. At one end was a large desk with nothing on it but two phones and a blotter. At the other end armchairs and a couple of sofas were arranged around a coffee table for informal meetings. On the walls were movie posters, prints from the Los Angeles Museum of Art, and photographs.

She looked around for some way out. If this was a movie, she couldn't help thinking, there'd be a lower rooftop outside the window with a safe drop into some convenient haystack, or a truckload of mattresses that happened to be passing. But this was not a movie, and there was no way out. Nor was there, so far as she could see, much place to hide.

Then, at about knee height and marked only by a hairline in the clean white paintwork, she saw a hinged panel in the air-conditioning duct beneath the window. She found the tiny white-painted handle, yanked it open, and rolled into the confined darkness.

The panel had a fine filigree pattern carved into it which gave her a limited and fragmented view of the room. Almost at once she saw the door open and two men enter. They made a quick search – checking behind furniture, curtains, connecting doors – then went out. She realized she had been holding her breath, crouched, with her legs tucked under her. She exhaled gratefully and tried to shift her position, wondering whether she should stay put or make a run for it. Before she could decide, the door banged open again.

'Shit! This is all we need.' She recognized the man she had bitten. He had a plaster on now, but was massaging the wound as though it was still painful. 'Bitch nearly bit my hand off!'

'You okay, Al?' The question came from a younger man who followed him in. His voice and manner marked him out as some kind of gofer.

'Yeah, I'm okay. Get out there and help find her.'

'Merrill says will you talk to the client? He's real upset.'

'Yeah – ask him to step in here, will you?'

The gofer left. She watched as the one called Al, the one she had bitten, paced the room anxiously. Once he came and stood right in front of the dusty cubbyhole where she was hiding. She

19

held her breath until she almost burst and was sure she would give herself away; but then there were footsteps in the corridor and Al crossed over to the door. It opened and the man she had taken for Jack was shown in by the gofer, who left them alone.

'Sir, I'm truly sorry about all this,' Al began, making an effort to sound more in control of things than he'd seemed a few moments ago. 'I apologize, and we're doing everything possible to get things back on track just as fast as we can.'

'What the hell went wrong?' Jack demanded. For some reason she still thought of him as Jack even though he so obviously wasn't. Everything about him was wrong, from the belligerence of his voice to the squat, stocky frame that it came from. She fought back a wave of disgust as she remembered what she had done with this ugly little man.

'We have to remember,' Al was saying, 'that we're dealing with something organic here, therefore by definition not entirely predictable. If you think about the process—'

'I know all I need to know about the damn process,' Jack snapped. 'I saw that movie a million times on TV when I was a kid – the one about cloning those dinosaurs from their own DNA. Shit, if they could do it back then, how come you can't get it right now?'

'In fact they couldn't actually do it in those days. That was just a piece of fiction. However, in recent years—'

Jack interrupted again with a wave of his stubby hand. 'Look, I haven't got all day. Why don't you just get another one up here? You've got others, haven't you?'

'None available, I'm afraid. At least, none that can be ready for this scenario in the time we have.'

'Then just what the hell do you propose?'

'As soon as we find her we'll have everything back to normal in no time. All we have to do is—'

Jack waved his hand again, bored with the details. He took a cigar from a case in his pocket and clipped it with a silver cutter as he spoke.

'I'll tell you what I'm going to do,' he said. 'I'm going to take a walk around, look at some of the exhibits you have here – and if you get this show on the road inside an hour, let me know. Otherwise I'm gone.' He touched a flame from some kind of lighter to the end of his cigar.

'I'm sure there'll be no problem, sir. Make yourself comfortable, and of course the hospitality wing is entirely at your disposal.'

'Find her, fix her . . .' Jack inhaled his cigar, blew out a cloud of smoke, and gave Al one of those sly, dirty, between-guys kind of smiles. 'And leave the rest to me.'

She didn't see them leave because her head was down and her eyes shut tight. She didn't know whether she was holding something in or keeping it out. Distantly, she heard them walking away, still talking, though she couldn't catch what they were saying.

For some time she remained absolutely still, replaying in her head the conversation she had overheard. In the end it was the sheer physical discomfort of her position that made her move. She pushed open the panel, crawled halfway out, stopped, and listened hard. She could hear nothing. It seemed that the whole building was once again empty.

The first thing she saw when she stood up was her reflection in a mirror. She looked like she'd been pulled through a hedge – which, come to think of it, she pretty much had. But there was nothing she could do about that now. The most important thing was to get hold of her agent, her lawyer, her analyst if need be – whoever and whatever it took to get her the hell out of here.

She ran to the large desk and picked up a phone. She had started to dial before she realized that the line was dead. She picked up the other phone. The same. She jiggled the cradle. Nothing.

'That won't help you.'

The voice came from behind her, making her spin around with a gasp of surprise. Al was standing in the door, watching her from behind those strange dark glasses.

'Those phones are just museum pieces, baby,' he said, coming into the room and closing the door behind him. 'Like this whole place. A tribute to the past. To the days when they made movies the way you remember them. Long gone faraway days.'

She backed away from him, still holding the phone like a weapon to defend herself.

'I figured you must be somewhere in this block,' he said. 'Only place you could be after we checked everywhere else.'

'Don't come near me,' she warned, feeling foolish, as she always did when she tried to threaten somebody, which anyway wasn't often.

'It's okay,' he said, spreading his hands so that she could see the palms. 'I told you – nobody's going to hurt you.'

'What's happening?' she said, her voice trembling with rage as much as fear. 'What the fuck is going on here? Tell me!'

He sighed, then walked over to one of the sofas and sat down, crossing his legs, oddly relaxed compared with how he'd been before. It was as though the fact of having found her made everything all right. She noticed for the first time how well his clothes hung on him. It wasn't just the way they were cut, loose but form-fitting; it was something in the material itself, a texture, natural but somehow resistant to stretching or creasing.

'There's no way you can understand what's happening. You're better off not asking. In a while you won't even want to. Trust me.'

'Fuck you.'

He made a little gesture, a kind of shrug, to show that he wasn't offended. There was something condescending in it that puzzled her as much as it angered her. Who was this guy she'd never seen before to treat her this way? Nobody treated her this way. Nobody! Not any more.

'Answer my question.'

He was looking up at her, his head slightly cocked to one side, as though something about her provoked his curiosity.

'What the hell!' he said eventually, as though making a decision. 'I'll answer it.'

He placed his hands on his knees and levered himself upright again. He was still looking at her, and she at him. She was unused to being stared at by someone in dark glasses. Usually it was the other way around; and if the star wasn't wearing them, nobody wore them. But she didn't say anything. She felt that what she was about to hear was more important. She knew how to listen when she had to.

'What you are, baby, is a Living Legend. The biggest of them all. Others come and go, but you just keep on getting bigger. You're a phenomenon. You're the only one they want.'

She hadn't taken her eyes off him. Still she didn't. He'd warned her that she wouldn't understand. Perhaps she wouldn't. Yet in some odd, hidden part of herself she felt she might. Perhaps she did already, just didn't know that she did.

He walked away, was silent for a moment, then turned.

'"Living Legend". That's a brand name. We own it. As a matter of fact I thought it up myself, registered it offshore, before this whole thing came out into the open. Not that it altogether has, but you know how it is – once people know that something can be done, then sooner or later it will be. The world finds a way of living with these things. A *modus vivendi*. You know what that means?'

'Yes. I know,' she said in a small, flat voice.

'Don't let it worry you,' he said. 'In a few minutes you won't even remember that we had this conversation.'

She tried to speak again, but her mouth was dry. It was a moment before the words came.

'That man . . . He wasn't . . . He isn't . . . Who is he?'

'That's client confidentiality. But no, he isn't who you thought he was. None of them were.'

It was just as she'd thought. None of them were the people she'd first taken them for.

'Then who . . . Why . . . ?'

'That's what they pay for. These are the hard-core fans, baby. Knowing all about you isn't enough for them. They want to know *you*. They want to play some part in your life, whether it's hair-stylist, make-up artist, dresser, whatever. What they play depends on what they pay. For some of them it's just the one time – thrill of a lifetime. For others – well, there's one guy, for instance, comes in here every week to play your shrink.'

23

She was perfectly still, trying to work out what she felt, what she thought. But nothing came. She felt empty. Dead. It was a moment before she realized that she had sunk on to the edge of a chair, her knees and feet together, her hands playing nervously in her lap.

'Why me?' she said at last, in a barely audible whisper.

'You tell me, baby,' he said with a casual half-laugh. 'You wanted what you wanted, and you got it. You created yourself. All we did was make copies. I've lost count how many. You're everywhere. And they're always wanting more – in spite of the occasional little problem, like today.'

He had walked across the room again, and regarded her now from a far corner.

She looked back at him through the tangle of hair that had fallen over her eyes. She had begun to shake and couldn't stop. It was worse than a shake; it was a bone-twitching, teeth-chattering shudder that ran through her whole body like a series of electric shocks.

'All right,' he said to somebody over her shoulder, 'take her down.'

She gave a cry of alarm and sprang to her feet, but before she could turn she was seized by two pairs of strong hands. She had a glimpse of two men, one bald and in a white coat like a doctor, the other younger, broad-shouldered and muscular. Then something was jabbed into her arm. It didn't feel like an injection, in fact it didn't hurt at all. But almost at once she felt herself starting to lose consciousness. She fought it, but knew, even as she did, that she had lost.

★

'Here, honey. Take these.'

She opened her eyes and realized she was lying down. When she tried to get up she found her movements were restricted. She started to panic, but the woman with her put out a reassuring hand.

'Careful, honey. We just got you sewed into this thing – don't ruin it.'

Of course. The dress. The damn dress. She let the woman help her into a sitting position. She was in her dressing room backstage at the Garden.

'Take these now. You'll feel better.'

She took the two pills that the woman was offering, then the glass of water that she handed her.

'What are they?'

'They're your prescription. It's okay.'

She swallowed them, one after the other. As she did, she became aware of a handful of people standing around, watching her. She wasn't sure she recognized them. Then she remembered that they were the people they'd got in for just this one show in New York.

The hairdresser came forward, flicked his comb, sprayed something on her.

'Perfect! I'm so proud. We all are. You're going to be wonderful.'

'Come on, let me help you. Everybody's ready.' It was the woman again, helping her gently to her feet.

She stood upright. She felt fine. She couldn't remember why she had been lying down. Had she passed out? Had she been asleep? It didn't matter. All she knew now was what she had to do.

Then she saw an open bottle of champagne in an ice bucket. 'Give me a glass of that, will you?'

'Sure.'

The woman handed it to her. She took a sip. Another. It tasted good, gave her just that little extra charge she needed. She'd be all right now.

There was a knock at the door. Someone opened it, then turned to her. 'They're ready. Joe here'll take you to the stage.'

She looked. A page-boy waited. She finished her glass, held it out, someone took it.

'Let's go,' she said. She felt nervous, but it was the right kind of nerves. Good nerves. Someone placed the wrap around her shoulders. She pulled it closer and started out in short, carefully measured steps which were all she could manage in that dress.

The corridor was long and dark, underground. In the distance she could hear applause, laughter. Somebody was talking on a mike.

'Excuse me . . .' It was the page-boy at her side. He sounded timid, cleared his throat. 'D'you mind if I tell you something, Miss Monroe?'

'Mm-hm?' she murmured absently, her mind on what she had to do, rehearsing the moves and the words, but not wanting to seem offhand. 'Go ahead.'

'I just want you to know – this moment, being here with you right now, is the biggest thrill of my whole life.'

Hollywood Lies

Artie Fleischman had long since passed the age when, according to popular myth, American men take stock of their lives and face up to the fact that they are never going to become president of their country. That was a fact that Artie had come to terms with a long time ago. Indeed, he had gone further and admitted to himself that he was unlikely, at his age and at this stage in his career, even to become president of a motion picture studio.

As an independent producer he had a dozen or so pictures to his credit over the last twenty-odd years, some of them better than others, none of them huge hits, few of them total disasters. His logo, 'An Arthur J. Fleischman Production', was known to audiences in the way that things can be familiar without being remembered. He did not make any specific type of picture, nor was he associated with any particular star or noted director.

His best picture had been *Tripwire*, an expensive, star-cast cold war thriller that might have done big business – were it not for the collapse of the Soviet Union just after the completion of principal photography. Audiences no longer wanted stories in which the Russians were the bad guys, so the film was released to an indifferent world and sank without trace inside two weeks. Artie had got drunk with a couple of fellow producers in a small, dark bar just off the Paramount lot. Between them they had a fortune in time and money invested in cold war scripts which were now valueless. They raised their glasses to old times, and cursed the triumph of capitalism.

By contrast, Artie's most successful picture had been something he had backed into by accident and without any planning or development. He had taken a chance on a spec script which everybody in town had turned down. It was a knockabout comedy thriller about two cops called *Cash and Carrie*, and made stars out of its two leads, who had until then played only in television. Unfortunately the deal Artie had been forced to make to get the picture financed left him badly placed on profits. He had then spent more than he had earned in trying to rush through another picture which repeated the formula – unsuccessfully.

All in all, however, it was a respectable career. He had passed his sixtieth birthday a few months earlier with surprisingly little pain, discovering that it felt far less close to death than he had imagined it would when viewed from the lush foothills of youth. He had energy and experience, and had never been a man to make a lot of enemies. Perhaps he should have been, he sometimes told himself; perhaps then he would have had the drive to make something exceptional of his life.

'Forward a little, Mr Fleischman, if you would.' The radiologist's assistant gently touched his elbow; the machine hummed.

'The thing about this town,' somebody had once said to him, 'is you have to be grateful to be working with thieves and liars, because the alternative is idiots.'

The line had made Artie smile, but he didn't believe it. There were many decent people in the movie business. Why shouldn't there be? What made them different from the rest of the world was that there was a little bit of passion in all of them. Being an assistant cost accountant with a shoe factory or some engineering firm was one thing; doing the same job with a movie on location was something else. In the movies you could still come from nowhere, start wherever, learn the business, and wind up rich and famous – maybe even married to a movie star. Other lines of work, even at their loftiest, offered scant competition.

'Okay, that's fine,' the radiologist said. 'There doesn't seem to be any problem there. You can get dressed now.'

It was the end of the routine annual check-up that Artie got automatically under his industry health fund insurance scheme. He hadn't been worried about it: he knew he was in good shape. In fact physically he'd never felt better. He went through to the changing room, where he put on the monogrammed shirt, the well-cut silk suit and the carefully chosen tie. The shoes were Italian, hand-made. This was the way producers used to dress – and, he felt, still should. Even were he a younger man, he would never be tempted to adopt the jeans and bomber-jacket kind of Hollywood chic that had become fashionable in recent years. The Spielbergs and the Geffens and their kind were billionaires, but they dressed like kids on their way to a softball game. By their standards Artie made a modest living, but dressed like one of the great moguls of the past. That was the way he was. He couldn't fake it and pretend to belong to a generation where producers wore pony-tails.

In his soul Artie knew he was a man of the 'forties and 'fifties. That was when the magic had first touched him. He grew up on Hitchcock and Billy Wilder pictures. His heroes were Cooper, Cagney, Stewart, and Fonda. He laughed at Hope and Crosby, Abbot and Costello, Martin and Lewis. He got his first girlfriends into bed with the help of Sinatra and the Nelson Riddle Orchestra. Rhonda Fleming was the woman of his fantasies. The titans of his early days in Hollywood were Kirk and Burt and big John Wayne. Those days and the movies that came out of them had set, for him, the standard by which all were subsequently judged. He didn't feel out of date because he knew what he was talking about. Story structure hadn't changed merely because special effects could blow up whole galaxies with total plausibility or because dinosaurs could walk across the screen like living creatures instead of jerky puppets with black lines around them. Characters still had to be conceived in the round and given an arc of development if your audience was going to care what happened to them. There was nothing old-fashioned about the rules of story-telling. They were timeless. The rest was dressing.

So why wasn't he more successful? He sighed as he drove back to his office on the Warner Hollywood lot at the corner of Santa Monica and Formosa. He had little cause to complain: in many ways he was a lucky man. Molly didn't seem to resent the fact that other wives had more couturier clothes, were taken on cruises twice a year, and didn't have to arrive for lunch with their friends in a five-year-old BMW. The house was paid for and, despite a recent property slump, he still had a decent equity in it. His kids by his first wife – they had been divorced more than twenty years – were married and had their own lives: Jane as a violinist with the Chicago Symphony Orchestra, and Steven as a doctor in Boston. They had never forgiven Artie for falling in love with Molly and leaving their mother. Fortunately she had subsequently married a New York banker, and none of them ever had problems on a material level. His children had shown no interest in staying in touch with him, though he sent them lavish gifts at Christmas and on birthdays. He received a printed card informing him that he was a grandfather (Steven's wife had given birth to a daughter eighteen months ago), but he was sent neither an invitation to any family celebration, nor even a photograph of the child. He didn't hold it against them. Artie Fleischman, despite his acquired patina of sophistication, came from simple stock who didn't impose themselves where they were not wanted.

He pulled on to the lot with a nod to Joe, the grandfatherly security guard who came on duty at midday. He parked and locked his bottle-green Jaguar in the space with his name stencilled on it, then walked over to the shabby ground-floor office that was part of his deal with the studio. They gave him that and his overhead – basically a secretary and his phone bills – in return for first look at any projects he developed. The agreement came to an end soon, and he had a feeling it wouldn't be renewed; they had shown no interest in anything he had offered them over the past two years. In fact he hadn't had a bite even from television or the smallest of the cable companies.

Still, he had one property, a comedy called *Conjugal Wrongs*, that he had been developing with a young writer for the last six months. It was Artie's idea, but the writer had done wonders with it – particularly considering that Artie was only paying him Guild minimum. But the money was coming from Artie's own pocket because this and every other studio had turned the idea down. Convinced the idea was good, Artie had decided to back his own instinct and put his money where his mouth was. Besides, it was deductible. Now the script was ready. He was going to give it to the studio and try to get it on everybody's reading list for the weekend.

His secretary, Becky, looked up indifferently from the paperback she was reading and handed him a sheet of paper listing his phone calls: only two in the four hours he had been gone. He murmured his thanks and went through into his office. A moment later his voice came over the speaker, casually asking her to get him Ned Ross on the phone.

The corners of her mouth turned down with involuntary scorn. What made Artie Fleischman think that the president of the studio would have nothing better to do than take his call? He would be fobbed off as always with some junior executive who would grudgingly spare him five minutes between more important meetings. The trouble with people like Artie, she reflected as she dialled, was that they never knew when the game was over and it was time to go home. She reminded herself that she must start looking seriously for another job.

★

'What d'you mean Ned Ross couldn't see you! Who does that little jerk think he is?'

Molly's indignation arose from the fact that when she and Artie were first married, Ned Ross had worked for her husband. 'Without you he'd never have got started in this business.'

'I know that and Ned knows that,' Artie agreed wearily. 'It doesn't alter the fact that he's head of the studio now, and I'm not.'

'It doesn't alter the fact that showing a little courtesy wouldn't kill him.'

'Molly, I've told you a million times, it isn't a personal thing. Don't be fooled by friendships, don't be hurt by rejection. This business works on who you need and who needs you. When you're hot – enjoy! And when you're cold – don't bitch. The wheel turns. It all comes around.'

'All I can say is your wheel's coming around pretty slow right now.' Molly stacked their plates and took them through the open-plan living room to the kitchen. Artie leaned back and took a sip of Californian Cabernet. Their house was high on a small street off North Doheny. The view of LA's lights was obscured by outcrops of land and several other houses that had sprung up over

33

the years, but it was still an agreeable prospect. It wasn't a place he was ashamed to have people come to for meetings or dinner. When they had a big party they hired help. Normally they just had Doris come in three days a week. It used to be five, but money was tight and Doris was happy to do only three without putting her rates up. Molly didn't seem to mind.

Artie picked up a couple of dishes and carried them over to the kitchen counter. 'Molly, the important thing is that Ned reads the script, not whether he returns my call or whatever the hell. He'll read it and I think he'll like it. I've known the guy a long time. I know what he likes. I know the pictures he's made and the pictures he wants to make. This is a gift for him.'

'And what about the rest of the studio – all those twelve-year-olds in running shoes? Isn't *Conjugal Wrongs* a little short on car wrecks and shoot-'em-ups for them?'

'It's Ned's decision. And even if he doesn't like it I can go elsewhere. It's only a first-look deal.'

To Molly, that sounded like Artie preparing himself for disappointment, but she made no comment. It was Thursday evening, and by Monday they would have the studio's verdict. 'Why don't we go somewhere for the weekend?' she said. 'Joan and Mike are going down to the Springs. They want us to join them.'

'I don't know about this weekend. I've got some stuff I want to work on.' The truth was that Artie didn't like to be around people when he was on the edge, waiting for a decision. 'You go. I'll stay here.'

Molly knew full well what Artie was thinking: if he spent the weekend sifting through old projects, thinking about new ones, generally putting two and two together and hoping to make five, he would at least persuade himself that the future still held some promise. It would soften the blow if *Conjugal Wrongs* were turned down on Monday.

'No, you're right,' Molly said. 'I don't feel much like the desert either.' She looked into his eyes and gave his cheek a little tug between her thumb and forefinger. 'Besides, I wanted to go over and help Kelly fix up her new apartment.'

Kelly was Molly's daughter by her first marriage, a bouncy

twenty-six-year-old of whom Artie was very fond. She had lived with them most of her life and was far closer to him than his own daughter. She wasn't particularly pretty, but she more than made up for that in high-octane energy and confidence. Artie had got her a job with a small agency that already found her indispensable. It wouldn't surprise him if she became somebody of real consequence in the business one day.

So it was settled: a weekend at home, maybe dinner out with Kelly and her boyfriend on Saturday. And they wouldn't discuss the script.

★

Becky was so surprised that she got up from her desk and put her head around Artie's door with her mouth open and her eyes wide. 'Ned Ross's office on the line,' she managed to say.

'Well, put 'em on, for Chrissakes!' he snapped, managing to suppress an impulse to throw something at her.

'Yeah, sure.' She ran back to her desk, and a moment later Artie heard the familiar high, fast-talking voice in his ear.

'Artie, you old son of a bitch, you did it! You goddamn did it, didn't you!'

'What did I do, Ned?' Artie said, trying to contain the prickly feeling of excitement that was beginning to mount from his ankles. 'I parked in the wrong spot or something? Forgot to turn off the lights? What?'

'Come on, you fuckhead, you know what I'm talking about. *Conjugal Wrongs* is a sensational script. It's the best damn comedy idea I've seen in years. It's exactly what this studio ought to be making, and we're going to make it!'

Artie stopped fighting to suppress the prickly feeling and let it mount as a warm glow suffusing his whole body. 'I'm glad you like it, Ned,' he said, keeping his voice steady. 'I thought you would, but I'm happy you've proved me right.'

'You and me have to talk, old buddy. Listen, what're you doing for lunch? You want to come and have a bite to eat?'

'You mean today?' Artie couldn't believe it. A studio head's lunch dates were booked up weeks ahead – dates that could not

35

be broken except for major stars in emotional states, a handful of big agents or top producers with a solid gold package that needed an answer by sundown, and maybe if the studio got sold.

'Sure I mean today. When d'you think I mean? You think I'm going to let you take this script some place else? If word about this script gets out, the whole town's going to be on you like a rash.'

Artie wondered who was getting bumped from lunch to make way for him. Somebody's day was going to have a big hole in it. Maybe their week. Maybe their whole year. But what the hell, it was their turn. God knows it had been his turn often enough these past few years. But things changed. Things always changed in this business. You could never tell. He told Ned Ross he'd be at his office at twelve forty-five. Then he called Molly.

She could barely keep the tears out of her voice. 'Artie, I'm so happy for you. You really deserve this. I'm so happy.'

'Come on, honey, don't cry. Put some champagne on ice, and I'll make a reservation at Spago. We'll have a real old-fashioned celebration, just the two of us. I've got to go now. I love you.'

The studio that Ned Ross headed was a twenty-minute drive across town. They kept space on the lot where Artie was based for people they couldn't accommodate on the main lot. It was a beautiful, clear day, and Artie was feeling euphoric by the time he pulled in through the impressive gates where a drive-on pass was waiting for him. Ten minutes later he was sitting in an over-stuffed armchair in the president's huge white and cream office.

Ned Ross was a short man with a round face and thinning ginger hair. He kept himself in trim with workouts and a sensible diet, and looked younger than his forty-five years. 'Of course, the script needs some work,' Field was saying. 'Not a lot, but some. It's not a problem. Every script needs some work.'

'I hope you're not planning to put another writer on it,' Artie said quickly. 'The kid's worked his ass off on this project. He deserves the credit.'

'Don't worry, we'll cut a deal for the kid. Whatever needs doing, he can do it. With you behind him, I have total confidence.'

Artie was relieved. The truth was he'd got far more work out of the kid than he'd any right to for the money he was paying. But you could do that with young writers; they'd do anything for a shot at something that might be the big breakthrough for them. On the way over he'd called Kelly – who was the kid's agent – from his car with the good news.

Field was on his feet now, arm around Artie's shoulders, steering him to the door. 'I thought we'd eat in the commissary. You'll see a few old friends down there. How's that sound to you?'

It sounded just fine to Artie. Lunch at Ned Ross's table in the executive annexe of the commissary was an announcement to the whole industry that Artie Fleischman was back in the game: a player. It felt better than he'd ever let himself imagine it would.

After the ritual greetings, handclasps, bear-hugs and promises to have lunch soon exchanged at almost every table as they crossed the room, Artie faced his powerful host over a Caesar salad and glass of mineral water. Ned Ross toyed with a crouton and a piece of chilled, crisp lettuce, seeming for a moment to be uncharacteristically at a loss for words. 'Artie,' he began eventually, 'I want to say something. For a long time now, I haven't seen as much of you as I'd have liked to. You know how it is, business, problems, deals . . .'

Artie assured him that he knew exactly how it was, noting inwardly that Ross must really love this script to be turning on the taps of sentiment so fulsomely.

'The thing I've never forgotten, Artie,' Ross went on, 'is you gave me my start in this business, and you taught me more than anyone I know. And for that I'll always be grateful to you.'

Artie made a self-deprecating gesture, but Ross persisted.

'No, let me finish, Artie. I want to say this. There's one thing you taught me about this business that I've always remembered and treasured. You once said to me, "Kid, this is a phoney business. The stars' teeth, tits, and hair are phoney. The sets are phoney. The stories are phoney. The happy endings are double-phoney. Even the music's phoney. But let me tell you one thing that you have to understand if you're going to succeed in this business: you can't fake phoney."'

Artie threw back his head and laughed politely. He remembered giving the advice. He also knew that Ned Ross had claimed the remark as his own ever since. It had even been quoted to Artie several times over the years as an example of Ross's shrewdness. But that was all right. Today everything was all right. Artie decided to have a glass of Chardonnay with the grilled sea bass, and was already adding zeroes to the sum he was going to have his lawyer, Joe Cross, negotiate for the deal.

As though reading his thoughts, Ross suddenly said, 'By the way, you're probably thinking that you and me should sketch out some kind of parameters for this deal. Which we can if you like. Or we can just have Business Affairs and – who's handling you now? Still Joe Cross? – I'll have Business Affairs give him a call and get something down on paper, then you and I can talk again. Incidentally, while I think about it, there's a suite of offices coming available down the far end of the corridor from me. You won't be able to move in for a couple of months, but I'd like to have you there. You and this studio are going to be doing a lot of business over the next few years. To start with there's at least two sequels in this story of yours. I want to talk to you about them.'

For the rest of lunch they discussed the script and the possible sequels. Artie had another glass of wine and an extra-large, double-strength, non-decaffeinated espresso. He drove back to his office feeling twenty years old and on the verge of life all over again.

Becky handed him a list of twenty calls already awaiting his return, and the phone was ringing off the hook for the rest of the afternoon. The word was out.

★

Lars Hanssen was a big Swede with the build of a heavyweight boxer. He was pleasant and slow-moving, and had absolutely no sense of humour – which was surprising, because he had directed the three biggest comedy hits of the past few years.

'"Funny" isn't funny,' Lars liked to say. 'It's trying not to be funny that's funny. A man falls in a hole – that's not funny. He walks around a hole, thinking he's smart, and falls in the ditch –

that's funny.' Still, it didn't make Lars laugh. 'Funny guys don't laugh,' he said. 'Funny guys do funny stuff, the audience laugh. The funny guys are too busy looking for more holes to walk around.'

As a theory it may have been questionable, but nobody argued with Lars Hanssen's grosses. The truly funny thing was that, contrary to what one might have expected from listening to Hanssen talk, he was a director of subtle comedy in a direct line from Lubitsch, Sturges and Billy Wilder. Artie was ecstatic that he had committed to the script after one reading.

'You know what I think?' said Lars expansively in the vast living room of his sprawling house on Mulholland. 'I think we should get Greg Warren to play Ed. Greg would be good for Ed.'

Jesus, thought Artie, that's twelve million minimum above the line, plus a piece of the gross from dollar one. But he was worth it. Greg Warren was currently one of the few stars who could 'open' a picture worldwide – meaning lines at the box office from the first weekend.

'Let's give it a try,' he said. 'The worst he can do is say no.'

'He won't say no,' Lars announced with conviction. 'He says no, I throw him through the fuckin' wall.'

In the event, no such tactics were needed. Greg Warren was in town, either from his ranch in Wyoming or his duplex on Park Avenue, and met with Artie in an office provided by the studio. He wore scuffed cowboy boots, old jeans, a crumpled tweed jacket and a wristwatch that might have cost all of ten dollars. It was a star's way of showing how unimpressed he was by his own wealth and power.

'It's a good script, Artie,' he said, sipping a diet Coke from the can. 'That's why I'm gonna do it. But I want to tell you why I'm happy it's a good script and why I'm happy I'm gonna make the picture. I'm happy,' he paused, coming closer and poking a forefinger at Artie's chest, 'because you're gonna make it. I'm happy to be working with you, Artie.'

'That's a very nice thing to say, Greg. It makes me very proud to hear that.' Artie knew how to play these scenes. He was out of practice with big stars, but nothing ever really changed.

'I want to remind you of something, Artie. Something that happened a long time ago that you've probably forgotten.'

Artie felt a flicker of unease and searched his memory. He had no idea what the actor could be talking about.

'Ten years ago,' Warren droned on, 'you tested a bunch of kids for the juvenile lead in *Stone Marathon*. You remember making that picture?'

'Sure I do,' Artie said, frowning. Was it possible he'd tested Greg Warren and didn't remember? No, Warren was too old. Besides, he was already known, though not a big star, ten years ago.

'One of those kids was just starting out in this business,' Warren was saying. 'He wanted to be an actor so bad that if he couldn't be an actor he wanted to die. You know what it is to want something that bad? I think you do, Artie, because you felt it in that kid. You didn't give him the part because he couldn't do it. He had no technique, no experience – nothing. He didn't even have a proper agent, but you said you'd help him out, you'd make a call and find him one. And you did. You made that call, Artie. And the kid got an agent.'

Artie's mind was racing. It was perfectly possible that he had done what he was hearing, but he had no recollection of the incident. 'So what happened?' he asked. It was all he could think of.

The star shrugged. 'He got a couple of roles, some television. He worked hard, real hard. Gave it all he had. But in the end he didn't make it. Didn't have the juice – you know what I mean?'

'What was his name?' Artie asked, more puzzled than ever. 'Is he still in the business?'

'Yeah, he's still in the business, in a way,' said the star, glancing out of the window at an overcast sky and taking another sip of his Coke. 'His name's Mickey Wallace. He's my driver.'

★

Artie was concerned by the way that Molly seemed to be taking two sleeping pills every night now before going to bed. 'Why d'you do that, honey?' he asked. 'You have a problem sleeping? You getting sick, or what?'

Molly hadn't realized he was aware of her habit and reacted defensively. Would he for Chrissakes stop worrying and mind his own business? If she couldn't sleep, that was her affair. Anyway, how was she supposed to sleep when they had all this excitement going on around them? It was a wonder, she said, that he could sleep. But the fact was he slept like a baby. He was a very happy man.

One morning about a week later Artie was leaving the house early for a meeting with Caspar Grenville. Caspar was officially retired, but Artie had persuaded him to sign on as production designer for the picture. The production designer was as responsible for the overall look of the film as the director, if not more so. Caspar had won three Oscars, and if he hadn't just announced his retirement Artie would probably have had trouble getting him, even for a picture this important. But Caspar had the time, and it wasn't as if the picture were a vast epic requiring monumental sets or extravagant location work. It was simply a matter of doing it right, making sure that everything was perfect. Caspar told Artie that *Conjugal Wrongs* would make an elegant and satisfying swansong to his long career.

Artie was just getting into his Jaguar – he had already picked out the model he was going to trade it in for when the bulk of his producing fee came through – when he heard a car coming up the hill at high speed. He paused, waiting to see what fool was tearing around those blind corners like the final reel of some B-movie – and was astonished to recognize the midnight blue Mercedes that screeched to a halt at the end of his drive. Jack Leonard, Artie's personal physician, got out.

Normally Jack Leonard was an elegant man, tall and slim with short-cropped greying hair and the haughtily benign expression of a prize-winning Afghan. This morning he was tripping over his feet and had the dismayed look of a man who has just discovered he is on a flight to Jakarta when his ticket said Newark. Artie turned to meet him, feeling a sudden chill of quite irrational foreboding. 'Christ, Jack, where's the fire?' he said. 'You trying to kill yourself or what?'

Jack Leonard was out of breath more from nervousness than any physical exertion, and there was something shifty in his expression, as though he was avoiding making direct contact with Artie's gaze.

Artie, a man who prided himself on looking straight down both barrels when trouble threatened, realized he was going to have to drag out of Jack whatever it was that he had come to say. 'What's wrong, Jack? You look like shit. Somebody dead?'

The doctor shook his head.

'Somebody sick?'

This time the doctor made a movement somewhere between a nod and a shake, which came out like a man trying to loosen up a stiff neck.

'For Chrissakes, Jack, will you say something? What is this?'

'Is Molly home?'

'She had an early appointment with her hairdresser. Is Molly sick? Is there something I should know?'

'No, Molly isn't sick.'

'Then what the . . . ? Jack, if you don't tell me what's going on here, I'm going to—'

'It's you, Artie.'

'Me? There's nothing wrong with me. I'm fine. What d'you mean it's me?'

'That check-up you had the other week . . .'

'The check-up was fine. Everything was fine. What are you talking about?'

'Everything wasn't fine, Artie. They found something.'

Artie was staring up into the taller man's grey-blue eyes, which were now looking into his. He felt the cold fingers of mortality reach out of the soft morning air and wrap themselves around him. 'What did they find?' he heard someone say, and realized it must have been himself.

'They found a very rare condition of the blood. It's a kind of leukaemia, but an unusual one. There's no treatment for it – no chemotherapy, nothing.'

'Jesus!' Artie barely breathed the word as he sank on to the seat of his car and leant against the open door.

'Artie, listen to me. It's not what it sounds like. They think they made a mistake.'

Artie looked up, trying to focus through the fog of racing

42

thoughts and fears that every human being knows they'll have to confront one day, but with luck not for a long, long time. 'What d'you mean, Jack? Am I dying or am I not? You said there's no cure. That sounds a lot like dying to me.'

'They think they made a mistake. They think now that you probably don't have the condition. That's why I'm here.'

'Wait a minute – just back up here, will you? First you tell me I'm dying, then you tell me I'm not. Now what the –?'

'Somehow a test that had nothing to do with you got fed into your data on the computer. It was a simple error. I got a call half an hour ago when I was driving to my office. I called your house, but there was no reply. I thought maybe you were in the shower or something. Anyway, I decided to come by and see if you were here. Artie, you've got to come with me right now to the hospital.'

'The hospital? If I'm not sick, why do I have to go to the hospital?'

'To make sure. Artie, we know there's been a mistake, but we still have to make sure. It's a ten zillion to one chance that you have the condition. I mean, to be misdiagnosed, but then to turn out to actually have the condition – it's just not possible. But we have to make sure. You can see that, can't you?'

'Yeah, I guess, but . . .' Artie looked at his watch. 'I've got a meeting with –'

'Whatever it is, it'll wait. This is more important, Artie. Come on, I'll drive you.'

Ten minutes later they were travelling down the long ski-jump-like stretch of Doheny Drive south of Sunset. As the dust of Artie's discomposure settled, he began to discern through it certain inevitable questions. 'Did Molly know about this – that I was supposed to be dying?'

Dr Leonard shifted uncomfortably behind the wheel of his car. 'Sure she knew, Artie. She was the first person I talked to when I got the news.'

'What made you decide not to tell me?'

'What made me, or what made her?'

'Both of you.'

'Frankly, Artie, the prognosis was so bad we figured, what the

43

hell. Inside four, five weeks you'd start to lose weight. Inside two months you'd be in coma. Some cancers are slow, some are fast. This one's like lightning. We figured, let you get sick before we told you what was wrong.'

Artie was silent a while. 'Poor Molly,' he said eventually. 'No wonder she needed sleeping pills. What a thing to have to live with.'

Dr Leonard glanced over at him. 'I hope you're not upset, Artie. She thought about it long and hard before deciding not to tell you.'

'No, I'm not upset.' He settled back against the smooth, rich-smelling leather and gave a long sigh. 'Jesus, what a time it would have been to die,' he said. 'Just when everything's coming up roses like it never has in my life before. How about that!'

'Would've been a bitch,' Dr Leonard agreed.

'Fuckin' A,' breathed Artie. Then he tensed. 'Hey, you don't think there's any chance I've really got this—?'

'Not in this universe,' said Jack Leonard, with a physician's absolute finality. 'It's like I told you, Artie – this test is just for the record.'

★

An hour later it was over. Artie had been pronounced in perfect health, his immediate future unblemished by the shadow of death.

The first thing he did was call Molly at the hairdresser's, but they told him he'd just missed her. He left her a message on the machine at home, brief and to the point and telling her he loved her. Then, as an afterthought, he called Kelly, figuring she must have been in on the whole thing too, and may even know where to contact her mother.

Kelly wept for joy when she heard of Artie's reprieve. He was touched by the genuineness of her feelings for him. It made him think of his own kids. Funnily enough, they hadn't crossed his mind until now. Had they known? Had they cared?

But then why should they? He was the bad guy who'd abandoned their mother and left her to marry a Wall Street banker who brought them up in luxury. What was it to them if their biological father lived or died? He put them out of his mind and concentrated on his own life: Arthur J. Fleischman, the man who was back from the dead – professionally and personally.

He took a cab back to the house and picked up his car. On the way to his office he called Caspar Grenville to apologize for having missed their meeting. Caspar wasn't home, so he left a message with his wife to say he would explain later what had happened. He knew that Caspar would understand.

In the office he forced himself to focus on pre-production details, checking technical availabilities, fleshing out a rough below-the-line budget – what the actual physical making of the film would cost as distinct from the fees for stars, the director and script. He tried several times to get Molly on the phone, but there was still no reply. Then, on a whim, he called Ned Ross.

Ned came on the line within seconds. It was still an enjoyable novelty to be able to get through to a studio head with so little humbug. 'How's it going, old buddy?' Ned's cheerful voice came down the line. 'Hey, isn't that great about Greg Warren? He's going around saying he loves this project so much he'd do it for nothing. I told him he's got a deal – his agent's having a shit fit!' Ned roared with laughter at his own joke, and Artie joined in. Then he cleared his throat and adopted a more sober tone for what he had to say next.

'Listen, Ned, there's something I want to tell you before you hear any kind of half-assed rumour from somewhere else – you know what this business is like. I want you to hear it from me first.'

'Go ahead, pal – shoot.'

Artie shot – from the moment that Jack Leonard had pulled up with a smell of burning rubber, to the point where Artie's blood test had been pronounced one hundred per cent healthy.

When he'd finished there was a long silence from Ned Ross. Artie let it run on. It was a lot to take in at one go; Artie knew that better than anyone.

Eventually a strange noise came down the line. A strange, strangled kind of noise, as though something were obscuring the mouthpiece of Ned's phone. It sounded like he'd said something, though it was hard to make out what. It was a monosyllable and it sounded like 'Shit!', but Artie wasn't sure.

'I'm sorry, Ned, I didn't quite catch that.'

There was another strange sound, but this time it was just a kind of gurgle coming from Ned's throat, no words of any kind.

'You okay, Ned?'

Slowly the gurgle became words. 'Listen, I can't discuss this now. I'll get back to you.' Then Ned hung up.

Artie stared at the phone in his hand before replacing it. He thought back over the conversation and tried to make sense of its abrupt conclusion. Maybe Ned Ross was one of those men who simply couldn't bear to talk about illness. Or maybe what scared him was the very possibility that Artie had called to forestall – the start of a rumour that Artie was sick and the studio's prize project rudderless.

He tried calling Caspar Grenville again, but his wife said he was still out. He tried home again, but got his own voice on the answering machine. He was beginning to be worried about Molly. Somehow he had to find her and let her know that he was all right. He tried Kelly; she was out of the office. He called Lars Hanssen's office; an assistant said he was out of town on business. Artie wondered what business. It couldn't be movie business, because Lars was committed to *Conjugal Wrongs* as his next project. He was about to try the house on Mulholland when Becky announced that Joe Cross, Artie's lawyer, was on the line. He sounded sombre.

'I just talked with Ned Ross, Artie. He was in quite a state.'

'Joe, there's no problem. Everything's okay. I'm not sick.'

'I'm afraid you don't understand, Artie. I'm afraid there is a problem.'

'What problem? What problem is there, Joe?'

'Artie, I'd rather not do this over the phone. Can you come by the office?'

'What's wrong with the phone, Joe? Half the business in this town is done over the phone. You got something to tell me – tell me now.'

'I'm just trying to make it easier for you, Artie. But if that's what you want ... I'm afraid there's no deal. The studio isn't going to make the picture.'

Artie felt the air go out of his body as though somebody had landed a blow. It was a sensation with which he was familiar, something that came with the territory in a business of ups and downs, manic highs and desperate lows. But this was hard. This was the worst yet. There had been no disappointment quite this brutal in his whole professional life.

'Okay, Joe, let me just make sure I'm getting this straight.' Unconsciously he was positioning himself in his chair, feet apart and planted firmly, like a man about to absorb the shock of a crash landing. 'You're saying the studio is backing out of the deal to make *Conjugal Wrongs*? Why?'

'They're not backing out, Artie. There never was any deal.'

'I don't get it. It was all agreed.'

'I wish you'd come and talk this through face to face, Artie.'

'Fuck face to face!' Artie exploded. He ran a hand across his eyes which were stinging with something wet. He felt humiliated. He swallowed hard to keep the pain out of his voice. Hide the pain, turn it into anger, threaten to sue, punch, kill – anything! – just hide the pain, never let them see how much it hurts. 'What the fuck's going on, Joe?'

'Artie, I have to talk to you. I can't do it like this.'

'What can't you do, Joe? You can't tell me the truth?'

'No, Artie, I can't.'

'Fuck. I'll be there in twenty minutes.'

It was the longest twenty minutes Artie had ever driven, and it turned into an even longer half-hour because traffic was backed up the whole of Santa Monica from Burton Way to Wilshire. He called in to say he was on his way; then he called Molly and left another message.

At last he stood in Joe's office on the fortieth floor of a Century City skyscraper. The place was dark-panelled and had heavy furniture, which contrasted strangely with the floor-to-ceiling windows on two sides of the room. It was like being in an old country club and a fish tank at the same time.

'You're sure you won't have a drink, a cup of coffee, anything?'

'Just talk to me, Joe. That's what I'm here for.'

Joe Cross was trim, slightly more than average height, with thick dark hair greying slightly at the temples. He'd lost a little weight since his wife died of cancer two years earlier, and it made him look younger than his fifty-six years.

'I have to tell you, Artie, it was the worst thing that had happened to me since Anne-Marie was diagnosed. Molly called me in a terrible state and said she'd just heard from Jack Leonard that you had only two months to live, three at the outside. It was a few days after you'd had your check-up, last Friday. You'd just submitted *Conjugal Wrongs* to the studio, they were reading it over the weekend. Molly and I talked about it, and I made a call to Ned Ross.'

'Oh, Christ!' It was a low moan, little more than a whisper, as Artie began to see what was coming.

'If they liked the script, fine. If they didn't, it was only a question of playing the game for a short time. What harm could it do? Ned owed you, Artie, from way back.'

Artie was sitting on the edge of a deep sofa, his head in his hands. 'What about Lars Hanssen? What about Greg Warren?'

'People have their reasons. You once did a favour for some kid Greg's fond of. Lars . . . I don't know . . . Maybe he owes Ned.'

'Christ!' Artie said again. This time it was barely audible. Then he looked up at Joe. 'What about my kids? Did you talk to Steven and Jane?'

'I got Steven in Boston. Jane was on tour with the orchestra, but he tracked her down. They said whatever we decided was okay by them.'

Artie let this sink in a moment. Whatever their stepmother and some lawyer decided was okay by them. All Artie could think was, how could he have been a better parent? He knew he should have in some way, but he didn't know what way. He just knew he should have been.

'Tell me, Joe,' he went on, his voice breaking slightly, 'what was going to happen when I got sick? What were you planning to say, all of you? "Gee, Artie, what a bummer, dying just when you made the biggest score of your life"?'

'You were never going to know how sick you were. Jack Leonard said that when this thing kicks in you go inside days. He and Molly had it all planned that you'd go to the hospital thinking you just had a virus. You'd never know what happened.'

Silence. Then: 'Joe, isn't there some law says a doctor has to tell the patient the truth about his condition?'

'They did it because they love you, Artie. We all did.'

'ISN'T THERE SOME FUCKING LAW?!' Artie screamed.

'No, Artie. There's no law.'

'WELL THERE FUCKING SHOULD BE!'

He wrenched open the door just as a young assistant who had heard the shouting was about to knock and check if he could be of help. Artie thrust him aside and strode through the outer office. Joe chased him, calling out, 'Artie, wait, there's more. We have to talk.'

But Artie was gone. He drove home through Beverly Hills to avoid the traffic, criss-crossing the quiet, lush avenues, across Sunset at Foothill, then the back way to North Doheny. Molly's car was in the drive. He didn't know whether he was glad to see it, or whether he needed more time before facing her.

She had heard him arrive and came into the living room to meet him. He closed the door behind him and they stared at each other across the intervening space. Her face told him that she knew everything; Joe must have called. She spoke first: 'I'm sorry, Artie.'

He studied her expression. She seemed to mean it. There was real regret there. And what else? A readiness to comfort him? Could he bear to be taken in her arms and told it was all right, he was a loser but he was going to live?

'I guess you were right,' he said after a while, his throat dry and gravelly. 'You never thought *Conjugal Wrongs* was much of an idea, did you? I guess it would've always needed some big element to get it set up. My judgement's pretty piss-poor these days, huh?'

She tried to say something but didn't find the words. He watched her twisting a small handkerchief and wondered if she was going to tear it. At last an awkward, sobbing gasp came from

49

her, and she turned from him and went quickly into their bedroom.

After a moment he followed her. She hadn't shut the door, so even before he got there he could see that she was bending over something on the bed. It was only when he got inside the room that he saw she was filling an open suitcase.

'What's going on? Molly?'

She didn't reply, just kept her back to him, shoulders hunched, as though afraid to brush up against the world around her.

Artie looked over the room. The drawers that were open were all her drawers, and the things in the suitcase were all her things. 'Molly, will you please tell me what's going on?'

She stopped what she was doing but didn't turn. 'I can't stay here, Artie. How can I? It's impossible.'

He didn't move. He thought about it for a while, tried to stand outside the whole situation, make sense of it like an objective observer. But what he saw from the outside was no clearer than what he saw from the inside – and yet just as appallingly obvious.

'You're leaving me? Because of what's happened?'

'No, not because of what's happened.'

'But you're leaving me?'

She nodded, her back still to him. He took a step towards her, reached out, touched her shoulder. She pulled away with a perceptible shudder. It was a shock to him that she reacted to his touch like that.

'Molly, I don't understand. I don't understand a lot of things. But this . . .'

She made an effort, turning three-quarters of the way towards him. She still had the handkerchief crumpled in her fingers. It had been there all the time she was taking things out of drawers and putting them in the suitcase. 'It's been going on for a long time, Artie. I've known I couldn't stay since . . . I don't know . . . How d'you know these things?'

'Is it something I did? Something I didn't do? Something I should've seen, something I should've known?' She didn't answer. 'Talk to me, Molly. Tell me something.'

'It's just our life, Artie. Our *lives*. Two lives in the same house, going nowhere. I can't take it any longer.'

'You mean my career. Is that what you mean? I can't get a picture made any more, so I'm not worth living with. Is that the problem?'

'No, Artie. It's not your career, it's you. If you had something to live for besides this stupid business, I'd know who you were. I could relate to you somehow. But you don't. You're nobody except what you do. And now you don't do it any more, I don't know who you are.'

He looked at her steadily for some moments. 'That's what I said – it's my career. My career's in the toilet, and it's taken our marriage with it.'

'No. It's my life. I want a lot of things I haven't got. Not material things, it's nothing to do with money. I've known for a long time I couldn't stay, Artie. It was just a question of when, and how. Then, when Jack told me you were sick, I suddenly didn't have to decide any more. You'd never have to know.'

'So you cooked up this scam to let the bozo die happy. Brother!' Artie turned away, shaking his head slowly. 'That must have made you feel real good about everything, huh? Nobody hurt, no harm done – just one happy stiff in the cemetery.'

That was when he saw the man standing across the living room where he himself had stood moments earlier. He hadn't heard the car pull up or the door open. It was Joe Cross.

'What the hell are you doing here, Joe?' Artie's voice was weary. 'Go home. This is private – all right?'

The rest happened with three looks: three small movements of three pairs of eyes that unmade and remade the world. Joe looked past Artie at Molly. Artie looked at her. She looked at Joe.

'Oh, no . . . !' It was a groan. Artie's legs felt weak, but he didn't want to sit down. Instead he leaned against the door frame and closed his eyes. When he opened them nothing had changed. 'How long has this been going on? Since Anne-Marie died, or before?'

'Nothing happened till long after Anne-Marie died. Six months, more.' There was a note of righteous indignation in Joe's voice that made Artie smile in spite of everything. At least it felt like a smile from his side. He had no idea what it looked like on his face.

They were both watching him now, waiting for some reaction. The thought went through his brain like a knife. Christ, he said to himself, I'll give them a reaction. I'll give them something to fucking remember me by!

He pushed himself off the wall, sprang across the room with a speed that startled both of them, and disappeared into his den. They heard him lock the door.

Joe looked over at Molly. She saw fear in his face. 'Does he have a gun?' he asked.

'I don't know. Yes, I think he has. He used to have.'

For a moment Joe seemed undecided. 'Listen,' he said, 'I think you should get out of here. Take your bag and go wait in my car.'

'I'm not leaving you,' she told him firmly.

'Please, Molly. He could be dangerous. It'll be better if you're not here.'

'What are you going to do?'

'I'll talk to him. Get your bag.'

'I'm staying here.'

Joe drew breath through his teeth, but didn't argue. It was pointless. He debated whether just to leave with Molly, or knock on the den door and try to reason with Artie. He took a step towards it.

The door swung open violently. Artie stood there, wild-eyed, and with a gun in his hand.

'Artie . . . Artie, get a hold of yourself . . .' Joe's voice shook as badly as the hand he held out to ward off attack. 'Violence is no solution, Artie. Nobody wanted this to happen, but it's just the way things are.'

Artie shifted his gaze from Joe to Molly, then moved between the two, alternately pointing the gun at whichever he wasn't looking at. 'Just get out of here,' he said. 'Both of you.'

They exchanged a look. 'Come on,' Joe said.

Molly hesitated, turning back to the bedroom where her suitcase lay open and half full.

'Later!' Joe hissed at her, exasperation and fear mixed in his voice. He was holding out his hand. She took it and they ran for the door. Artie, watching them, was irresistibly reminded of some childhood fairy tale: Handsel and Gretel running through the dark and dangerous woods. He gave a bark of sardonic laughter. 'Wait!' he ordered them.

They turned and saw the gun aimed at them from the end of his outstretched arm. Molly seemed to accept what was going to happen. There was a sudden passivity about her, no longer even a question in her eyes.

But Joe was nakedly terrified. His voice was high and there was sweat running down his forehead. 'Artie, for God's sake! Don't be crazy! Please, Artie! Don't be crazy!'

Very slowly Artie lowered the gun. He clicked on the safety. He'd known he wouldn't shoot. Why should he? What would it achieve? But he'd had to go to the edge. He needed to know that he'd been to the edge.

'Take this with you. I don't want it in the house.' He tossed the gun across the room and it fell with a clatter on the wooden floor. Joe bent down and picked it up gingerly, as though afraid that it might still go off. 'Now get out,' Artie said. 'Get out and don't come back.'

He didn't even hear the car drive off. Nor did he register that it was growing dark and would soon be night. He pulled a chair up to a window that looked out over the partially obscured view of downtown Los Angeles, and he thought about things.

★

'Artie? Are you there? If you're there, Artie, please pick up.'

It was Kelly's voice coming from the answering machine. Artie stirred and realized it was dark. He had been sitting for almost two hours and had not even consciously registered that the phone was ringing.

'Okay, if you're not there, I just want you to know that I called. I know about what's happened with you and Mom, and I just wanted to check you were okay. I'm home if you want to call me, and—'

'Kelly, I'm here.' Artie had levered himself to his feet and hobbled stiffly to the phone. He arched his back and stretched as he spoke.

'Artie, how are you?'

'I'm okay, Kelly. It's nice of you to call.'

'Jesus, Artie, I feel so bad about this.'

'It's not your fault.'

'Yeah, but . . . I love you, Artie. You know that.'

'I know. I love you too, Kelly.' As he spoke the words, he realized how much he meant them. People said they loved each other too often to mean it – especially in California. It was something to do with the endless psychobabble, the constant but shallow self-analysis in which they all lived; 'I love you' wound up being used as a plaster to stick on relationships where you'd successfully scratched the problems but didn't have time to get down to the truth. It was a jolt to find an occasion when the words exactly fitted the sentiment.

'We've come a long way together, big guy. I'm not going to let you go now.'

He swallowed hard to get rid of the lump in his throat. 'Me too,' he said. Kelly had been only five years old when he'd married her mother. Since then Artie had served as both a barrier and a conduit between Kelly and her mother, depending on what one or the other felt was needed at the time.

'I don't like to think of you up there on your own,' Kelly was saying. 'I could come by. Or we could go out and get some dinner – it's not so late.'

'I'm all right, truly. I'd rather be on my own. I mean, I'm grateful, but . . .'

'I understand. But call me if there's anything you need – promise?'

'I promise. Oh, Kelly, there is one thing. Christ, I've only just thought about it – no wonder writers bitch about how badly they're treated in this town. Somebody better tell Mike what's happened.'

Mike Swift was Kelly's client, the writer whom Artie had hired to do the screenplay of *Conjugal Wrongs*.

'That's okay, he understands.'

There was something in the way she said it that tipped him off.

The silence that neither of them broke for a few seconds was enough to confirm it. 'He was in on it, wasn't he?' Artie said eventually.

She sounded embarrassed. 'Artie, he did the best he could with the idea. It's a good idea, and it's a good screenplay. But they don't want movies like that any more. They say they do, but it's not true. They talk about Gable and Lombard and Hepburn and Tracy, but when it comes down to it they pay an Austrian weightlifter fifteen million to play an android.' She was silent a moment. Then: 'I'm sorry, Artie. I'm sorry we lied to you. We meant well, but I'm sorry.'

'Don't be,' he said. 'It's kind of a tribute in a way. I feel flattered. I guess it made things easier for your mom and Joe, but it was nice of Ned Ross to go along with it.' He paused. 'There's only one thing I don't understand. I can kind of see why Greg Warren went along, and Caspar, of course – Caspar's a mensch. But why Lars Hanssen? I mean, what the hell difference did it make to him if some producer he'd never heard of died happy or not?'

She hesitated before answering, then seemed to make a decision. 'D'you want the truth? Dumb question – of course you do. Okay. When Hanssen heard what was going on, he said it was the funniest idea for a movie he'd heard in years. He played along in return for a development deal at the studio. Mike's already working on the first draft – about a guy who doesn't know he's dying.'

The silence lengthened as Artie looked out into the night. The thump of a helicopter came and went overhead.

'Artie? You still there?' The sound of her voice was suddenly very close and intimate in his ear.

'Yeah, I'm here. I was just thinking ... isn't this business something?'

'Artie, if I may presume to give advice to an experienced old warhorse like you, it's only because I'm quoting something you once said to me. D'you remember when I told you that I wanted to go into the business? Mom wasn't too happy, but you and I talked a while, and then you said, "Well, kid, if that's what you want, go ahead. But always remember one thing: the hours are long, but it sure beats work."'

★

Ever since he turned forty, Ted Long had been wondering when the mid-life crisis was going to hit him. He had seen signs of it in some of his friends as much as five years ago; either that, or the mistakes they'd made as younger men were coming home to roost. Dan and Harry, for instance, had both married for what Ted considered the wrong reasons: Dan for lust and Harry for money. It was inevitable that those relationships would break down in time. Maybe that's all the so-called 'crisis' was – a forced adjustment to realities you had tried to ignore.

Ted didn't claim to have made anything special out of his life, but he knew that here and there he'd made some crucially right choices. He loved Linda in a way that, if anything, improved with the years. She was as attractive to him now and after four kids as she had been that night he first saw her in Greenbaum's Bowling Alley twenty years ago. She still looked ten years younger than she was – or had done until four days ago. Now she sat by his bed in the hospital and held his hand, looking at him with the dark-ringed, staring eyes of shock.

'What was the guy's name again?' Ted asked her.

'Fleischman. Arthur Fleischman.'

'I don't want to see anybody.'

'Sure, okay.'

'What does he want from me, anyway?'

Linda shrugged vaguely, her blank gaze wandering off down the length of his bed and over the monitoring machines alongside it, seeing nothing. 'I don't know. I just told you what he told me – that he'd like to come visit you.'

In fact, the man in the expensive-looking suit, who had called on the phone and then stopped by the house to see her, had spent about an hour gently asking questions and finding out all he could about the family. Artie could tell that she wasn't taking anything in, and his heart had ached for her. The three kids who still lived at home had been at school. He had listened to her soft voice against the casual sounds of the suburban neighbourhood.

'He seemed like a nice man,' Linda said, straining to remember something of their conversation and feeling strange that she couldn't. Ted felt an unbearable pang of sorrow for her; any way you looked at it, this whole thing was worse for Linda than for him. He didn't even feel sick yet, not really. A little weak, but nothing more. And they had told him that when it happened it would be fast. He gave her hand a squeeze.

'Okay,' he said. 'If you like him, tell him I'll see him.' She returned the squeeze and managed a faint smile. For some reason she had liked Mr Fleischman. Whatever it was he had said, it had seemed to come from the heart. He had been a brief, companionable presence in a painful time.

Two hours later, Ted Long was looking at the shortish, dapper man with the slicked-back thinning hair and the thoughtful eyes who sat where Linda had been sitting. The man seemed a little uncomfortable now that he was actually there.

'Why don't you tell me what you want, Mr Fleischman,' Ted began, breaking the silence. 'I know the hospital mixed up my records with yours for a couple of days, but that hardly makes us brothers. How did you find out my name, anyway?'

Artie smiled apologetically. 'I greased a couple of people. The hospital was afraid I was going to bring a suit, but as a matter of fact I don't think that would be very easy in the circumstances. How about you? Have you thought about it?'

'My union lawyer said it was a possibility, but it could drag on for years. That wouldn't be any help to Linda. Anyway, I hate lawyers.'

'You and the human race.' Artie gave a nervous smile. 'No, you're right – I don't think lawyers are going to do us any good.'

'So – why are you here? My wife says you're a producer. You going to make a movie about this, or what?'

'Hell, no.' Artie gave a nervous laugh. 'To be honest, I don't know why I'm here.' He paused. 'I guess it's got something to do with coming to terms.'

'With what?' Ted's eyes were hard, unimpressed. 'I'm the one who has to come to terms with it, not you. You're a lucky man. You're off the hook. That must make you feel good.' Bitterness built in his voice as he spoke.

'No, it doesn't make me feel good.'

'Well, it should!' Ted was openly angry now, shouting. 'If going on living doesn't make you feel good, then fuck you!'

Artie sat in silence a moment, humbled. Then he began, tentatively: 'I just, for some reason, thought I should come here. It wasn't a rational thing. I just felt that, I don't know, fate or something had made some kind of connection between us. I guess I was wrong. I'm sorry. I've intruded on your privacy.'

He got up and started for the door. Ted Long watched him, trying to make sense of the warring emotions going on inside him, and still oddly fascinated by this man from Hollywood who'd so much wanted to come and see him, then had nothing to say when he did.

'Wait a minute,' he heard himself say abruptly, his tone changing from anger to weary resignation. 'I shouldn't have said that. You didn't have to come here. I think I know what you mean. I think I'd have felt the same if it was you. Only I'd have been scared to go near a Hollywood producer.'

Artie turned. 'It isn't as impressive as it sounds.' He went back to his chair and sat down. 'Tell me, Mr Long, what do you do? Your wife said something about firefighting.'

'I run a warehouse. We make – I mean the company makes – firefighting equipment. Everything from domestic extinguishers to emergency foam for airport runways. Not as exciting as the movie business.'

Artie made a self-deprecating gesture. 'It's just a business, like any other.'

'Tell me some of the movies you've made. Maybe I've seen some.'

It was the inevitable question, the moment when Artie braced himself to reel off his mediocre list of modest hits and near-misses. Most people had never heard of them, and Ted Long was no exception, although he did remember that his kids had liked *Cash and Carrie*, and he himself had seen about half of it once on television. The film had, however, registered in his consciousness as a hit, and it lent an added lustre to the man who was sitting by his bed. 'I'm impressed,' he said.

Artie felt a little glow of satisfaction. It was more than just his ego being stroked. In some odd way that he would never dare put into words, not even to himself, he was giving this man's death a touch more meaning than it would otherwise have had. Ted Long was not, as it were, dying in place of a nobody.

But no, he must not think such thoughts! They were absurd, and they made him, Artie, even more absurd than he already was. He must make amends at once.

'I guess you've heard of Greg Warren, haven't you?'

'Who hasn't?'

'And Lars Hanssen?'

'That Swedish guy? Yeah, I saw his last picture. It was funny.'

'I've just been having meetings with them both. We're talking about a project together.'

'Sounds like that should be a hit. I'm sorry I won't see it.' Ted fell abruptly silent, staring straight ahead into something he still couldn't relate to even when it faced him like a wall.

Artie shifted in his chair. He suddenly knew what he was going to do. It had crossed his mind, but in the way that a million things cross your mind all the time and you know you'll never do anything about them. Fantasies. But suddenly he knew with absolute certainty, though without having the first idea why, that he was going to make this a reality.

'How about if I give you a piece of it?'

'I don't understand.'

'A piece of the picture.'

'Why would you do that?'

'Like I said – I feel some kind of bond between us. At least it would be something for your family. What d'you say?'

Ted Long was staring at him with something between suspicion and incomprehension. 'It's your money, Mr Fleischman, to do anything you like with.'

'Call me, Artie.'

'Ted.'

Automatically, impulsively, they shook hands, not lowering their gaze from one another. 'Looks like we have a deal, Ted,' said Artie.

'Are you for real?'

'I'm here, aren't I?'

'How do I know you're not crazy?'

Artie laughed. 'You'd better hope that I am.'

Ted still looked at him, running through the possibilities in his mind – anything rather than accept that this could really be happening. 'How much would we be talking about here?'

'Hard to say.' Artie pushed his chin out and tipped his hand, palm down, this way and that. 'Depends how well the picture does.'

'Give me a ballpark figure.'

Artie made a quick calculation. There was an absolute limit to the amount of money he had to play with. After selling the house and settling half the value on Molly – not only was that California law, but she had a right after all these years, and he wasn't going to argue about it – and after paying a couple of outstanding but fairly small tax bills, he would probably wind up with around a quarter of a million in his own pocket. That would be a fortune to somebody like Ted Long. It would pay his mortgage and help put his kids through college if they chose to go. That would be good. That would make Artie feel that everything had not been in vain after all.

'Let's say . . .' He pretended to pluck a figure from the air. 'Let's say, just to be fair to everybody else, which I have to be . . . Let's say we agree on two per cent of net.' In Hollywood, net profits was a euphemism for nothing. Studios routinely manipulated their books so that even a smash hit never showed any net profits, everything being magically drained away into mushrooming overheads and other assorted expenses. But Ted Long didn't know that. Ted Long didn't even know there would never be a film; at least, not one that Artie had anything to do with.

'How much would that come to?'

Artie gave a little shrug, as though hazarding a shrewd professional guess. 'Around a quarter of a million.'

Ted's whistle was long and low. 'You know, Artie,' he began, 'it's kind of hard to say that anything good has come out of all this – my illness. But if it has it's for my family's sake, and it's you.'

60

Artie didn't speak. He just patted Ted's hand where it lay on the blanket. He was feeling good. Very good. So good that he didn't trust himself. He had to make sure that he didn't screw up. He had to get this right.

'I'll tell you what I'm going to do, Ted,' he said after a moment. 'Just to set your mind at ease so you know I'm not bullshitting you, I'm going to guarantee that money right now.' He reached into his jacket and took out his cheque-book and gold fountain pen. 'I'm making this cheque out to your wife, undated, for a quarter of a million dollars. Of course she can cash it any time she wants, but I'm going to ask her to hold it for about two months.'

'Will the movie be out then?'

'We won't even have finished principal photography, but I'll take the money out of production funds and repay it from the percentage of the profits that I've set aside for you.' He marvelled inwardly at his snake-oil salesman's fluency, and wondered vaguely if he would ever succeed in using it again to his professional advantage in the future. Something in him told him that he wouldn't. In some way that he didn't understand, at least not yet, that part of his life was over.

The perforated paper made a clean ripping sound, and he handed the cheque to Ted with a flourish. Ted looked at it for some moments, his eyes glistening with bafflement and gratitude. 'I don't know what to say, Artie. Goddammit, I just don't know what to say.'

'You don't have to say anything, pal. Not a damn thing.'

★

Artie started to drive back towards Doheny, but after barely a mile he realized that he didn't want to spend the rest of the morning there, and he didn't have anything else to do. He remembered a little café and patisserie on Robertson that he'd always liked the look of whenever he drove past. It reminded him of holidays in France. He found a parking space right by it, fed the meter, and sat down at a table on the terrace. He ordered a coffee and a croissant, and reflected on his situation.

Basically, he told himself, he owned his car, the clothes he wore, and the money in his pocket. That was it. Sum total. Fat zero.

To his surprise, he found that the realization brought him a quite extraordinary sense of liberation. He had no idea what he would do next or how he would live, and he didn't want to know. He looked at the busy passing traffic, at the people coming and going from the interior of the café, some of them carrying brightly wrapped boxes of confectionery that they had bought at the long glass counter.

Then something curious happened. It wasn't disagreeable and it wasn't alarming – partly because it was so like a shot he had seen used often in films. Some part of his consciousness detached itself from the rest of him and hovered above him like a camera on a crane. It proceeded to pull back, effortlessly and slowly, high into the sky, until he saw himself in his mind's eye as just a dot surrounded by the restless fibrillations of the city.

Way down there on the café terrace, beneath the unwavering gaze that was his own and yet not entirely his to control, Artie began to laugh. Quietly at first, and gently. Then more loudly.

People looked.

Remember Me?

The cab dropped us off a few blocks east of Highland, about halfway between Hollywood and Sunset. The entrance to the place I was looking for was up a kind of alley and you could only get to it on foot. It didn't look like any sort of entrance to anything – no lights, no name, just a chipped red-painted door and a brass handle polished by the hands of all the people who'd gone in and out of there over the years.

Not just anybody could get in. It wasn't a private club, but it was run like one. Everybody knew everybody else, and the only way an outsider would ever even find the place was if some regular took them, the way I took Christopher that night.

I pushed open that old red door and told him to watch his step because the only light was a reflected glow around a corner from the main interior. It was late and we must have been drinking for about three hours, so I wasn't surprised that he stumbled and fell over, or that I was a touch slow catching him, but I apologized for that and helped him to his feet. He dusted himself off and said he wasn't hurt. After that I made him walk ahead of me – partly to watch out for him if he fell over again, but also to see the look on his face when he finally saw the whole thing. I'd only given him the vaguest hint of what to expect.

He was impressed. I could tell that from the way he stopped and looked around to take it all in, and said 'Wow' and 'Gosh' and stuff like that. He was English. Nice kid. Well, must've been in his mid to late twenties, but when you get to my age that's still a 'kid'.

I took him by the elbow and steered him over to a booth from where we'd have a good view of the action, such as it was. There were quite a few of the regulars already in, but it wouldn't really get going until later. Christopher slid behind the table and along the polished dark red leather, then sat there swivelling his head this way and that like a ventriloquist's dummy – and with a bit of the same kind of dopey grin on his face.

'This is absolutely amazing,' he said. 'You told me I'd never have seen anywhere like this, and you were absolutely right!'

We'd met in a place way down off Overland where I was ten days into a four-week booking. When I finished my act he came over and asked if he could buy me a drink and chat for a while, and I said sure, why not? He told me he worked for some English newspaper and he was writing a book about Hollywood. I laughed, and told him he'd picked some place to start, hanging out in a low-class joint like that with pot-bellied beer-drinkers, bottle blondes, and maybe the worst band I'd ever worked with. He said the book was more about the fringes of Hollywood than Hollywood itself. There were already enough books about Hollywood, he said, so he was trying to do something different.

We'd talked for a while. Then, at my suggestion, we moved on. I admit to the thought having already crossed my mind that, if I played my cards right, I could find I'd lucked into something useful here. This might be the break that I'd been looking for, him being a journalist with some big English newspaper that maybe wouldn't share the prejudice and bias I'd come up against at home. Anyway, I figured I was in with a chance, and a chance was all I needed.

He didn't even look up at the waiter who brought over the drinks that we'd ordered – martini straight up with a twist for him, beer with a vodka chaser for me. He drank without taking his eyes off the scene, staring over at a corner of the bar where a guy in a white tuxedo stood smoking and generally looking like he owned the place, which in a sense he did. He took a long drag on his cigarette, caught my eye and gave a nod of recognition. He barely even glanced at Christopher, just acknowledged that he was there, and with me. Then he turned to the two big men – I mean *big* – who sat perched on stools a little further along the bar. He watched with a wry smile as one of the men pointed to a shelf behind the barman's head.

'Pass down that bottle, will you, Sacha?' the man said.

'Which bottle, Mr Welles?'

'Right there, just below the light.'

The barman reached up and took down a bottle of wine with a simple, eye-catching label. His gargantuan customer took it and twirled it with surprising dexterity between thick pink fingers. 'One of the best wines in California,' he boomed to the man in the stetson on the stool next to him. 'Check it out, any of the wine writers – that is, the ones who know what they're talking about. I'm telling you, Duke, this is a world-class wine.'

'I believe you.'

'Sold to Mr Wayne. Sacha, a corkscrew if you please.'

'Hey, wait a minute, I didn't—'

'Trust me. You're going to thank me the rest of your life for introducing you to this wine.' He appealed to the man in the tuxedo who was still watching with amusement. 'Am I right, Rick? Tell him.'

'You're right, Orson,' the man in the white tux said, stubbing out his cigarette and showing his teeth under a tight smile that pulled his mouth up to one side.

'But I'm a bourbon drinker, for Chrissakes!' protested the big man in the stetson.

The man called Orson beamed widely through his greying beard and his eyes twinkled wickedly. He leaned forward and patted his companion on a massive knee. 'Think of your friends,' he said.

Christopher laughed and slapped the table with the flat of his hand. I reached out and stopped him doing it again. 'This isn't a show,' I said. 'Watch by all means, but don't treat it like a show. They don't like that. Now sit back, relax – let's get another drink.' I snapped my fingers and the waiter headed over, round pink face wreathed in smiles under a cap of snow-white hair.

At a table across the room a puffy-looking guy with a bulbous nose and eyes that peered out through folds of flesh nudged his companion. 'You see that?' he said in a high, wheezily sing-song voice. 'Orson just conned Duke into buying another bottle of that Cabernet that he drinks by the barrel.'

A broad-shouldered man with glossy dark hair and a trim

moustache followed the other's gaze. An eyebrow twitched in amusement and his lips parted over perfect, pearl-white teeth. 'Son of a bitch did that to me one time. And that stuff's not cheap.'

'Orson's a magician,' wheezed the smaller man, and drained his glass. 'One night I sat across from him at dinner and watched him spinning some unlikely yarn to a woman next to him, keeping her enthralled while he stole the food off her plate because he'd finished his own. She never suspected a thing. That's why I've always said he should have run for Congress.'

His companion chuckled and winked at the man in the tuxedo by the bar. Then he caught the eye of the waiter who had just brought the drinks over to our table and said, 'Same again for Mr Fields and me.'

'Right away, Mr Gable,' came the cheerful response in Hungarian-fractured English.

'Isn't this something?' Christopher was saying, more to himself than to me. 'Isn't this abso-bloody-lutely something?'

There was a movement in the corner of the room where we'd entered, and a shimmering blonde crossed over to a table where a man awaited her – a man with dyed hair parted in the middle, wire glasses and a greasepaint moustache. He was smoking a cigar, deep in thought, with his chin resting on one hand. She began to pull back a chair, then stopped when he did not move.

'I thought a gentleman got up when a lady joined him,' she said in a breathy voice that was more playful than reproachful.

The man glanced up at her and removed the cigar from his mouth. 'A gentleman only gets up to go home to his wife,' he said. 'Sit down and have a sarsaparilla. Garçon!' He signalled the waiter, then leaned closer to his companion and, lowering his voice, said: 'You see that guy at the bar in the white tuxedo? He thinks he's Humphrey Bogart playing Rick in *Casablanca*.'

The blonde looked toward the bar and then back to the man with the cigar. 'Isn't he?' she asked, with an air of mild surprise.

'You mean he is?' The man with the cigar thought about this for a moment, frowning. 'In that case, I must be somebody, too.' He brightened at the thought, then jabbed his cigar in another direction. 'Hey, look at Duke over there with his nose in that glass like somebody's trying to poison him.'

She looked and gave a girlish giggle. 'He's cute. I really like him.'

'He may be cute, but he isn't too smart. He thinks we don't know he's bald under that stetson.'

She looked at him, puzzled that this man could be so misinformed. 'He isn't. He has his hairpiece on.'

The man with the cigar blinked, drew on his cigar, and blew out a cloud of smoke. 'I have no answer to that. But it reminds me of a story. Did I tell you about the actor who was killed by his wig?'

'Killed by his wig? That's ridiculous. How could anyone be killed by his wig?'

'It blew off in the wind, and in racing to retrieve it before anyone noticed he was bald, he got hit by a location catering truck.'

'So he was killed by a catering truck, not by his wig.'

'Ah, but the truck was being driven by his co-star, who shall be nameless, because to accuse a murderer of murder is bad for business in this business ... Where was I? Oh, yes, the wig business. The best part of the story is that everybody already knew he was bald, but they never let him know that they knew – in the hope that one day his wig would blow off in the vicinity of a catering truck. The man was so vain that when he had to play a bald guy in a picture one time, instead of just taking off the wig he always wore, he made them fit a bald wig over it. On another picture he even—'

An elegantly gloved hand broke his concentration by reaching over his shoulder to tap a cigarette from its holder into the ashtray before him. He placed his cigar in his mouth, drew on it, and looked up.

'You know, Bette,' he said through a haze of blue smoke, 'if you smoke enough of those things, it's a statistical fact that they'll shorten your life by eight days, three hours, five minutes and six seconds.'

'No, darling, you're quite wrong.' Her voice gave a distinctive crack to each word she spoke, and she enunciated as though addressing a whole audience. 'It's not that you live longer by giving up your vices. It just seems longer.'

Her gaze swept to the blonde companion. 'Hello, sweetie, how's tricks? And I choose my words carefully.' She turned in a well-timed swirl of taffeta before any riposte could be launched. A few springy, flouncing steps took her to where a tall man stood, a light already in his hand for the fresh cigarette she had fixed in her holder.

'Why thank you, Cary. How very kind.' She surveyed him with something bordering on amused disdain from beneath arched eyebrows. 'And to think, there are those who claim you don't like actresses – unless they're men in drag.'

'You are right as always, my dear,' he said, lifting her free hand to his lips and beaming her a smile that disarmed all criticism. 'There are indeed those who say that.'

'But you're not still sleeping with that dreadful cowboy actor, are you?'

'Now, Bette, a gentleman never tells – something for which you more than most have had good reason to be grateful.'

She gave a throaty gurgle of amusement and slipped her hand through his arm. 'Darling, I do love you. Now fasten your seat belt and buy me a drink.'

'Ollie,' came a not very discreet stage whisper from nearby, 'if we talked to our wives the way Cary Grant talks to Bette Davis, we wouldn't have any problems any more.'

'You're absolutely right, Stanley,' replied his plump companion with a decisive nod of his head. 'Now why didn't I think of that?'

The smaller of the two men looked puzzled and scratched his scalp as he tried to work out the answer.

Christopher leaned over and hissed a question in my ear. 'These people are fantastic,' he said. 'Who are they?'

'Who do they look like?' I answered.

'It's obvious who they look like. Just like it's obvious who you look like. But you've got an act, you do a show. What do these people do except dress up like their idols? I suppose they do charity appearances, the opening of a new retirement home or something. But they must have day jobs.'

70

I turned my drink on the table and watched the ice clink. 'I'll try and explain something to you,' I began to say, but before I could get started he interrupted me.

'Wait a minute!' He was pointing across the room at the waiter who had served us. 'I know who that is!' His mouth worked soundlessly a couple of times as he strove to recall the name, then he got it. 'It's "Cuddles" Sakall! He was in all those old movies – he was in *Casablanca*. And this . . .' He was looking around now, at the walls, the ceiling, everything. 'For God's sake, this is the set from the movie! This is Rick's American Bar, or very like it. I thought there was something familiar about it at first, but it only just hit me . . . And look, look, over there . . . There's Ingrid Bergman coming in with . . . with Henry Fonda!'

It was true, the place was starting to fill up. I could see George Sanders with Veronica Lake and some redhead I couldn't place at first; then I realized it was Lucille Ball. David Niven came in with Errol Flynn and the whole bunch got into kisses and bear-hugs like they hadn't seen each other in months. Gary Cooper and Marlene Dietrich had appeared at the bar, and over in a corner I spotted Spencer Tracy playing gin with Peter Lorre and Sidney Greenstreet.

Christopher was loving it, sitting there rattling off the names like one of those old-time radio shows – you know that impersonator schtick: 'I went to a Hollywood party, and who do you think I met? Well, look who's coming over this way,' and then they do all the voices.

Radio featured big in my early life. I was a lonely child, too young to be brought up on television, so I listened to the radio a lot. Mainly it was music, 'Grand Ole Opry' and such like, but that's all history. What most people don't know is that I discovered movies on the radio. I used to sit looking out the window at that sad, bleak wasteland out there, and listen to this programme about the week's new movies – and this was before I'd ever seen a movie or even a movie theatre. But I used to listen to those bits of soundtrack that they'd play, and I realized that movies *sounded* different from anything else. There was a kind of space around the words that wasn't there with other things – soaps, variety shows, all that. When you listened to these movie clips you could hear that people were moving about and doing things. When you heard people talk you could always tell whether they were outside or inside, in a big room or a small room, up close or far off. Sometimes you could hear their clothes move when they got up and crossed a room. On the other shows they were supposed to be moving around and doing things too, but you could tell that really they were just standing at a microphone and talking, with some guy in the background opening doors or tapping shoes on something to make footsteps. It never sounded real. But in the movies everything sounded real. More real than real life.

'Of course,' I heard Christopher saying, 'the more you look at them, the more you can see they're just doubles. I mean, look at that guy doing Bogey. I mean, it's close, but it's not him.'

I chuckled. 'Let me tell you, kid,' I said, 'I met Bogey. I've met everybody one time or another. And *nobody* looks like themselves if you look at them long enough. No matter how famous they are, when you get to know them, after a while they start to look maybe a little like somebody you once saw in a movie – but only a little.'

'I know what you mean,' he said. 'And I'm not saying they're not good. They're terrific. I mean, this must be the biggest get-together of look-alikes you'll ever see under one roof. I have to get a photographer in here.'

I looked at him, then looked away, kept my voice kind of casual when I spoke, because I didn't want to scare him off. 'So you think they're just look-alikes, huh?'

'Well, of course they are. I mean what else—?' He broke off because Burt Lancaster was standing right by our booth chatting with a young Joan Crawford. 'That's amazing,' he said. 'Really quite amazing!'

'Haven't you noticed one thing?' I asked after a moment. 'One thing that everybody in this room has in common?'

He looked a little blank. 'Well, they're all movie stars,' he said.

'Something else.'

'Well, they're all . . . They're all *dead*, if that's what you mean. Including you.'

'Right,' I said. 'That's it.' I was looking at him now, smiling. I could see he was relaxed and I wanted to keep him that way. 'So tell me, Christopher,' I said, real easy, like it was no big deal, 'what d'you make of that fact? That we're all dead, I mean?'

Again he looked blank for a second, then brightened. 'Nostalgia night?'

'That's one possibility,' I said. 'On the other hand, suppose I were to tell you that there used to be a studio here, right where we're sitting now, one of the first ever built in Hollywood? Only it got the reputation of being haunted, and after a while people wouldn't work in it any more so they pulled it down. Turned out it was built on some Indian burial ground. It's still there, that Indian burial ground, right under our feet as we sit here. Doesn't that make you feel that maybe there could be a little more to what's going on here than just a gathering of look-alikes?'

He looked at me for a moment without blinking. Then his face split into a grin. 'Hey, these are the first ghosts I've ever met who make martinis this good.' He picked up his glass and drank.

I picked up mine and winked over the rim, letting him off the hook. But I'd had him for a second there. I'd really had him. Maybe it was going to be easier than I'd thought.

'The curious thing is,' I heard him saying as I drained my glass, 'that of all the people in here, you're the one who's – how can I put this, not wanting to cause offence, you understand – least qualified.'

I didn't know whether to spit out, chew or swallow the piece of ice I'd got in my mouth. It wasn't that I was upset. On the contrary, I was encouraged. He was getting to the point before I'd barely started leading him to it.

'I made thirty-three movies,' I said, casual and matter-of-fact. 'That's more than some people in here. It doesn't necessarily make me a movie star like Bogey or Wayne, I agree. But I was big.'

'I'm not questioning that you – he – was big. In fact huge. But movies aren't what he was really known for – d'you know what I mean?'

He waited for me to respond, but when I didn't say anything he went on. It was obvious that the alcohol had scrambled his brains a little. I could tell he was having trouble getting his thoughts into focus. He planted his elbow on the edge of the table and spread out his fingers, opening them and closing them as he spoke, as though he was constantly catching something but letting it go again because it wasn't what he wanted.

'I mean, what he really was, really, was a *phenomenon*. I mean, almost the last thing people think of in association with Elvis is . . . movies. Don't you agree? I mean, they think of music, of rock and roll, of . . . God, I don't know . . . T-shirts with his picture on them, the whole . . . you know . . . *thing*.'

Again I didn't say anything, just nodded in a way that suggested I was taking in what he said, but neither agreeing nor disagreeing.

'I mean,' he said, 'he was just the King. He was . . . Elvis!'

'Yes,' I said. 'I was the King.'

'And by the way,' he said, almost as an afterthought, 'you do him brilliantly. I mean that act of yours – really good!'

Inwardly, I was wondering to myself how I was going to handle the next step. It was tricky, and I had to be careful.

'Of course,' he went on, ' – and this isn't meant to be a criticism or anything – as far as looks go, you're older than he was. Though in fact, in a funny sort of way, that adds to it. It makes you more like, you know, more like he might have been now, if he'd lived.'

'Well,' I said, hitching myself around slightly to look at him full face, 'that's not all that surprising considering that . . . I'm him. I am Elvis.'

He laughed. 'Yeah, sure. I know. Of course you are.'

I didn't say anything. Just looked at him. For a long time. Then repeated, very quietly, 'I *am* Elvis.'

This time his laugh was a little less sure. 'Come on . . .'

I kept my eyes on his, didn't even blink. I was willing him to see the truth. 'I *am* Elvis,' I said again.

He looked back at me for quite a while, not saying anything. There was something in his eyes, a certain apprehension, that hadn't been there before. But there was interest, too. I could see it. He sensed a story.

'That's the big difference,' I said, 'between me and all the other people in this room. They're all dead, but I'm not.'

His eyes widened very slightly. I checked myself, taking care not to go too fast. I reached out and touched the sleeve of his jacket where his arm lay on the table. I felt him jump, but he didn't move.

'Look,' I said, 'for all I know and all you know, these people in here could be the ghosts of the real thing, or they could be look-alikes. What I'm trying to say is that I'm neither. I'm not dead, and I'm not somebody else. And I want to tell you my story, because you may be able to help me. I'd like that. I'll be honest with you, Christopher – I could use a little help.'

He didn't interrupt, and he still didn't take his eyes off mine. They were getting wider. I had his attention and the rest of the room was forgotten.

'I didn't die in '77,' I said. 'I'll skip the details for now – let's just call the whole thing a misunderstanding. The man they buried was not me. I will say no more than that. At the time of my so-called death, I was actually in hiding. All those stories about me being seen around the country, working in some drugstore or travelling on a bus – they were true, some of them. I had to go into hiding and use many different names all for reasons which I will describe in detail at some future time. I will just say for now that there was a conspiracy of great and amazing dimensions of which I was the victim. The main point of this conspiracy was to persuade me that I was not the person I knew for a goddamn fact I was! By the way, I didn't used to swear. That's something I've picked up with the accumulated frustration and bitterness over the years.'

He still didn't take his eyes off mine even when Cuddles took our empty glasses and replaced them with the refills I'd discreetly signalled for. I raised mine in the gesture of a toast. Christopher didn't do anything, just kept on staring at me, waiting for me to continue my story.

'Cutting to the chase,' I said, 'it became obvious after a few years that the conspiracy had run out of steam and fallen apart. So with the threat over, I decided it was time to resume my rightful place in the world and pick up the threads of my life. Naturally I imagined that there would be some celebration at this news – among the fans of course, but especially among those people who'd been most near and dear to me.'

I broke off to shake my head in resigned sadness, and take a sip of my drink.

'What I found was something I could never have imagined in my wildest dreams. The ranks had closed against me. I found myself frozen out of my own life! Elvis was officially dead, and that was the way people wanted him to stay. Nobody was willing to even listen to me. I tried to get them to take blood samples or fingerprints or any of the things that would prove who I was, but they wouldn't. Family, agents, doctors, lawyers, managers, friends – they all turned their backs on me, claimed I was some kind of nut. Now I'm not going to say anything about that, but you have to ask yourself what their motives could be for doing something of that kind, and I'm pretty sure a smart young man like you could come up with a plausible explanation without too much trouble. Sometimes a legend is more valuable dead than alive – you know what I mean?'

The look he gave me – sidelong and knowing – convinced me that he understood what I was trying to tell him. I returned a conspiratorial wink.

'I knew you'd get the point,' I said. 'And now you see why I need somebody like you, with influence on a big newspaper, an *English* newspaper that's independent of all the conspiracy in this country to keep me dead. You see why I feel fortunate that I ran into you tonight.'

There was no question but that he was mindblown by what I had told him. He tried to speak, but words failed him. He just spluttered something I couldn't make out, but I could tell that he was sincerely moved.

'I'm glad that you can appreciate the dreadful irony of my position,' I said. 'I mean here I am, the real thing, forced to make a living as my own look-alike. Having to work in two-bit clubs like that one you saw me in tonight as an Elvis impersonator. I mean, this thing has reached ridiculous proportions. Why, I've entered more Elvis look-alike contests than you've had hot dinners – and I've never once come in better than third! Can you believe that?'

He spluttered some more, sympathetically.

'Why,' I said, 'it's reached a point now where the only place that I can be myself is here, with all these people who think I'm one of them! Now I'm going to level with you, Christopher. I don't know whether the people in this room are goddamn martini-drinking ghosts, or whether they're a bunch of jackass nobodies pumping gas by day and working stag nights, smokers and Shriners' conventions in their time off and on weekends. Furthermore, I don't give a flying fast fuck! This is a place where I'm treated like who I am instead of like a piece of shit. What I want, and what I need, is for the outside world to do the same. Then maybe I can finally get back where I rightly belong and lay claim to what is mine.'

I looked him straight in the eye now, and moved my face a tad closer to his. 'Christopher,' I said, 'I believe you are the one man who can help me achieve that goal.'

He took a pull on his drink, but it must have gone down the wrong way because he started coughing. He'd turned white and, frankly, didn't look too good. I clapped him gently on the back.

'You okay?' I asked.

He nodded quickly.

'Listen to me,' I said, keeping my hand on his shoulder and trying to create a sense of intimacy shared just between the two of us. 'I'm talking from the heart, Christopher. Do you know the word "yearn"?'

He nodded again. I took hold of his wrist with my other hand, applying gentle pressure – just enough to impress on him the importance and sincerity of what I was telling him.

'It's a beautiful word, "yearn",' I said. 'And a sad one, too. That's what I do, Christopher. I yearn. For what's mine. For who I was and who I should be. For what I should have. I yearn.'

I looked into his eyes, and I do believe I saw tears in them. Or something close. I let go his wrist.

'Listen,' I said, 'why don't we get out of here, go some place we can talk more quietly?'

'Well, I . . .' His voice was hoarse, but he looked at his watch, so I knew what was on his mind.

'Where are you staying?' I asked him.

He named a hotel in West Hollywood, not far from where we were.

'No sweat,' I said. 'We'll get you a cab back there later. Right now, I want to take you to where I live, because I got some stuff there that'll blow your mind.'

'You mean drugs?' He looked wary.

'Hell, no. Memorabilia. Stuff that'll prove I'm who I say I am – prove it, I mean, to any decent, open-minded individual like yourself. From there on the information's yours to do with what you will.'

'Well, look . . . perhaps tomorrow . . .'

'I'm ten minutes from here, fifteen outside, straight down the freeway and off at—'

He cleared his throat and started to say something, then seemed to change his mind. 'If you'll excuse me,' he said, 'I have to go to the bathroom . . .'

'Sure,' I said, taking my hand off his shoulder as he slid out of the booth. 'It's back there, near where we came in. Try not to fall over this time – okay?'

He gave a kind of nervous laugh, then added: 'Oh, look here, let me pay the bill – get the check, I mean.'

I told him not to worry about it.

'No, really,' he said. 'I can put it on expenses.'

'Hey, listen,' I said, and winked. 'They're ghosts. Your money's no good here. You haven't even been drinking – you just think you have. Soon as you're outside you'll find yourself stone sober, and we'll have to go get drunk all over again.'

He hurried off, holding himself in some peculiar stiff way that seemed to help him keep a straight line.

A few moments later I was waiting for him in the little vestibule by the exit. From where I stood I could see the door to the men's room. Eventually it opened a crack and his face appeared, but as soon as he saw me he stopped.

'Just . . . just a moment,' he said. 'I forgot something.' Then he stepped back and shut the door.

Forgot what? His pants? To flush the toilet? Sounded peculiar to me. I hoped I hadn't misjudged him. I'd be very upset and disappointed if I had.

There was a crash, like something breaking. I went over and pushed open the door into the men's room.

Sure enough, a window high in the wall over one of the stalls was open. The cover of the cistern lay smashed on the floor where he must have dislodged it climbing out.

I pulled myself up to see if there was any sign of him. I don't know if I intended to go after him or not at that point. Truth to tell I was more hurt than angry. I'm not normally a violent man, but I felt betrayed.

At first I couldn't see much. It was pretty dark out there. Then I saw something move. He was trying to climb a wire fence that separated the back lot of the building I was in from the next one. He was having trouble getting over. It was pretty high – maybe eight feet. Several times he tried to swing himself over the top, but he couldn't make it. I could hear him grunt; it must have been painful.

Finally he got over, but his jacket snagged. He tried to get out of it so that he could climb down, but he didn't make too good a job of it. In no time he was snagged worse than ever, hanging helpless from the fence like a prisoner on some medieval dungeon wall.

I don't remember leaving the building, but all of a sudden I found myself outside in the open air, walking down that empty, silent alley. The only sound was a hum of traffic in the distance the only light the reflection of the city from the sky. We were in a dark, deserted no man's land with nobody to see us – myself and this man who had just delivered me a profound and humiliating insult.

It was obvious that he thought I was crazy, a pathetic hanger-on of fame, replacing my own lack of identity with that of an icon. It was also obvious that he didn't know the first thing about fame. Fame doesn't change people, only the way other people look at them. I know this from what happened to me. I was a lonely kid, but suddenly, through fame, that loneliness was turned into something else. It became a kind of privacy, something that everybody wanted to break down. Instead of being outside everybody else's world, I was suddenly the centre of theirs. That too, let me tell you, has its drawbacks. All of which I would have gladly talked to Christopher about, if he hadn't done this rotten thing.

I stepped over the low wall into the yard of the next-door building. It was the office of a small production company, empty at night. I approached the wriggling mass that was Christopher, hanging there like something to scare the crows off a cornfield. His eyes were on a level just above mine, and they glazed over with fear when he saw me standing right there in front of him.

'Guess you lost your way coming back from the men's room,' I said. I kept my voice low, its tone neutral – which wasn't easy, considering the way I felt inside.

His answer was mostly coughing and spluttering with occasional words coming through in no particular order. I felt in my pocket for the familiar polished wood handle that I knew was there. My fingers closed around it.

'Or maybe,' I suggested, 'you suddenly remembered that you had to be somewhere else. Was that it?'

'Um . . . Well . . . Um . . .'

'You know,' I said, 'I talked to a journalist once before.' I was still trying to keep the emotion that I felt out of my voice. 'She disappointed me, too. D'you want to know how she described me in the article she wrote? "A symbol of the ongoing identity crisis that is Hollywood." That's what she said.'

I paused to let the words sink in, then added: 'What do you think that means, Christopher?'

'I don't . . . I really don't . . . I don't think I . . .'

My fingers were running over the smooth wooden shape in my pocket, feeling for the catch that would release the blade.

'I've only got one question for you,' I said. 'For you personally, Christopher. Just one.'

'Yes . . . Yes, of course . . . What?'

'Who am I?'

'Who? Why, you're . . . You're . . . Elvis . . .'

'Elvis who?'

'Elvis Presley.'

There was an utter stillness between and all around us, as though the universe had stopped. The only sound I could hear was the gathering of a dreadful pain-filled roar within me. It began distantly, then surged upward like volcanic fire until it burst from my mouth in a single word.

'Liar!'

I whipped out the knife and pressed the catch in one clean movement. The long blade snapped into place.

'No! No, please! For God's sake!'

He screamed as I slashed upwards, and then down – making a single neat incision across the back of his pants. There was a ripping sound as he fell from the fence and hit the ground like a sack of potatoes. I didn't try to break his fall. I didn't even move.

By the time he'd freed his arms and struggled to his feet, he seemed to have lost the power of speech. With exaggerated care I folded the knife away, watching his eyes stay on it until I'd dropped it safely in my pocket. Then he looked at me.

'If you come inside,' I said, managing a thin smile, 'I'm sure we can find you another pair of pants – from wardrobe.'

He stared at me as though I were a lunatic, despite the fact that he looked the part far more than me, standing there in his boxer shorts, with his jacket in rags and his hair on end. That's how he was when he turned and started sprinting down the alley toward Sunset, going like a rabbit with a pack of dogs after it.

Sooner him than me, I thought, trying to stop a cab looking like that. Most likely the cops would pick him up. I hoped they'd throw him in the drunk tank overnight.

It had been a close call, but I'd stayed in control. I'd hung on to my dignity and faced down the urge to take revenge for my life on that pathetic, unimportant individual. If ever I let the anger and the pain I sometimes feel take over, there's no imagining what I might do. It frightens me. So I try to rise above it.

As I turned to go back inside, I felt a real pride in that achievement.

I'd remembered who I was.

Scribbler

The plain fact is that most writers believe themselves to be the sanest people in the world. When pressed, some will modestly deny it, but with the knowing smile of one unwilling to discuss a secret with the uninitiated. Others will admit there may be some truth in the proposition, accepting it as a simple consequence of the reflective life. Yet others will be awkwardly divided, knowing themselves with certainty to be the equals of God in wisdom and the higher understanding, while being forced to dismiss the greater part of their professional colleagues as dullards, lunatics and pretentious hypocrites.

As a writer myself, I suppose I come into the second category. You may ask what is particularly 'reflective' about being chief writer on a soap opera, and it's a fair question. But even when all you do is turn the prism of some finite group of everyday relationships, searching for a thus far unexplored perspective to provide a few new episodes, much goes on in your mind that does not go on, I dare say, in the minds of haulage contractors, pharmaceutical salespersons, captains of industry and presidents of nations. All of these latter live more in the world around them than in their own heads; with writers it is, of necessity, the reverse. We plot and we plan, in the darkness of our imaginations, the shadow lives that will live out their time on the screens and stages, and occasionally pages, of the world. If our public does not unhesitatingly suspend its disbelief and swallow whole what we are offering, then we would be well advised to seek another line of work. We have our tricks of persuasion, used equally to reveal truth, expose humbug, or sell frivolity. We are, in some sense, conjurors. And we do not believe, therefore, that we ourselves are easily fooled.

All of which is by way of explaining that nobody could have taken a more sceptical view of the following events, at least initially, than I myself. I would not want you to think that you are in the hands of what is known in the literary trade as an 'unreliable narrator'; what follows is fantastical, but not a fantasy.

I live with my business partner. She is strikingly attractive, smart, ambitious, and a few years younger than me (I am thirty-nine). We met when I became a staff writer on the network's biggest drama series, which was, after four years, finally running out of steam. Claire had been a lowly production assistant when the show began, but by the time I joined the team she had risen to producer. Shortly after my arrival, using that subtle sense of timing that marks out junior executives as the stuff of future legend, she had taken a year off to explore new projects. We didn't go to bed together until a few weeks after that. We'd both sensed for some time that it was going to happen, but only her departure from the power structure in which we were both involved had freed us sufficiently to have sex. We needed to be sure that there was nothing to it except personal pleasure. That having been established, she told me – after our second night together – her idea for a new show.

It was a good idea, but hopelessly underdeveloped. Like most people who are not writers, she had never truly understood the difference between a premise and a story. A premise is what you can describe in two lines in the TV guide to capture your audience's interest; a story is what holds them for however many hours you have to. I worked with her on it, and eventually it was launched as a joint venture.

From the first episode it was a hit. It broke the rules sufficiently to be interesting, yet stayed safely enough within them to be universally accessible. Critics took to it as much as audiences. Within weeks we had an order for a second season and an option on the third, which would guarantee us enough episodes to go into syndication indefinitely and make a fortune. Our lives became gilded with the knowledge that we would never have to work for money ever again. In Hollywood that makes you part of an elite: not the top drawer, but still a smaller group than you'd imagine.

You don't have to worry about your next job, wait for the phone to ring, or pray that somebody important is going to wave to you across a restaurant that you cannot afford to be eating in anyway. I always knew it would be a nice feeling to be out of all that, and I was right. Claire and I began to talk about having a baby, getting married, settling down; her biological clock, she said, was striking eleven, so she had little time to waste. Although I'd been married once in my twenties, I had no children, and the idea of having some was beginning to appeal to me.

We had just wrapped the final episode of the first season when a totally unknown actor to whom we had given the role of chief villain decided that he wanted out. Of course by then he was no longer unknown. His name was Alan Kemp, and he had become a victim of that dizzying spiral of success that only worldwide television recognition can bring about virtually overnight. To his credit, he knew that there was something empty and dangerously transitory in all of it. He had to change gear decisively and soon if he was to capitalize on his sudden fame. Several major movie stars had started out in television, but for one reason or another their careers had transcended its limitations and they had become icons of the big screen – where all TV stars, to their chagrin, know true greatness lies. It was largely a matter of timing, and Alan realized that for him the time to make the break was now.

The character he played was called Clay Granger. Clay had looks, charm, and a dazzling smile. Think of the young Robert Redford in *The Great Gatsby*, if you ever saw that picture. In fact, the character was marginally based on Gatsby. His origins were humble, though shrouded in mystery. He lived in a world of private jets and titled friends; his clothes were made in Europe, and his wines imported from a château he owned in Bordeaux.

In fact he was a psychopath. He'd murdered his business partner, driven his first wife to suicide and his second wife insane. Having got control of her money, he'd set himself up in the investment business in Los Angeles. In the course of our first season he committed massive fraud, slit the throat of an IRS investigator in a dark alley, lost his entire fortune, and made it back tenfold.

Alan Kemp suddenly found himself on magazine covers, talk shows, mobbed whenever he appeared in public, written up in serious editorials as some kind of symbol for the times. It was heady stuff for a man who, only eighteen months earlier, couldn't get arrested in Hollywood.

Neither Claire nor I blamed him for his ambition; on the contrary, we thought that he was right to want to make his move now. We never dreamed, however, that his contract might allow him to do so. But his agent had long had faith in Alan's future – a rare enough thing in itself. Even rarer was the skill with which he had stitched into his client's contract a construction which had entirely escaped the scrutiny of our lawyers as well as the network's. The result was a smokescreen of ambiguity that left us with no actionable grounds for insisting that Alan, in the face of so many offers from elsewhere, return tamely to our fold for a second season. It was good agenting, and will certainly never be allowed to happen again.

For us it was a potential disaster. The security and clout of having a hit show running three, four, maybe five seasons, everything we'd just got used to taking for granted, suddenly looked like being snatched away. We had the choice of replacing the actor, or writing out the character. I tried everything I knew to make a replacement possible: ideas like having a car crash in the opening show, followed by plastic surgery, then the removal of the bandages around show four or five. The sixth show would be the one in which, scar tissue fading with each stroke of the make-up artist's brush, the new actor would make his bid for Alan's mantle.

Claire knew before the network that it wouldn't work. It was corny, the critics would kill us, audiences would laugh. Better to write the character out, make what dramatic mileage we could out of his disappearance, and try to come up with a new character who was sufficiently the same and yet sufficiently different to be – what's the phrase I'm looking for? – virtually identical. It was a tall order. I started making notes for an ex-astronaut accused of child molestation to take his place. And that was when this whole chain of events started to happen.

Most mornings I got to my computer around eight thirty and worked till lunch. On this particular morning I booted up as usual and sent the cursor down my work directory in search of the file still called simply 'Replace', meaning the replacement character I was working on. Like most people who use computers, I couldn't have told you what was in half the files listed without dipping into them to refresh my memory. They were familiar daily landmarks, accumulated over months and years, that I would eventually need again, or finally delete. But on that particular morning one that was unfamiliar caught my eye. It was labelled 'Help!' I glanced across at the two columns on the right, one giving the number of bytes in the file, the other the time that the file was last exited. Strangely, the file appeared to be empty, and the exit was 23:51 the previous night.

I had done a little work the previous night, though I didn't remember it being so late. Anyway, I checked out 'Help!' to make sure it was as empty as the directory said, and it was. Clearly, I must have had something in mind, but it hadn't stayed long. I deleted the file.

Now we flash-forward twenty-four hours. It's the following morning, I'm sitting at my desk, I boot up the computer – and what do I see? 'Help!' is back.

This was particularly strange, because I hadn't been working the night before, and certainly not at two in the morning – 02:07 to be precise, when the file was logged in. Even more strange was the fact that there appeared to be something in the file this time. I retrieved it, and this is what I read:

You can't let this happen. You have to help me out of this mess. I have nobody else to turn to.

Sometimes writers jot down a few phrases that are absolutely meaningless in themselves, but which they know will tug on the strings of memory and bring a complex series of associations tumbling forth. This, for me, was not such a memory-jogger. I knew I had not written those words. True, I was under pressure to save the show; I was worried, maybe even a little panicked, my concentration sometimes fragmented; but I had not written those words.

Casually, without making an issue of it, I asked Claire if she had been using my computer. She said no, as I expected; she had her own office and her own computer. I didn't tell her why I'd asked the question, because I wouldn't have known how to explain. It was baffling.

Let me say something about me and computers: I use them, but I don't understand them. I mean, I understand them in theory. I know that they feverishly manipulate ones and zeros in patterns of mind-bending complexity to accomplish what we want of them. I am not a stranger to words like 'algorithm', 'neural net' and 'biochip'. But on a technical level I am an infant, totally reliant on Bob at the computer store to install my programs, instruct me in how to use them, and sort out my various foul-ups. Without Bob, I would still have nothing more mechanically complex than a pencil-sharpener on my desk. I debated calling him, and decided against: it was too trivial. With great deliberation I deleted the file, made sure there was no back-up copy listed, and got on with rounding out the character of my ex-astronaut.

Flash-forward another twenty-four hours. Not only was 'Help!' once again listed the following morning, but the file was considerably longer than before.

> Whichever way you look at it, you're taking a life – my life. You're doing it without reference to any moral or legal sanction, and you don't even give me a chance to plead on my own behalf. Now that's murder, and according to you, murder's wrong. That's what everybody said when I was accused of it – though, I might add, nobody was ever able to prove anything. But it seems we have a double standard operating here, and that is neither fair nor right.

There was no question whose voice it was, of course. It was Clay Granger. And I don't mind admitting that I was spooked. If somebody was playing games with me, I didn't like it. The other

90

possibility – that I was writing the stuff myself and forgetting about it – was even more disturbing.

That day I didn't get much work done. I called my doctor, who was a good friend, and he found a few minutes to see me before lunch. I laid out the problem: could I conceivably be writing stuff and nor remembering? He checked me over and asked a few questions, chief among which was, 'Been doing any drugs lately?'

'Christ, no Gary,' I protested indignantly. 'All that was years ago. Nobody does that stuff any more.'

'Try doing my job for two weeks and see if you still believe that,' he said drily.

'Well, not me,' I said, sounding a touch more priggish than I liked. Then, more worried: 'D'you think I could be having some kind of delayed reaction from stuff I did when I was a kid?'

'It's possible,' he answered, 'but I don't think it's likely.'

'How about Alzheimer's?'

'There'd be other signs. Roll up your sleeve.'

I obeyed glumly.

'I'm going to give you a vitamin shot and a booster course to be taken orally.' He swabbed my arm. 'This stuff's industrial strength. In a couple of days, you'll feel like a ten-year-old.'

'What if I don't?' I said.

'Let's worry about it then. Maybe somebody's playing games with you.'

'I don't see how,' I said. 'First of all, they'd have to break into the house in the middle of the night, which isn't easy. The only other possibility is Claire – and that makes absolutely no sense.'

The third possibility, after ruling out amnesia or nocturnal pranksters, was one that I was doing my best not even to think about. But there was, finally, no way to avoid it, absurd though it was.

Superstition, by definition, is something that does not go away simply because you know it's nonsense. Persistent 'nonsense' can be a very disturbing thing. I may be a hack scriptwriter, but I make a good living. I went to college, I am by any standards well read, I once had my IQ tested, and I don't want to boast but it was more than adequate. What am I trying to prove with all this? I don't know.

All I know now, and all I knew then, was that I had to be sure about a possibility that I refused to believe in, but which wouldn't go away.

The first step was to isolate my computer so that neither I, in some sleep-walking state, nor anybody else in whatever kind of state could get to it during the night. Accordingly, I locked the door to my office and placed the key in a music box that played 'The Star-Spangled Banner' very loudly whenever it was opened. Claire and I had won it one drunken summer evening at a fair in Austin, Texas, where we were shooting some scenes for the show. I fastened the box with strong adhesive to the top of a wardrobe in our bedroom, so that it could neither be removed from the room during the night nor opened without making enough noise to wake us both up. I took pains to ensure that Claire knew nothing of all this.

I didn't sleep well that night. I felt rather like a child on Christmas Eve: would Santa really come? Would I see him? Would I dare speak to him? Would I find out who he really was?

The morning was both an anticlimax and full of troubling possibilities. I knew that nobody had taken the key to my office during the night, so I retrieved it while Claire was watching *Good Morning America* in her bath, and went to check out my computer. I had taken the further precaution of stretching a fine thread of cotton across the door to my office, thus ensuring that nobody could gain entry either by picking the lock or using a duplicate key, if one existed. The thread was undisturbed.

I booted up the computer, entered my directory – and found no file called 'Help!'

Instead, I found one called 'Helpclay!' I opened it up, and this is what I read:

So now you know I'm here. And I know you know. And I have no intention of letting you off the hook for this responsibility that you seem determined to avoid. You're not God, you know. And you're sure as hell not the Devil. You're just some miserable scribbler hunched over a computer screen, taking orders from anybody who drops a couple of bucks in your lap. You're pathetic! The idea that I'm dependent on a creep like you for my survival makes me want to throw up.

Still, I guess I have to make the best of it. So from now I'm taking charge, and you're going to do what I say.

Otherwise you're going to be very sorry, scribbler!

★

Bob got to the house a little before noon. I did my best to explain what had happened without sounding like an hysterical fool. I told him simply that a file I had repeatedly deleted kept popping up again and I couldn't understand it. He nodded sagely and said something about main directories, pathways and rogue links. At least, that's what I recall. My principal memory is of that awful sense of dread around twenty minutes later when he told me there was nothing wrong with my operating system. He said that what I was describing was impossible; I must have been mistaken.

I knew too much (or too little) to argue. Bob had long since drilled into me the fundamental truth that computers do not make mistakes: people do. I thanked him for coming over and apologized for wasting his time.

'He's a great character, that Clay,' he said, as he was leaving. 'I'm going to miss him.'

I jumped slightly, unprepared for the remark. 'What? Oh, yeah,' I mumbled lamely, realizing that he had read the 'Helpclay!' file and had probably assumed that it was some discarded piece of dialogue from the show.

'I hear Alan Kemp's going to make a movie,' he went on. 'I reckon he's going to be a big star.'

'Looks like it,' I replied. I must have sounded less than ecstatic, because Bob patted me reassuringly on the shoulder.

'Don't feel bad,' he said. 'Remember when Shelley Long left *Cheers* everybody thought the show would go right in the toilet. Instead it ran another seven years, better than ever.'

'I'll bear that in mind,' I said. (It sometimes seems that everybody in this town is an archivist of showbiz trivia.)

When he'd gone, I sat down at the computer and went into

'Helpclay!' again. I don't know what I was expecting to find. A few more lines already added? Words actually appearing as I looked at the screen? My mind raced with unnatural possibilities.

But nothing had changed. That last sentence still hung there, a barely disguised threat: 'Otherwise you're going to be very sorry, scribbler!'

I knew Clay, because I'd created him. Villains are fun to create, much more so than heroes; heroes are a chore. But you would not, on the whole, want to meet one of your own villains on a dark night.

Filled with misgivings, as much about my own rationality as by the thought of what I might be going up against, I decided that I would try acknowledging Clay as a living reality, an independent consciousness in my computer. Hesitantly, I tapped in:

I don't understand how this can be, Clay.

There was a brief pause. I thought at first that nothing was going to happen. But my hands were not moving as a response appeared spontaneously on the screen:

What you don't understand, scribbler, would fill a lot more storage space than this or any other computer has available.

I swallowed, and forced myself to set aside the certain knowledge of how impossible it was that this was happening. I typed:

What do you want ?

Another moment. Then came the reply:

What the fuck d'you think I want? Am I talking to myself here? I told you – I want to stay in the show. I'm having a good time. I have plans. Jesus Christ, scribbler! First I just thought you were an asshole, now I see you're a moron!

I reflected, then responded:

94

Clay, the actor's leaving the show. There's nobody to play you.

His reaction to that was immediate, all three words appearing simultaneously:

Get another actor.

I snapped back, fingers pounding the keyboard:

That's impossible.

Equally abruptly came:

Nothing's impossible.

I responded more slowly, trying to communicate a feeling of conciliation and reasonableness through the gentler touch of my fingertips:

It's a network decision. It's too late.

He shot back:

Talk to them.

I had to laugh aloud at such naivety. I wrote:

That's impossible. Network decisions are irreversible. It's part of their machismo. You of all people can understand that, can't you?

A pause. Long. Worryingly long. I added:

I'm already working on the character that's going to replace you. Everything's been approved.

Another pause, then he responded with:

You know your problem, scribbler? You think like a loser. Which you are.

I did not intend to let him provoke me. I typed in simply:

That is untrue.

His reply was a cold:

Don't say I didn't warn you.

With that he fell silent. I did not like it. I did not trust that silence. I knew him, and I knew what he was thinking. I did not know what he was planning, but I feared it.

And I knew I had to stop him – by any means necessary.

★

The smoke curled up and vanished like an agent's promise in the evening air. I raked the ashes in which I had just burned all my back-up disks. It was a desperate measure, but nothing less would have sufficed. I had to be sure that he was hiding nowhere.

Of course, in a sense he still existed in the tapes of the show, but that was different. The show revealed some aspects of his personality, but not the whole. There were things that I'd been holding back for later use, secrets and surprises that only I knew about. But they were all on file. My files were his birthplace and his nursery. They contained his past and all the permutations of his future. They were his life. (Could it be pure coincidence, I wondered, that 'file' and 'life' were anagrams? Yes, probably.)

I turned to the square, grey shape lying at my feet. Cut off from its lifeblood, electricity, and displaced from its commanding station on my desk, there was an abandoned, melancholy look about my poor computer that, for a moment, made me feel remorse for what I was about to do. But I braced myself, picked up the heavy sledgehammer that I had dug out of my garage, and delivered a devastating two-handed blow.

Splinters of plastic, glass and circuitry flew everywhere, yet still it took a second and even a third blow before I exposed the thing that I was looking for, and which I knew I must destroy as finally as ever Van Helsing slaughtered Dracula. I picked up the hard disk in my fingers and regarded it with fascination: that so much life could lie within its inert form. Then I placed it carefully upon the stone I had prepared, and smashed it to a powder.

Only then did I know that it was over. The evil spirit's sanctuary was no more. Being, as I said before, a primitive in these things, I had never used a modem and I wasn't on the net; nor had I traded disks with other computer users. There was, therefore, no way that he could have escaped. I had given life, and I had taken it away. But I did not feel godlike. I felt frightened and relieved in equal parts.

I would buy a new computer. Bob would install it and set me up with newer, more efficient versions of the programs I had always used. Much of the information I had been storing was now lost for ever, though I had taken the precaution of printing out the files I absolutely had to keep – none of them connected with the character of Clay – and I stacked them alongside my typewritten scripts from pre-computer days.

At last I sat back and recuperated with a glass of Californian Chardonnay, wondering if I would ever understand what had happened, knowing that I could never speak of it to anyone; but strangely confident, for some reason I could not define, that the whole affair was finally over.

What an innocent I was.

★

There was a general agreement between myself, Claire and the network that Clay Granger's demise should take the form of an off-screen suicide. Certain of his guilty secrets would subsequently come to light to explain the event. I wrote the relevant scenes by hand, and had them typed up by a secretary.

One morning, as Bob was showing me how to use my new computer (I told him I had given the old one to an impoverished friend), my phone rang. It was Claire calling from the studio. She said she had just got a call asking if we could have lunch with the president of the network.

Strictly speaking, 'Can you have lunch with the president of the network?' is not a question in any real sense of the word. What it means is, 'Drop everything, because this is more important than your life.' Claire and I duly presented ourselves in the outer office of Ward Podomsky's personal assistant at twelve twenty p.m. precisely, and took our places in the comfortable waiting area until we were bidden forward into the inner sanctum.

Still neither of us knew what all this was about, though Claire told me in the elevator that she had made some discreet calls to find out whose lunch with Podomsky had been cancelled to make way for us at such short notice. It turned out to be Podomsky's own boss, the chairman of the whole damn global conglomerate who was in from New York. This mysterious event was taking on interesting proportions.

It is a fact of life in Hollywood that men who have acquired a certain amount of wealth and power tend to dress in one of two ways. Either they affect the casualness of the youngest recruit to the lowliest job in their mail room – jeans and sneakers, possibly a little designer stubble; or they look as though they've just stepped out of the window of a menswear shop on Rodeo – hair as thick and impeccably groomed as moulded plaster, teeth whiter than nature intended, manicured fingernails gleaming like large pink gemstones. Ward Podomsky's personal style conformed to the latter tradition. His clothes had a strange, unused quality, as though none of them – ties, shirts, shoes included – had ever been worn before.

Podomsky had been in his job for over five years, which, in terms of Hollywood executive turnover, brought him close to being a figure of historic significance. He had stayed the course because he'd made a lot of right decisions – including backing our show and the previous one on which Claire and I had met. We were welcomed with firm handshakes and a sincere smile. He took us straight through to his private dining room, where we lunched on pasta, salad and mineral water. A glass of wine was offered, but it would have been deeply unwise to accept. Occasionally a European could risk it without automatically flushing his career down the toilet, but never any home-grown talent. And two glasses would do it, even for a European.

'Something's come up,' he said, getting right down to business without wasting time, 'that the three of us have to think about very seriously.' To me, this meant he was about to tell us what decision had been made that we were going to have to get behind. But perhaps I was unduly cynical. I munched a lettuce leaf and listened.

'When Alan Kemp announced that he was leaving the show, we all – as you remember – thought it was a disaster. That loophole in his contract was an error that should never have happened. As you know, changes have been made in Business Affairs to ensure that nothing similar happens again.'

Those 'changes' were several abruptly terminated careers. I wondered what Podomsky was leading up to. He didn't keep us waiting.

'The thing I want to ask you both,' he said, 'is what would you think if Alan Kemp wanted to come back on the show?'

I stopped chewing. Claire swallowed, and looked from Podomsky to me and back to Podomsky, too stunned to speak. He continued with his spartan lunch, and filled in the silence.

'The reason I'm talking to you about this and not Tod, is that the suggestion came direct to me from Kemp himself. He called me yesterday. Naturally I've discussed it with Tod.'

Tod Weinberg was head of dramatic series at the network. He made all the decisions in that area except the important ones, which were passed up to Podomsky for a final green light or the big nix.

'What does Tod think?' I heard myself saying.

'Tod thinks like I do,' said Podomsky.

This came as no surprise. Tod liked his job; and, with two ex-wives and five children, he needed it. Claire and I waited to hear what Podomsky thought.

'When Kemp walked out,' he continued, 'we could've offered him two million a show, and he'd still have turned us down. My first thought when he said he wanted to come back was that he was going to want to own the network. But he says not, and his agent confirms it. He's willing to work for not much more than we could have held him to under his previous contract.'

There was a pause. 'I don't get it,' Claire said.

'Nor me.' It was Podomsky speaking. 'I called up Ed Pleskow-itz, who's producing the picture Kemp's supposed to be making at Fox. Believe me, they're plenty pissed off over there – like we were a few months back. They don't understand it any more than we did then.'

'The man's obviously unbalanced,' Claire suggested. 'He never struck me that way. But there isn't any other explanation.'

I, very deliberately, said nothing.

★

Flash-forward twenty-four hours. Alan Kemp took his seat opposite me at our table at Le Dome – the back room to the left as you enter, where you sit when you want to talk uninter-rupted and without being too easily overheard. I had never seen him so nervous, not even eighteen months earlier when he was still awaiting final confirmation that he had got the part of Clay.

'I've made a terrible mistake,' he said as soon as he sat down. 'All I can do is admit it and say forgive me, please!'

The outcome of our meeting with Podomsky had been that I should have this conversation with Kemp alone. To the network, the attraction of having him back on the show was obvious. We had a solid hit which had many seasons of life in it yet. But Podomsky, to his credit, smelt something wrong. So did Claire, who felt we had moved far enough along to put the whole Kemp episode behind us and prove it was the show that worked, not any single actor in it.

For myself, I was more suspicious than either of them, but for my own reasons could not say why. My indecision at Podomsky's lunch had been mistaken for sagacious fence-sitting. I was to report back to Claire, and then Podomsky, who would make the final decision about readmitting Alan to the fold, or pressing on with the ex-astronaut.

100

'Alan,' I said, 'we've gone a long way towards replacing your character. I've written story-lines, we've talked to actors – we've done everything but sign a deal. We need to know – *I* need to know – what's made you change your mind.'

His words came out in a rush. 'It just suddenly hit me that I was being a damn fool,' he said. 'I should never have left the show. But everything happened so fast I didn't know where I was. I guess I got big-headed, and I'm sorry . . . I'm sorry, truly sorry. I know now I'll never in my life be offered a better part than Clay. I don't want to make movies. I don't want to do anything except play this part for as long as you'll have me. Take me back, please! Let's go on like all this never happened.'

'You've got to understand,' I said, picking my way carefully around his obviously deep-felt emotion, 'that we never wanted this to happen either. You remember how hard we fought to keep you.'

'I know, I know.' He passed a hand across his forehead, as though wiping away nervous perspiration.

'If we take you back, we have to be sure that the same thing won't happen again.'

'It won't! It won't! I swear it won't! I'll sign anything you want.'

There was a barely controlled hysteria about his passion that made it futile to demand too much explanation. I made some anodyne promise to consider very carefully, discuss with utmost seriousness, etcetera. It was an effort for him to talk about anything else until the coffee, which we both decided to skip. I paid the bill, and we walked out together, pausing to greet acquaintances at tables on the way.

I think there had been a vague plan half-formed in my mind; but, when the moment presented itself, I acted more on impulse than design. We were waiting on Sunset for our cars to be brought up from the parking lot behind the plaza. Alan had put on his sunglasses and was taking a few bucks from his wallet for a tip. For a moment there was nobody immediately around us. I was about a yard behind him, slightly to one side, watching him. That was when I spoke.

'How did you do it, Clay? How did you get out of my computer and into him?'

He whirled around as though I'd hit him. I couldn't see his eyes behind the sunglasses, but he could see mine. And he knew that I knew. Very slowly, the poised-for-action hunch of his body relaxed. The angry, tight line of his mouth loosened into a smile. He even laughed: that gentle, detached laugh that Clay always used when he was most dangerous.

'Hey, scribbler, that's pretty swift,' he said. 'But what are you going to do? Beat his head in with a hammer, like you did your computer?'

I didn't have an answer. And before I could think of one, his car arrived. He handed over his money and got in. Even though my own car had appeared and the door was being held open for me, I stood there watching him. He gave a casual wave, a broad, self-satisfied and mocking grin.

It was Alan Kemp's car, but Clay Granger who drove off in it.

★

It was easy enough to block his wishes. Bringing him back into the show required a unanimous decision between Claire, myself and Podomsky. The way that I had been manoeuvred, even by Claire, into making the final decision meant that, if the show failed without him, I would be blamed. But that didn't worry me. I was actually becoming convinced that Clay's malign influence would destroy the show, and I was beginning to like my ex-astronaut a lot more. I thought he had a depth and authenticity that Clay didn't have. Clay was a concoction, an assembly of traits and characteristics pulled together from all over. He wasn't centred. There was a hole at the heart of his being. He was a dramatic device, nothing more: a two-dimensional villain, who only got away with his wickedness because we needed to keep him running through the show week after week. But not any more.

Both Claire and Podomsky accepted my view without argument. To my relief there were no reports of violence or hysteria when Alan Kemp was given the news. Perhaps he, or the part of him that was Clay, realized that there was nothing to be done. Would this 'possession', this 'spell', this 'entity' that had somehow migrated from my computer and lodged in a man's brain, would the thing fade now, like a memory, losing its power to influence and control?

I could only guess, but my guess was that it would. I felt in my bones that life was a pretty – how shall I put it? – ordinary affair. That doesn't mean I'm unaware of the wonders of nature or the miracles of science: in my business, 'quantum uncertainty' has become the routine explanation for every bit of showbiz hokum from time travel to flying pigs. But how often do you meet a flying pig outside of fiction or the movies? You see what I mean? I knew that what had happened was real; but I also knew it was an aberration. I felt, deep down, that it had gone away; that it was over.

Once more, what an innocent – what a fool! – I was.

★

Two weeks later, I was up in San Francisco for a seminar on writing for television. It was the kind of thing I did half a dozen times a year at campuses around the country, partly out of a near-superstitious belief that it kept me in touch with 'the audience out there'. It was nonsense, of course; the 'audience out there' would no more attend a writing seminar than sign up for classes in basket-weaving. I and my fellow panellists spent three days answering questions from the usual group of hungry kids and middle-aged wanabes who wanted our jobs and expected our advice on how to get them. Still, we always told them what we could as constructively as possible ('Don't give up your day job till you make a second sale!'), and went home feeling like big-hearted celebrities.

I decided not to stay the night after the final session, and flew back to LA. I picked up my car at the airport and got home around midnight. I had tried to call Claire from my car, but my cellular phone wasn't working for the second time in a month. Claire and I lived at that time off Coldwater, just beneath Mulholland and overlooking Beverly Hills. The house is built on the highest point of the lot, with decks and open living spaces making the most of the view. It is connected by steps to the garage, which is considerably lower than the house and shielded from view by an overhang of rock and dense foliage. I used my remote to open the gates and swung into the drive. My headlights picked out a car parked on the forecourt of our garage. I knew at once whose it was. It was Alan Kemp's.

My first reaction was alarm. Claire knew nothing of his recent state of mind. I blamed myself for not having found some way to warn her. She did not know that Alan Kemp had become only a mask worn by Clay Granger; and that Clay Granger had been prepared to stop at nothing to get what he wanted.

I have never thought of myself as a physical coward, but I wished at that moment that I could lay my hands on a gun. Alan Kemp was a well-built man, and, like most actors, worked out a lot; I wouldn't have chosen to go hand-to-hand with him. Unfortunately, the only weapon in the house was a .38 that I kept in a drawer by my side of the bed. So I snatched up a tyre-lever and crept quietly and quickly up the covered steps to the house. At least, I told myself, I had the advantage of surprise.

In the event, I was the one who was taken by surprise. I don't know how long I hid in the shadows, watching those two naked bodies thrashing and heaving back and forth across the mattress on the main deck of our house. It probably wasn't much more than a minute. I didn't move, I didn't breathe. I didn't make a sound. I was too numb even to think. Eventually, I turned and crept back the way I'd come. I didn't know what I was going to do, or where I was going to go. I just got into my car, and drove off into the night as silently as I had arrived.

★

I didn't blame Claire for what had happened. If the man had been anyone else, I would have been mortified. But this was not a straightforward betrayal, not a time for tears and accusations. Normal emotions played no part here – not in him, not in her, not in me. There was, for want of a better word, some kind of spell at work, and it had to be broken.

104

When Alan Kemp's car pulled into his drive, I glanced at my watch and saw I had been crouching in the bushes for a full three hours. Time, like so much that I normally took for granted, had become unreal. I shifted my weight painfully from one haunch to the other, preparing to straighten up. My fingers groped for the tyre-lever that I had brought with me. I was not planning to hit him with it, but I was reassured by the feel of that length of steel tucked down the back of my trousers and hidden by my sweater.

He got out of his car and crossed to the door of his house. The echo of his footsteps was replaced by the electronic beep of his alarm system as he punched in its deactivation code. I was afraid that he would hear the creaking of my joints, stiff after such a wait, as I came up behind him. But he didn't.

'Hello, Clay,' I said softly. He tried not to let me see that I had made him jump, but I noticed the quick hiccup of his shoulders, immediately suppressed as he recognized my voice.

'Well, look who's here,' he said, turning slowly with an arrogant leer. 'Hello there, scribbler. What are you doing out this time of night?'

'You know, Clay,' I said, taking a step towards him, 'I don't like that word.'

'What word? Sorry, scribbler – I don't know what you're talking about.'

'You know what word,' I said, very calm, very quiet. 'Don't call me "scribbler". I don't like it.'

He looked at me a long time without saying anything; then tipped his head back and gave a slow, deliberate scornful laugh. All the time his eyes stayed fixed on mine, ice-cold, unamused.

If it hadn't been for that laugh, I wouldn't have done it. But it was too much to bear. My hand whipped around and under my sweater to the small of my back – and I don't know how it happened, but the damn tyre-lever slipped out of my fingers and fell down my trouser-leg, hitting the Italian tiles with a loud, metallic ring that echoed for some time in the night air.

What to do? His eyes still held mine, and mine his. I couldn't bend down to retrieve the weapon, because that would have exposed the back of my head to a potentially mortal blow. All I could do was shake my right leg, like a cat that had just stepped in a puddle, to detach the wretched instrument from my clothing.

Suddenly something happened to Clay's face: it became Alan's face, as though the sound of steel on terracotta had somehow brought him back to himself. He looked strangely disoriented for a moment. Then his eyes filled with such sadness and despair that I almost wanted to take him in my arms and reassure him.

'I don't understand what's happening to me,' he said, his voice trembling. 'Help me.'

We went inside and sat across from each other in his vast living room, he in a huge white armchair, I in the middle of an overstuffed white sofa, with pools of strategically placed light dappling the darkness between us. He had bought the place a few months earlier, when he realized just how big a star he was about to become.

He leaned forward, interlaced fingers pressed between his knees. He had already offered me a drink, which I had refused. Now I began to think I should have accepted: the displacement activity would have helped him gather his thoughts. As it was, he faced me unprepared, awkward and unsure of himself.

Suddenly his head slumped forward, and his shoulders started to heave. His voice, in between heart-rending sobs, was a barely audible whisper.

'It's a nightmare. I should be on top of the world, but I'm in hell. I don't know who I am. I'm famous, but I'm nobody.'

His hands came up from between his knees and covered his face. I felt inadequate.

'Alan,' I began falteringly, 'it's partly my fault, I know that.'

'No, no,' he interrupted. 'It's not your fault. You didn't create him out of nothing. He was always there. He's the rottenest part of all of us – of you, of me, of everybody who watches him. He's alive, that's all that matters. He's alive, and he's living in me, and I can't get rid of him. It's like a punishment for all the terrible things I've ever done.'

'What terrible things?' I asked, trying to sound as though I didn't believe him capable of such behaviour.

'Oh, I don't know. We've all done terrible things. Had terrible thoughts.'

106

'Doing and thinking are not the same,' I demurred, but he ignored me.

'He won't ever let me go,' he said, his voice taking on a whining, tearful quality. 'I won't ever be able to play another role. I know that. He won't let me. And he makes me do things – things that I don't want to do. But I have no choice. You've no idea.'

'Alan, listen to me,' I said, leaning forward and holding out a hand, but not touching him. 'We'll get help. We'll get you free. We'll do whatever we have to do, but we'll find a way—'

'No!' He shot out of his chair so abruptly that I ducked back and threw up my arm to protect myself. He laughed – and I knew that he was Clay again.

'You dumb creep,' he sneered, looming over me. 'Just what d'you think you can do, scribbler? You and that dumb actor together! I could chew up the pair of you and spit you out before breakfast any day of the week.'

His hands were on my sweater, pulling me up off the sofa. I thought of the tyre-lever that I had left outside, and looked around for a replacement. There was nothing. I was gearing up to fight him any way I could, when I saw the change come over him again, that same look of startled incomprehension in his eyes. He let go of me, and I fell back, floundering amidst the lush upholstery. His hands went to his head, as though fighting to hold his skull together against some awful pressure from within. He screamed. It was an awful sound, a trapped animal in pain.

'No! No! No! Don't, don't!' It was Alan's voice again. He turned and ran. I lost him in the darkness. By the time I'd scrambled to my feet and found my bearings, he was gone.

A door slammed in the distance. I followed the sound. Only a few months ago, the proud new owner, he'd shown Claire and me around the place. I remembered the layout vaguely, not in detail. The door to his bedroom was open and a light on. I went in. One wall almost entirely of glass opened on to a large wooden deck; two more doors led to a bathroom and a dressing room respectively.

There was a crash from the direction of the dressing room, which was dark. I ran towards the noise, stumbling over something he had knocked down in his flight. A light went on in the distance, showing a corridor turning to the right. I remembered that it connected with a gym that he was having installed. There was another crash, heavy and metallic. I got into the gym just in time to see a door on the far side slam shut. A bench press lay on its side, barbells still rolling on the floor.

I knew that the door across the gym led only into a large storage space from which there was no escape. I tried the handle, but it was locked. I banged on it and called his name: 'Alan, open the door. Listen to me, don't do anything foolish.'

Why I said that, about not doing anything foolish, I still don't know. I think it was that awful animal-like cry he'd given in the living room. There was only one end to that kind of pain.

'Alan!' I shouted, slamming the door with my shoulder and nearly dislocating it. I tried again, this time kicking the lock with the heel of my shoe. There was a splintering sound and it swung open. I saw Alan in the semi-darkness. He was facing me. He started to raise his hand in what, for an absurd moment, I thought was going to be a Nazi salute. Then I saw that he was holding a gun.

I backed away, and he came towards me, into the bright light of the gym with its shiny chrome and black leather equipment, and mirrored walls that spun out our reflections infinitely about us. I was in the final reel of *The Lady from Shanghai*.

Just as the thought hit me, I stepped on one of the barbells and fell noisily on my back. He started to laugh. It was Clay's laugh.

'You're not cut out to be Action Man, scribbler. Take my advice, stick to your typewriter.'

'I don't use a typewriter,' I said coldly, picking myself up with what dignity I could muster, 'as you should know better than anyone.'

'Just a figure of speech, scribbler,' he replied, still eyeing me with amusement. 'Figures of speech don't mean shit – as you should know better than anyone.'

I ignored this last piece of sarcasm, dusted off my trousers, pulled down my sweater, and turned to face him.

'Sit down,' he said, gesturing with the gun. There was no trace of a smile on his face now, not even a sneer: just a cold, flint-hard determination.

'What's the matter with you? Are you crazy?' I heard myself saying. 'Put that thing down. You'll never get away with this.'

He blew a little scornful puff of air out of his nose. 'Jesus, scribbler,' he said, 'your dialogue sucks – you know that? Some of the stuff you write for me's bad enough, but your own stuff – boy oh boy! Now, sit down!' He gestured with his gun towards the seat of an arm-curl machine. I lowered myself on to it. He stood with his feet a little way apart and looked at me, shaking his head. 'You and me need to get a few things cleared up, scribbler.'

I took a deep breath, trying not to let him see that it came in unsteady little gasps. 'You know, Clay,' I said, 'this isn't between you and me. There are three of us here, not two. Alan's here as well, and I'd like to know what he thinks.'

He looked at me a while in silence, the gun held loosely, pointing at my chest. Then he gave a short laugh. 'I don't see no Alan. Don't see nobody – 'cept you and me.'

I don't know what made me do it: some instinct about where the cracks between the two parts of him might lie. I pointed to the mirrored wall. 'Look right there,' I said. 'Tell me who you see.'

He followed the direction of my finger automatically. He shouldn't have. I knew at once from the way his eyes focused on and held their own reflection that I had found the weakness I was looking for.

'Who d'you see?' I said, keeping my voice low, steady, under control. 'Who d'you see looking back at you? Alan? You see yourself, don't you, Alan? And you don't mean me any harm, any more than I mean you.'

He blinked. Then, with his free hand, he reached up and touched his face, feeling experimentally around in search of familiar landmarks. My eyes went to his other hand, in which the gun hung forgotten now, pointing at the floor.

'Alan,' I said, 'why don't you put down that gun. Then you and I will take care of this problem like a couple of good friends should be able to.'

His fingers continued to play across his face. He stared through them as they fanned his eyes. Very cautiously I got up from my armchair and took a step towards him. 'Alan,' I said, 'I'm going to take the gun. Do you understand? I'm going to take the gun from your hand and put it somewhere safe.'

That's all I would have done, nothing more. His only response to my words was a grunt which I took for assent. But when my fingers touched his gun, I saw how mistaken I was – not for the first time in this sorry tale.

He turned with the speed of a beast surprised in its lair. The breaking of contact with his reflection seemed to reassert Clay's dominance instantly. They were Clay's eyes, not Alan's, that looked into mine, burning with the rage of one who has been tricked into humiliation. The gun was already raised, ready to fire point-blank into my face. Time froze. I faced my death in slow motion. I did nothing. I looked on from outside as hands that were mine, yet somehow didn't belong to me, reached out to turn the gun away. We struggled. At least, I assume that we struggled. Where I stood, there was no sense of movement. It was like nothing so much as descriptions I had read of the out-of-body experience; and perhaps, being so close to death, that is what it was. I saw his finger tighten, squeezing infinitely slowly on the trigger.

A jet of water hit me in the face. It felt ice-cold, and the shock of it took my breath away. I thought he was going to have to sit down he was laughing so hard. Instead, he did what I had just done: slipped on one of the barbells and fell backwards like a stone.

I heard his head hit the sharp steel corner of the bench. It was a horrible sound – a brittle crack with a wet, soft undertone.

I knew he was dead. But I didn't know what to do about it. I could hear my own breathing; then my heart thudding like some huge bird taking to the sky. My thoughts swam. For a moment I thought I was going to faint, but instead, impulsively, I knelt by him. I don't remember touching him, but I suddenly found that my hand was wet with blood. I wiped it on my sweater, then realized at once what I had done. I straightened up again and backed away.

There was no sense in calling the police – I knew that for sure. There was that kicked-in door: that looked bad. Inevitably, the whole episode of Claire and Alan on the deck of our house would come out, and that would lead to a nightmare of misunderstandings and accusations.

I realized I must leave him exactly where he was. At the same time I decided to remove the water-pistol, tugging it from his fingers and putting it in my pocket. If he were found with it in his hand, together with the smashed door behind him, the whole situation could be badly misinterpreted. It could be seen, for example, as a desperate attempt to defend himself against some attacker with the only thing resembling a weapon that came to hand. There can be a terrible ambiguity about certain objective circumstances, as we writers know at least as well as any detective.

There was no reason why my fingerprints should not be found in the house. After all, I had been there more than once as a legitimate visitor in the company of others. All the same, I used a handkerchief to let myself out of the front door and to close it after me. I retrieved my tyre-lever from where it had fallen in the drive, and slipped over the fence at the place I had climbed in. The house was in a canyon above Malibu, and I had left my car some way off so as not to arouse his suspicions when he returned. I got in, pulled the door shut, and drove off. I realized that my face was still wet from the water he had squirted at me, but when I licked the dampness from my lips I tasted tears.

Poor Alan. Poor brave, bewitched Alan. Nobody would ever know what he had been through. Nobody would ever understand his death. Nobody but I. And I could never tell.

It was almost dawn. I drove north on the Pacific Coast Highway. Luckily, I had a nearly full tank and a can of gas in the back, so I didn't need to stop at a filling station, which would have run the risk of somebody remembering me. After a while I pulled off into the hills, stopped, got out, and took off my sweater. I poured some gasoline on it and lit it with a piece of paper ignited from the cigarette lighter on my dash. In moments it was dust.

After that I drove around aimlessly for another hour or so, finally stopping for a cup of coffee at a Starbucks in Santa Monica. From a window I watched a city refuse truck pick up the trash can into which I had dropped the water-pistol.

I called Claire from a payphone. She sounded upset. She said she had just heard something awful on the news: Alan Kemp had been found dead by his maid that morning. The police were treating it as a possible accident.

I didn't like that word 'possible'.

★

Claire didn't even ask. She took it for granted that I had stayed the night in San Francisco. We were both in shock at Alan's death, which covered any awkwardness there might have been between us.

We didn't go into the office that morning. We stayed home and made calls, starting with the network. Tod Weinberg had got the story from Alan's agent. In so far as it went, it was accurate. He had been found in his gym, fully dressed, with a terrible gash on the side of his head. Tod said he had a feeling that something was being held back, something that pointed towards a more sinister explanation than a simple accident.

I knew what it was: that smashed-in door in his gym. There could have been some innocent reason for it, just as there could have been for the things he had knocked over in his flight through the house; but it raised questions.

Then I thought about the tyre-lever in my car. When I picked it up outside Alan's house, had I used the hand smeared with Alan's blood? Could there be traces? Even invisible ones detectable only by forensic tests? I must get rid of it.

Our incoming phone rang constantly, but we screened all the calls on the machine, only picking up the ones we wanted to or felt we should. One was from an LAPD detective. I saw Claire look at me, wondering if one of us should take it, and if so which one. I realized it looked suspicious not to, and picked up as the detective began to leave a message. He said he needed to come up to the house to ask a few questions. I said we'd expect him around eleven. As I put the phone down, I saw Claire still watching me oddly.

'What is it?' I asked.

She was playing with her fingers nervously, something she rarely did. 'I . . . I have to tell you something,' she began haltingly.

My stomach turned over. I feared I was going to be the recipient of a confession that I had no wish to hear. 'Go on,' I said.

'He was here last night,' she said, looking at me anxiously.

'Here?' I echoed, eyebrows arching in surprise.

'He called up, asked if you were home, and when I said you were away he begged to come over and talk to me. He said his life depended on it.'

'What did he want to talk about?' I asked, figuring the only way to handle this was one step at a time.

'He wanted me to intercede with you to get him back on the show.'

'Did you tell him you would?'

She didn't answer at first. My eyes strayed through the window to the deck where I had seen them together last night. She was too wrapped up in her own thoughts to notice.

'As a matter of fact, I did,' she said, after a while. 'I don't know why. He was just so . . . desperate.'

I let a moment or two go by in silence. 'I suppose what you're wondering,' I said eventually, 'is whether you should say anything to the police about this.'

She nodded, watching me, saying nothing. I paced up and down a few times, hands in pockets, eyes on the Mexican rug under my feet. This was tricky. If our house featured on Alan Kemp's last itinerary, there were going to be questions and routine checks – such as whether I actually had spent that night in San Francisco or not. It would be awkward if they discovered that I hadn't.

'What time was he here?' I asked eventually.

'Oh, it wasn't late,' she said quickly. 'Nine, nine thirty, something like that. He just had a drink, then left.'

She had turned away and was looking out towards the haze over Beverly Hills. I watched her. I could see no signs of hidden grief, no aching sense of loss. She had not loved him, even briefly. It was just the spell: that awful spell that was now broken. I took a deep breath.

'Did anyone know he was coming here?' I asked.

'Oh, no,' she said, too quickly. Then added, 'Well, I don't know for sure, of course, but I doubt it. I mean, why would they?'

She looked at me, as though fearing I might think of a reason.

'I don't honestly see,' I began, 'what coming here has to do with his having an accident later.'

'Possible accident,' she said.

'Okay,' I shrugged, '"possible", whatever that means. If you think it's relevant that he was here, tell them.'

'You know what they say,' she said. 'It's for them to decide what's relevant and what isn't, not the witness.'

'You're hardly a witness,' I said.

She was silent for a while, then said, 'It's bound to come out that he wanted to go back in the show and we turned him down.'

'So?' I said.

Again she was silent. 'Suppose,' she said eventually, 'just suppose that, for some reason, somebody did know that he was here last night. If I said he wasn't, that would look like I was hiding something, wouldn't it?'

She was right, of course. It all hinged on whether anybody else could have known. But my guess was that Clay would have kept it to himself. He was instinctively, preternaturally secretive. Clay acknowledged no division between truth and lies; there was just expediency. If it was not positively in his interest to do a thing, he did not do it. How could it have been sufficiently important to him to tell somebody that he was coming to our house last night? I could not think of a reason. Therefore I decided to take the risk.

'Look,' I said, 'you must do whatever you feel comfortable with.' I took a step towards her. 'But you know what this town's like for gossip. Even if there's no scandal, people invent one.'

'Like what?' she asked, failing to hide a flash of defensiveness in her eyes. I pretended not to notice.

'I don't know,' I said casually. 'There's a lot of jealousy, people who'd like to hurt us, hurt the show. People make up stories out of nothing.'

'So what are you saying?' she asked, looking at me very directly for a moment.

'I'm saying,' I said, taking another step closer, 'that if you felt you didn't want to say anything about him being here, I don't think anybody could blame you for it.'

She looked at me a moment more, then dropped her gaze and nodded almost imperceptibly. 'You're right,' she said. 'It's better.'

I put my arms around her, and she relaxed against my body. I could tell that she was as relieved as I was.

★

We went to his funeral, shook hands with his family, and collaborated on a touching tribute in *Variety*. I felt tears prick my eyes as I gave the words a final polish, because I genuinely regretted Alan's loss. But it was Clay, not I, who had killed him; just as surely as those pods from outer space killed off the humans they replaced in *Invasion of the Body Snatchers*.

All the same, I had followed through my resolution on the tyre-lever. After we had spoken to the detective, who accepted without question Claire's statement that she hadn't seen Alan since he left the show, and mine that I hadn't seen him since our lunch at Le Dome, I drove out to Silver Lake. There I threw the tyre-lever as far out into the water as I could, and made a mental note to buy another at some place I wasn't well known.

Life moved on. The inquest decided that Alan had tripped and struck his head. The broken door remained an unsolved mystery, but not a decisive one. It would feature in future anthologies of death in Hollywood, but for now Alan Kemp was yesterday's news, and Clay Granger just a fossil in the ever-mounting bed of silt left behind by television's endless gusher. The ex-astronaut was cast, and we began shooting for the new season. We had high hopes.

Shortly after the funeral, I asked Claire to marry me, and she agreed. We held the ceremony up at the house with, as the Hollywood joke has it, a few hundred of our closest friends.

The new season was a hit, even bigger than the first. I bought a cruiser that I kept down at Marina del Ray. Sometimes we would sail to Catalina on the weekends. Claire got pregnant, and we appeared in *People* magazine. Soon after that we moved into a bigger house off Benedict Canyon; the view was less good, but the garden was spectacular, far better for kids.

A year passed. Deborah was born and beginning to crawl,

115

putting everything she could get her hands on into her mouth. The show was in its third season and huge around the world. We were becoming seriously rich. I had not known that it was possible to be so happy. I even ordered wine at lunch with Ward Podomsky: I felt untouchable.

And then . . . It began the way it had before. I found a file on my computer one morning that had not been there the previous day. It was called 'Clay', and I could see at a glance that it must be a page or so long.

It was as though a black hole had opened up inside me, draining everything away – blood, warmth, breath, and life itself. With a trembling finger I tapped the cursor down the page, then hesitated between 'Retrieve' and 'Delete'. But I knew I couldn't escape that easily. I had to face this thing the way I had last time. I brought the file up on the screen.

Hello, scribbler! How're you doing? Life's good – right? And you're pretty damn pleased with yourself, too. Don't deny it, I know you.

How's that pretty wife of yours? Nice lady. Smart, too. Fucks like a rattlesnake – but then you know that. Okay, okay, scribbler. Cool off. If it makes you feel better, I won't mention it again. I am nothing if not a gentleman – and I am far from being nothing.

The words scrolled up the screen and my eyes darted over the lines.

I know you killed that actor.

'That's a lie!' I protested aloud, as though he could hear me. The words continued scrolling up the screen.

If the cops found out he'd been at your house, and you'd been at his that night, they'd start digging around again. You'd be in a lot of trouble.

He paused a moment to let me think about this, then went on:

116

I could tell them what I know. I could, you know. Don't underestimate me.

Very slowly, as though afraid the keyboard would electrocute me, I stretched out my fingers and typed:

What do you want?

The answer came:

I want what I always wanted. You haven't delivered yet, scribbler. I'm waiting.

There it ended, for the moment. I sat back, and realized that my hands were shaking. I clasped them together, tight, until the fingers became dappled white and puce. My breathing, too, was shallow; I filled my lungs, deeply and deliberately, several times. I felt like I was trying to escape from a long, dark tunnel. I shivered, very cold. Then I deleted the file, and pulled the computer plug out of the wall.

I spent much of the day driving around, making calls from my car, avoiding people; I was sure they would see that there was something wrong, and I did not want to have to answer their questions. I was numb, the way you are when you're in shock and you keep telling yourself that everything's fine and you're going to be all right; then you realize that the strange sound in the distance is you, laughing insanely, or screaming, or sobbing. I know, because I laughed and screamed and sobbed in my car that day on the freeway – where, thank God, nobody noticed.

★

Back home I managed somehow to conceal from Claire the fact that anything was wrong. That night I took the same precautions as the last time: locked my office, then placed the key inside the kitsch music box that would play 'The Star-Spangled Banner' if anybody opened it, then fixed the box to the top of the wardrobe in our bedroom. The only difference was that this time I knew I would be a nervous wreck if I lay awake all night, so I took a

117

sleeping pill. In fact I took two, and didn't wake up till after eight. Claire was already up and having breakfast with Deborah and the nanny.

Nothing in my office had been disturbed, but I could see as soon as I booted up my computer that Clay had been there. There was another 'Clay' file listed on the directory. It was obviously very short. I called it up. All it said was:

Let's talk.

I tapped in:

All right – let's.

His reply popped up on the screen immediately:

You're just going to have to find a way, scribbler.

And so we continued:

Me: A way to do what?

Clay: To get me back in circulation, dammit! I'm bored and I'm really running out of patience now – which means you're running out of time.

Me: You can't threaten me.

Clay: Oh, yes I can, scribbler. Yes I can.

Then something happened that made me almost jump out of my skin. Somebody whispered, 'What are you working on?', right into my ear. Claire had entered barefoot, and was peering over my shoulder.

'Jesus Christ!' I yelled. 'Don't ever do that. You nearly gave me a heart attack.'

'Well, I'm sorry,' she said a little huffily. 'I just thought that since you'd been up working half the night, and here you are back at it before breakfast, it must be something good.'

I had that awful feeling of the blood going cold in my veins again.

'Up half the night?' I protested, turning to look at her. 'What are you talking about? I've only just got up.'

'For heaven's sakes, you woke me up at three o'clock with that stupid music box playing "The Star-Spangled Banner". Then you went shuffling off to your office mumbling about having to finish something.'

I stared up at her. 'Are you putting me on?'

'Of course not. Don't you remember?'

All I could say was, 'I took two sleeping pills. I couldn't possibly have been working.'

She shrugged her shoulders. 'Obviously your pills didn't work – because you did.'

I was silent for a moment, my mind racing towards some awful cliff-edge of panic. I asked her, 'Do you happen to know what time I came back to bed?'

'Don't you remember?'

'Should I?'

'It was around dawn. You woke me up, we made love. You can't have forgotten that.' Her eyes gleamed.

I felt a terrible hollowness open up inside me. 'We' had made love?

Not I, I was thinking, but dared not speak the thought. Not I.

'Are you all right?' she asked, starting to look anxious.

'Sure I am,' I said, not very convincingly.

'Maybe you should have a check-up.'

I turned towards her, taking her wrist. 'Listen,' I said, 'how long were you behind me just now?'

She looked puzzled, but answered: 'Not long. About a minute.'

'Did you see me type any of what's on the screen?' I indicated my dialogue with Clay.

'Most of it, I guess.'

'Most of it. So you saw *some* of it come up by itself, without me touching the keyboard – right?'

'Honey, what is this?' She was looking at me strangely now, her eyes searching mine. 'What's wrong? You're beginning to scare me.'

'There's nothing to worry about,' I said, summoning as much conviction as I could into my voice. 'I'm sorry, it's just that there's something wrong with the computer. Stuff keeps coming up on the screen that shouldn't. I'm going to have to call Bob.'

This seemed to reassure her somewhat. 'It can wait till after breakfast,' she said, taking me firmly by the arm. 'You need some juice and something to eat.'

I offered no resistance as she led me away.

★

I thought it through, long and hard, until eventually I was convinced that I had found the problem. It was that I had never really killed him off. Not properly. He had been alive at the end of the first season, and dead at the start of the second. He had died off-stage, undramatized, and therefore had never believed in his own demise – any more than you or I would if somebody came up to us at lunch and casually told us we were dead. We would dismiss the idea as absurd: a metaphor at best.

So he was alive. But where? And in what form?

He was a thought, a living thought, trapped in some loop between my mind and the world into which I had originally introduced him. There was no longer an actor to give him life; there was by then only me. He was alive in me as he once had been in Alan Kemp. As he once had been in the minds of all those millions who had watched him every week on television.

That, after all, was what he was: a Frankenstein's monster who lived in people's minds. In their imaginations. That was the world of any fictional character, the only atmosphere that they could breathe.

But Clay had been cut off from that world, and he held me responsible. If I did not help him get back into it . . .

There was no 'if'. I had to. I was too afraid not to.

120

But how? How was I going to get him into other people's minds, and therefore out of mine?

It was too late for television. That route was closed to him – definitively. How else could I help him escape from the narrowness of his present trap to the freedom of his natural audience, the world out there? After which he would, I prayed, leave me alone?

And then it came to me. I had the answer at my fingertips. It would take time, and there would be no guarantee. Certainly he would never reach the numbers he had become accustomed to through television. But even a handful would be better than nothing.

With luck, little by little, he would spread, like a virus . . . and slowly, gradually, I would become free of him.

It was my only hope.

As I say, I had the answer at my fingertips.

Now you have it in your hands.

The Fame that Dare Not Speak Its Name

'Do I have to explain what a wet shot is?'

'Um . . . no.'

'There's only two kinds of people – you know that? The kind who know what a wet shot is, and the kind who lie.'

'I guess that's true,' Tom said, hoping his unease didn't show, but increasingly convinced that he'd made a mistake in coming here. 'Except maybe my grandmother. I don't think she'd know.'

'We're not going for the grandmother market,' replied the man in the baseball cap, Ray-Bans, and overgrown designer stubble. He leaned back in his chair, crossed his running shoes on the edge of his desk, and gestured with a stubby finger. 'Pull up your pants, get some lunch, and be on set by two thirty. If you get a hard-on, you're hired.'

And that was how Tom got into the X-rated movie business. His friend Hal at the Singing Lobster on Melrose had told him they were looking for guys who could act, and who had the other necessary qualifications. 'What the hell?' Hal had said. 'You like girls, don't you? And you get paid for it. Good money. If you can beat that deal, let me know!'

At first Tom had dismissed the idea out of hand. Then, after a while, he realized he was still thinking about it. He went on thinking about it for some time before he made the call.

What pushed him over the edge was going up for a part on a small independent feature. It wasn't a big part, but it was the pivot of the picture. He knew so well how to play the role that in his head he was already rehearsing his speech of thanks to the Academy. Silly, he knew. But he also knew this could be the one. He just knew.

The part went to the star of a TV show who wanted to change his image, and who was also, as it happened, the boyfriend of the director's agent.

That same week the Singing Lobster finally closed in the face of the tidal wave of new and better restaurants opening around that time. It was 1978. The Lobster was old without having become a tradition like Musso and Frank's, The Palm, or Chasens.

Tom's search for work led nowhere – and that was just work waiting tables. Acting jobs were even thinner on the ground. When his agent suggested that he might benefit from alternative representation, Tom fished out the matchbook from the back of his desk drawer and called the number written on it in pencil.

Hal had been in three X-rated features by now. He had an apartment at the beach and was renting a Porsche, which Tom thought was a crazy waste of money; but then Tom came from Idaho, whereas Hal was native Californian.

All the same, Tom liked Hal and chose to believe him when he said that the audition was the only time that Tom would feel any embarrassment. After that it was plain sailing and money for, well, doing what came naturally. Tom looked at a couple of movies and had to admit that Hal and the other guys seemed to be having a pretty good time, which wasn't surprising considering the great-looking girls they were having it with.

Tom's sex life had not been exactly animated for the best part of a year – not since he broke up with his regular girlfriend. She left him to move in with a network executive, and was now appearing regularly on TV and being photographed at parties with celebrities. Tom, meanwhile, was confronting the inescapable truth that girls do not on the whole throw themselves at out-of-work actors in little aprons rattling off today's specials with an order pad in one hand and a pencil in the other. There were times when he wished he was gay: those guys were never short of a little action. But he wasn't, and there was nothing to be done about it.

So, at two twenty-nine he was on the set. At two thirty-two he was being rehearsed in a set of moves that made him think of a tag-wrestling match choreographed by Martha Graham, and at two forty-five he was performing on camera. At two fifty-eight he

126

was told that he had a future in this business, and was handed an envelope thick with dollars.

★

The best thing about having sex for half the day on camera, Tom reflected some months later, was that it pretty much took your mind off sex for the other half. That, he found, was a change for the better, and a great relief from the obsessive fantasizing he used to suffer every time he set eyes on an attractive woman. His social life outside work was still largely spent with people from work, but that was no different from any other kind of job. He was mildly surprised at how conservative some of their lives were, especially those on the technical side. Some of the girls, too, lived quietly, often with someone, and would organize cook-outs at the weekend. Others were harder to get to know. These were the ones who worked the burlesque circuits as well, constantly travelling around the country when they weren't making movies, pulling down every cent they could before the wrinkles, stretch marks and cellulite put paid to their earning power.

They all knew it couldn't go on for ever, and most of them had vague plans for the future. Tom secretly figured that he would get out by the time he was thirty, which gave him another three years. By then he would have enough money stashed away to start over and make anything he wanted out of his life. Within reason.

He knew, for instance, that he could never go back to straight acting. And even if he could, he didn't want to. It had finished with him, and he had returned the compliment. *Nymphos Get It Up* and *Hot-Rod Girls in Heat* would represent the pinnacle of his film career – which only served him right for thinking he had any real talent in the first place. Occasionally he found himself remembering the words of a producer who got lucky with a fluke hit after years of working out of the payphone in the men's room of the Singing Lobster: 'The only thing I thank Hollywood for is giving me enough money to leave it.'

Then, one day, he met Amanda. He was having a cup of coffee in a place near the location for the day's shoot. He was sitting in a booth at the back, wearing the dark glasses that he always wore in public now. They helped him slide through those moments when strangers glanced at him twice – usually men, though very occasionally a woman – and wondered where they'd seen him before.

The first he saw of her was in a mirror, because he had his back to the entrance. The place was pretty full and she was standing with a tray in her hands looking for somewhere to sit.

On an impulse he would forever after wonder about, he got up and offered her the vacant seat opposite his own. She hesitated. On another impulse, he took off his sunglasses, sensing that the implied hostility in them was putting her off. She smiled, thanked him, and sat down.

He looked at her. Her hair fell away from her face, on which she wore no make-up. Her cheek-bones were high, her nose straight and fine, her forehead sculpted above cool green eyes that were steady and inquiring. Her mouth was full, and her chin, which had a tiny cleft, gave a strength to it all.

'Do you work around here?' he started, because he had to start somewhere.

'No,' she said. 'I'm doing research.'

'Research?'

'I'm a sociology postgrad at UCLA. There's a team of us monitoring a study group of interracial families, their internal relationships, societal interactions, etcetera.'

'Cool,' he said. 'How are they all getting along?'

'They have their ups and downs. What about you?'

'Oh, I have mine too. Don't we all?'

Her look, as she munched her alfalfa sandwich and sipped her Calistoga water, gave no indication that she thought he was funny.

'I mean what do you do?' she said.

'I'm in the movie business,' he replied.

'Uh-huh,' she responded neutrally. 'What d'you do in the movie business?'

'I'm an actor,' he said.

'What have you been in?'

'Oh, you wouldn't have seen me.'

'Try me.'

'Actually, I'm more on the production side these days.'

'You're a producer?' She didn't seem impressed, just politely curious. Perhaps faintly disbelieving. Or indifferent. The long, loose sleeve of her long, loose coat opened up like a yawn as she lifted her bottled water once more to her lips. 'What sort of movies do you produce?'

'They're kind of specialist. You wouldn't know them.'

'What kind of specialist?'

His mind raced. After an age, he heard himself say, 'Marine biology. We make films about marine biology.'

To his relief she seemed to lose interest, and they talked in general terms for ten minutes until she had to go. He walked down the street with her to the corner. By then he had remembered who she reminded him of: Carol-Anne Leider back home.

'We all have a girl we left back home,' Hal had said once. 'That is if we're lucky. If we're unlucky, we're back home with her and the kids.'

Tom had ached for a future at home with Carol-Anne Leider and however many kids she wanted. The first time he saw her he'd flashed on their life together, down through the years to old age, still holding hands. He didn't know if that was always how it took you when you were seventeen, and it certainly never happened again. One time he had scraped up the courage to tell her how he felt. She had blushed and told him he was really nice, but she didn't feel that way about him. He could have died when she went off with a banker's son from Minneapolis who was over for the summer. That was one of the reasons he had gone to drama school. One day, he told himself, she would go to a movie theatre in Minneapolis and dream of the life she could have had with that guy up there on the screen. Big laugh.

Suddenly he realized that the girl was speaking to him. They were on a busy street corner and she was saying that she had to buy some things, and it was nice meeting him. She held out her hand, and he took it.

'Tom Shaughnessy,' he said.

'Amanda Higgins,' she said.

129

'See you again?' he asked, once more on an impulse, his third in a very short time.

She hesitated just perceptibly, then said she'd be around for a few days and she sometimes ate lunch in that café. He let it go at that, and watched her walk away. When she turned to cross the street she flashed him a smile that made him wonder how many cups of coffee he'd have to sit over in that café to be sure of seeing her again, because he certainly meant to see her. Then he told himself that this was stupid.

He realized suddenly that the driver of a garbage truck had spotted him and was gesturing excitedly to his colleagues, pointing in Tom's direction.

Hoping that Amanda hadn't noticed, he slipped on his sunglasses and walked quickly away.

★

The location they'd hired was a little grander than usual: a big mansion in Hancock Park with an indoor swimming pool. The place was empty, and they'd dressed it to look like some fantasy hotel where every time you rang for room service . . . well, the film was called *Lip Service*.

Tom was standing around in his robe as Zeb, the director, in his eternal sunglasses, baseball cap and permanently shaggier-than-designer stubble, was setting up the next shot at the poolside with the lighting cameraman. He turned to Tom and asked him if he'd got to know his co-star yet, 'Torrid Flame'. Tom said he hadn't.

There was a movement across the floor and a mirrored door opened. The girl who entered wore a robe like his own and walked towards him on red stiletto heels.

Her hair was more fluffed out to frame her face softly, but the extra make-up had been applied with the lightest touch and served only to emphasize her fresh and natural beauty. There was no mistaking Amanda Higgins.

'Torrid Flame.' Zeb made the introductions using stage names only. 'Dick O'Toole. Okay, you've both read your scripts, we go in five.' He went back to his set-up.

The two of them walked towards the far end of the conservatory that housed the pool and gave on to a lushly overgrown garden.

'Sociology,' he said drily. 'That's the study of human intercourse in all its varieties, isn't it?'

She cocked an eyebrow at him and said, 'I suppose marine biology is what we're about to do in this pool.'

He was silent a moment, his gaze, he hoped, suitably flinty to suggest a man who had not yet made up his mind about this woman. In reality, however, he feared that it was made up irreversibly and inescapably.

'Did you know who I was when you sat down in that café?' he asked.

'Of course I did,' she said, her lips parting in a spontaneous grin that revealed small, white, perfect teeth. The upper row extended fractionally beyond the lower to create a kind of smile within a smile that was utterly disarming. 'Zeb's assistant pointed you out from the door. I'm surprised you didn't see him.'

'Hm,' he said. 'Very funny.'

'I thought you'd probably recognize me,' she said. 'But I guess you don't watch much hardcore, hm?'

'I don't take my work home.' It came out too heavy, like a man with no sense of humour.

'No you're more of a 'Masterpiece Theater" type, I can tell.' She eyed him shrewdly.

Once again he felt his words dictated by an impulse which he had no power to resist, despite his long self-promised rule against getting involved with the girls he worked with.

'Okay,' he said with a smile that he hoped showed a good-natured readiness to take a joke against himself. 'You owe me one. Have dinner with me tonight.'

He had the impression that she looked him over from head to toe in a split second, but without moving her eyes.

'Okay,' she said.

'All right, everybody, ready to go!' The voice of the first assistant director filled the room. 'Everybody in your places please. Everybody ready now. Let's shoot it.'

Dick O'Toole and Torrid Flame slipped off their robes.

★

131

They dined at the beach in a windowless concrete bunker converted into a fashionable restaurant. Tom had become a good customer there in the last year or so, but was never quite sure whether the management welcomed his patronage or were embarrassed by it. They always gave him a table in the corner which was agreeably private, but also had the effect of shielding him from the gaze of fellow guests.

'The fame that dare not speak its name,' he whispered to Amanda as a couple of male diners followed their progress between tables, obviously trying to remember where they knew them from.

Amanda smiled. She knew about that look and the momentary blush of confusion that often followed it as the questioner made the connection. It happened to her infrequently, because she looked off-screen so utterly unlike her on-screen self. She dressed either with a perverse drabness, or, on social occasions like tonight, with a simple modesty. The lineage of her fashion sense stretched back to Kelly and Hepburn, not Monroe or any of the other bombshells.

They settled at their table, ordered, and began to talk as strangers do on a first date. Preferences in music, food, movies, people and travel were explored. Birthplaces and backgrounds touched upon. They agreed to differ on politics: she thought the President was underrated, he thought the opposite. Neither pried into the other's past relationships or inquired about current ones, nor did they volunteer details, though there was a tacit understanding in the air that they were both, at this time, unattached.

In the parking lot she thanked him for a lovely evening. He planted a kiss on her cheek, and asked her to come home with him.

She looked at him, he thought, with a slight sadness, and shook her head.

'I'd rather not.'

'Is that personal rejection, or on principle?'

'What do you think?' she asked him, with a hint of amusement softening her delicately solemn features.

'I'd like to think,' he said, 'that, like me, it's just because you've made a rule. Only I just broke my rule.'

132

'Maybe one broken rule is enough for one evening. Besides, we have an early call tomorrow.'

It was true. They both had to be on set for the orgy scene at ten a.m. And sexual energy was not something to be squandered lightly on the night before a heavy schedule – certainly not for the men.

He opened her car door, kissed her on the cheek again, and stood watching until her tail-lights had disappeared in the distance.

★

Something happened to him that following day which had never happened before. Seeing a co-star he had just worked with, even one he might have had lunch or dinner with a couple of times, being ravaged by three other men on camera was something he normally took for granted. She was simply doing her job, like Shirley Temple tap-dancing or John Wayne slugging the bad guy. Normally he didn't even watch. Like all filming it was pretty boring: mostly long waits, with occasional brief flurries of action. Usually he would find some quiet corner and settle down with whatever paperback he was reading at the moment.

So why, this time, was he turning the pages and taking nothing in? Twice he turned back and re-read the same passage before giving up. There were, he told himself, days like that, days not meant for reading. He didn't know why this should be, but accepted that it was.

He took a walk around the mansion garden and chatted to one of the girls coming out of the make-up trailer. She was spacy and smiling, and the pupils of her eyes were dilated. He didn't know what she was on – quaaludes probably, some of the girls found they helped get them in the mood – but if Zeb realized how stoned she was she'd be out on her ear. Drug use was forbidden on the set. Tom had only worked on one shoot where it was widely used, and the results had been so dire that the film was unreleasable. The director and most of the cast had never worked again in the A-stream of the business.

The girl was called to the set, and Tom continued walking. He pulled his towelling robe tighter as he felt a breeze stir the air and listened to the lazy slap of his leather slippers as he crossed the lawn.

He sat down on a peeling green-painted bench and crossed his knees, looked up into the pale blue-white sky, and let his mind go blank.

Except that it wasn't blank. It was filled with one thought. Amanda – in there having sex with all those guys. And him out here, in the cold, because he couldn't bring himself to watch.

Amanda.

Damn.

★

When he suggested that they drive up the coast to Carmel for the weekend, he felt her hesitation on the phone. Right away he wanted to pull back, to reassure her that he hadn't meant what she thought he meant, that he was taking nothing for granted. But it was too late.

Besides, he had meant what she thought he meant. He just hadn't meant it to be so obvious.

'Look,' he said, 'I'm sorry. That came out wrong. All I'm suggesting is if we . . . I mean, if you'd rather go some place not so far, some place we can go and come back in a day—'

'No,' she interrupted, 'that's all right. I'd like to go.' Her voice was soft but level, the voice of someone who had made a decision and did not wish to be suspected of uncertainty. She said that they could take his car. He could pick her up around ten on Saturday morning.

★

The murmur of the sea below the terrace where they dined was hypnotic and relaxing. Amanda turned her head to follow the moon's dappled spoor to the horizon. When she turned back, she saw that he was watching her. She smiled apologetically.

'I suppose it must seem silly. I'm sorry. It's just how I am.'

'I understand,' he said. And the thing that annoyed him most was that he actually did. And sympathized. A voice inside him kept saying that he would not have liked her as much if she had done anything else.

134

The conversation had started in the car only minutes after he met her in the lobby of the building on Doheny where she lived.

'I'm not going to sleep with you tonight. If that's understood, we can go anywhere you like – but single rooms. Otherwise, let's just have lunch at the beach, my treat.'

For a second some smart-Alec reply rose to his lips such as, 'Hey, you're right. We've been screwing all week – we owe ourselves a night off.' But he suppressed it, and was immediately glad that he had, because there was a curious refinement about Amanda that would have made such a crack sound even cruder than it was.

What was it, this quality she had? A kind of innocence, but not the little-girl kind that looked at you with big eyes and deferred to your wisdom. On the contrary, she was at least as smart as he was, probably smarter. But there was no cynicism in her. She did what she did for a living, and neither excused it, complained about it, nor hid a sense of degradation behind relentlessly extrovert behaviour like some of the girls. She was quiet, thoughtful, private, and good company.

Perhaps the thing that most disturbed him was that this quality in her made him reflect more than he cared to on the life that he himself was leading. When you're born in the Midwest, no matter how far you go or whatever you do, you carry some of that homespun Presbyterian morality with you for life. Even if you reject it, it's still there. Even if you manage to forget it for a while, it lies in wait, ready to spring out and fold you back into its suffocating small-town bosom the first moment you give it a chance.

Such a moment had happened to him when Amanda sat down opposite him in that café. His first thought had been that a girl like this was off limits for him. Oh, she might be amused to have a fling with a porno stud; some women were, but they wouldn't want their friends to know about it. And they certainly wouldn't want a relationship.

To put it bluntly, he had instantly felt that he wasn't good enough for her. She came from another, better world. And the irony was that, even now when he knew who she was and what

135

she did, he still felt it. He felt ashamed of what he'd done to her on camera. He had no right.

But the shame did not attach to her. She seemed not so much above it all as untouched by it. Not because she was barricaded into herself like some of them, but because there was a place in her that no one touched, unless she wanted them to. And she did not, it seemed, want him.

They parted outside her room with a gentle hug, a brushing of cheeks, a touch of lips. Then, before he knew it, she had slipped from his arms and closed her door behind her.

Minutes later he lay in his bath and reflected on what she had told him about herself. Born in Germany of an air force colonel who had been killed in a flying accident when she was six. Her mother had remarried a widower with three children of his own. She had been the odd one out. Money was short, and so was affection. She had survived because she had to. She didn't rebel but withdrew into herself. She dreamed, read, made up imaginary friends. She tried to convince herself that a prince would come and fall in love with her. More realistically, she made inquiries about acting schools.

At seventeen, when she left home, she had already experienced a lifetime of loneliness. She got a job selling cosmetics in a store in Sherman Oaks and took acting classes in her spare time. She struggled for a few years, but finally realized that her talent was at best limited, and the prospect of trading sexual favours for lousy roles in unimportant movies did not appeal to her.

One day a girlfriend she'd met in acting class, and whose career so far had followed a similar arc, told her about an offer she'd been made to get into the X-rated movie business. They talked it over, and decided that fucking for a living was more dignified than doing it for a couple of lines in some movie-of-the-week.

Tom felt they had a lot in common. His own background had been more stable, but crushingly dull. His parents, though still alive and married to each other, were capable of neither affection nor imagination. He too had known loneliness. He knew it still.

Why could they not share their loneliness? Why was it that the intimacy he sought with her did not materialize? Was it only their work that came between them? Choreographed, auto-erotic, actual yet unreal sexual acts? He didn't have an answer. He knew only that he wanted her desperately, like a pubescent boy in love for the first time.

He sensed his body stir in response to his thoughts. Glancing down the length of his torso, he saw his erection pointing back at him accusingly from the soapy water, bobbing just perceptibly with each pulse of his heartbeat.

Resignedly, he stretched out his hand, preparing to deal with the problem in the way that only loneliness knows how.

★

'Fluff girl' was a term that Tom had heard on the first day in the business. Zeb had smiled when he'd asked what it meant, and pointed to a girl with a mass of hair in a canvas chair in the corner reading a magazine. She wore shorts and a shirt tied at the waist. He would have taken her for one of the actresses, but Zeb explained that her job was to keep the male stars in the mood between takes: not too much in the mood, but enough to be ready to go when the cameras rolled.

Once or twice in the beginning he'd availed himself of the service, but less out of need than curiosity. The mechanical stimulation he'd received was effective, but left him cold; at least on the actual shoot there was some acting to go with it. So it was with reluctance that, on the Tuesday after his weekend in Carmel with Amanda, he found himself obliged to ask for help.

Nothing worked. First of all the crew just talked quietly among themselves; then they stood around with their arms folded, waiting. After a while the director – not Zeb this time, but an excitable Hungarian who had once worked for NBC – began to look nervous and glanced constantly at his watch. Finally he had the set cleared and called in two more girls. Tom showed not a spark of response.

'You've screwed yourself out, haven't you?' The director's angry face was pushed into Tom's.

'I swear I haven't had sex since Friday, when we finished the first scene.'

137

'You're lying. Or are you on drugs?'

'No, I'm not on drugs,' Tom protested. 'And I'm not lying. I've never had this problem before. I don't know what's wrong.'

The truth was that he knew exactly what was wrong. The scene he was due to play was with Amanda. It was the first time he had seen her since dropping her at her apartment on Sunday night. They knew that they were booked for work on Tuesday, and had arranged to have dinner afterwards.

'Look, this isn't going to work,' Tom said miserably. 'I think you'd better get someone else.'

The director's tirade about lack of professionalism and how he had worked with some of the finest in network TV, and how he wasn't going to carry the can for the overages occasioned by this fiasco, was nearing its third crescendo when Amanda walked on to the set.

She wore a black see-through gown that left nothing to the imagination. There was, as usual, barely a touch of make-up on her flawless skin, and her hair was pulled back in a pony-tail. She shoved the director gently aside, and fixed Tom with a clear, firm gaze.

'All right,' she said. 'Leave this to me.'

The director started to walk away, muttering in his native tongue and shaking his head.

'Bring in the crew,' she called after him. 'We'll be ready in five minutes.'

Tom felt panic tighten the muscles of his face.

'It's no good,' he hissed at her. 'I can't. I just can't do it.'

'Nonsense,' she said with quiet confidence. 'You'll be fine. Trust me.'

She kicked off her pumps, dropped her gown, and slid her arms around him.

The touch of her flesh, the smell of her hair and the taste of her mouth made him realize at once that she was right.

★

Tom poked morosely at his linguine with clam sauce and said he had no appetite.

138

'Come on,' she said in an effort to cheer him up. 'The scene was great. Couldn't have gone better.'

'That's not the point,' he grumbled. 'And you know it.'

'You are in a bad way, aren't you?' she said sympathetically, and stroked his hand on the table. He pulled it away with a sharp, 'Don't patronize me.'

She looked at him with a hint of reproach as well as understanding in her eyes. 'I'm just trying to make you feel better,' she said.

'No, you're not,' he said. 'You're just trying to avoid the issue.'

She sighed and sat back. 'I thought maybe it was better avoided.'

'I don't agree. I think we should talk about it.'

She continued to look at him, until he dropped his gaze to twirl a few more pieces of linguine limply around his fork.

'I think the best solution,' she said eventually, 'is that we don't work together any more.'

He nodded once in agreement. 'I agree we shouldn't. But that's not a solution.'

She saw pain in the eyes across from her as they searched her face.

'Amanda,' he began, 'will you please help me to understand what's happening here? Because I don't. We have sex on set – not the sex that we would have or could have between us in private, but it's still sex. Sometimes, at least for me, it's been good sex. What I mean is, we're not strangers to each other, or virgins or something. Yet you won't sleep with me. You'll have dinner with me, go up to Carmel with me, we have a good time, we enjoy each other's company – so what's the problem? I don't understand.'

She took a moment to gather all her thoughts before replying, first of all regarding him with her usual steady gaze, then looking down at her fingertips as they traced little patterns on the tablecloth.

'I do what I do,' she said, 'for a living. Right or wrong, good or bad. I have no illusions about it, but I do it.'

Here she paused. Her fingers stopped tracing, and she looked at him again. He braced himself for what was coming.

'What I do for myself,' she said, 'is different.'

Once again he gave a nod of acceptance, which was thrown into question by the frown on his forehead.

'All right, I can understand that,' he said. 'But why did you agree to go out with me at all if you didn't want to get involved?'

'Going out with somebody doesn't mean you're necessarily going to get involved.'

'I know. But if you go out with them several times, that's kind of a sign that you're willing to think about it. At least it is among normal people.'

She gave a faintly weary smile. 'There are no "normal" people. Everybody's different.'

'And some,' he said, 'are more different than others. Look at you. On-screen you're Torrid Flame, off-screen you're Doris Day.' An edge of anger had crept into his voice despite his attempt to suppress it. 'Are you deliberately trying to drive me crazy? Is that it? Are you some kind of secret man-hater and I'm your latest victim?'

Her face closed up, and he knew at once that he had gone too far. 'I don't usually have a relationship with people I work with,' she said coldly, making movements as though about to leave.

'Do you ever have a relationship with anybody?'

He knew now that he had gone further than too far. She looked at him with open hostility and started to get to her feet. He grabbed her hand as she reached for her purse. She glared at him.

'Amanda, I'm sorry. Don't go. Listen to me. Please,' he started to babble.

Her gaze was stony, but she stayed where she was, although coolly disengaging her hand from his.

'I can't help how I feel about you,' he went on, keeping his voice down so as not to attract attention. 'This has never happened to me before. Well, not for a long time. I want to be with you, alone, the two of us, like people who mean something to each other. We do, don't we? You know we do.'

There was, he thought, a softening in her eyes that gave him hope.

'Maybe,' she said. 'But you have to give me time, Tom. I can't just leap into a relationship. I'm sorry, but I'm not made that way.

I suppose I'm a little old-fashioned. It's true, I do love those old Doris Day movies on TV. She's strong, she knows what she wants, but she's also a woman. I admire that.'

Tom looked at her for some time without so much as the twitch of a muscle on his face or the blink of an eyelid. At last he said, 'Amanda, will you tell me one thing? Are you putting me on?'

She shook her head almost imperceptibly. 'No.'

He leaned back, apparently reassured.

'Okay,' he said. 'So we agree we won't work together any more. And I give you time.'

'I think that's best.'

A new flicker of concern crossed his face. 'I hate the idea of you working with anybody else.'

The corners of her mouth gave a little twitch that was both apologetic and philosophical at the same time. 'I think it's time I went home,' she said, getting to her feet. 'Good night, Tom. Take care of yourself.'

'When will I see you?'

'Call me in a couple of days. And don't look so unhappy – please.'

★

Tom had to go by a producer's office the next morning to pick up some expenses in cash. It was a routine arrangement benefiting all sides except the IRS. The accountant there was an old-timer called Hank, who had worked for most of the major studios over the years and was therefore, as he liked to boast, a thief trained by the world's best. Only on one unfortunate occasion had he made the mistake of stealing from the studio itself instead of from someone to whom it owed money, an error which had led to a surprisingly severe prison sentence, and thence to his current employment in a nondescript building off Ventura Boulevard.

Hank's duties were relatively light, though precisely defined, and he liked to reminisce about times past with anyone who would listen. On this particular morning Tom was a willing audience, having nothing particular to do and wanting only to take his mind off Amanda for a while.

In his former life Hank had never dealt directly with the stars, but he had been party to many an intricate deal on their behalf. 'If you know how to read a deal,' he always said, 'then you know all there is to know about somebody's life. Who they're sleeping with, who they're paying off, who they owe favours to and why. It's like a language, but in code. You just have to know how to decipher it.'

This led to a string of stories about famous names, some dead, some still around. Tom was only half-listening to this rattling of skeletons in distant cupboards when Hank's monologue took a turn towards the very subject that was weighing so heavily on Tom's mind.

'You know what I like about the women in this business?' Hank was saying. 'They're straightforward. They do what they do and get paid for it. There's no pretending they're something they're not – unlike some of those so-called movie stars giving blow-jobs to the producer because they want to play a nun in his next picture. And I'm talking big names! In this business, if a girl gives a blow-job, she does it on-screen, not in some guy's office to get the part. I tell you, these girls are a lot more honest than some of those snotty actresses picking up their Oscars and bursting into fake tears over Mom, Dad, America, and apple pie.'

Tom was pensive. 'Tell me about these girls, Hank,' he said. 'In this business – the girls you've known in it.'

Hank made an open gesture with his hands. 'You work with them,' he said. 'You know them better than I do.'

'Not really,' Tom said. 'When you work with people, you're kind of focused on other things – you know what I mean? – not who they are.'

'Well, I'll tell you,' Hank went on, warming to his subject, 'I've met them all. I've done deals with them, with their managers, their husbands, boyfriends – whatever. And they're the nicest girls you'll ever meet – honest, straightforward, no bullshit.'

Tom's head was nodding sagely, when he heard Hank saying, 'Take that girl you've been working with. Torrid Flame. She's exactly what I mean. Californian born and bred. Escondido – you know, down towards San Diego. Great kid. Stops by here for a cup of coffee and a chat sometimes – same as you.'

142

'You mean Amanda Higgins?' Tom asked, trying to keep the note of surprise out of his voice.

'Yeah – Amanda. That's her name.'

'Escondido? I thought she was born in Europe somewhere,' Tom said after a moment, not wanting to sound too specific, or too interested.

Hank shook his head. 'You must be mixing her up with somebody else. I had to get her details for some tax forms one time. Her folks still live down there. I've never met them, but they sound real nice from what she says.'

Tom thought fast, trying to look as though his mind was on nothing in particular. Amanda's story about being born in Germany, her father's death when she was six, her mother's remarriage, was plainly at odds with Hank's presumably accurate information.

All he said was, 'Yes, you're right, Hank. She's a nice kid, Amanda. Real nice.'

★

Rosalie Higgins had never felt easy about the way that driveway sloped down to the street. The first time she and Don had seen the place thirty years ago she'd known it was wrong: you couldn't see left or right with the wall at that height and the street bending around at the angle it did. But that was a problem they could fix; the house was perfect, exactly what they wanted.

For several weeks they'd discussed what they should do – either lower the wall or create a new opening if they could get planning permission, one where they'd have a less obstructed view in both directions. But then they'd had that unexpected problem with the roof, and by the time that was solved and paid for they'd grown accustomed to the driveway where it was. All you had to do was take a little extra care and warn people who came for the first time.

All the same, Rosalie had a moment of unease every time she took her car out. She would roll down from the garage, then brake and edge forward an inch at a time until she could see that the road was clear to pull out. Never in thirty years had she had a problem. But in her heart of hearts she knew that an accident was bound to happen one day, so that when it finally did she felt a strange kind of relief more than shock.

The young man who'd backed into her could not have been more charming. He accepted full responsibility and she had no reservation about asking him into the house to exchange insurance details.

Tom looked out at the well-kept houses opposite and their trim gardens. Children were playing in one of them up the street. Amanda's mother came back into the room with her papers. 'Let me get you a cup of coffee or something, Mr Shaughnessy. Make yourself comfortable.'

Adding a drop of cream and putting down the jug, Tom let his gaze drift with apparent casualness to a framed collection of family pictures on a cabinet. In fact the images of Amanda from childhood to the age of about eighteen were the first things he had seen when he entered. He took a step closer.

'Nice family, Mrs Higgins. This is your husband and daughter, I take it?'

'That's Don and Mandy,' Mrs Higgins responded proudly and with pleasure.

'Mandy?' he said. 'Nice name.' She was obviously, from the photographs, an only child.

'Actually it's Amanda, but we still call her Mandy.'

'She's beautiful,' he said. 'May I?'

He reached out to pick up one of the pictures, but waited for her permission before touching it. He held it toward the light from the window and studied the smiling teenager in her prom dress.

'My sister says it's difficult bringing up a teenage daughter these days,' he said. 'Do you find that?'

'Oh, Mandy isn't a teenager any longer.' Mrs Higgins gave a little laugh and crossed over to his side. 'She's grown up now.'

He wondered whether to use the line about looking too young to have a grown-up daughter, but decided against it.

'Gosh, isn't that something?' he said, shaking his head at the way of the world. 'How fast they grow up – suddenly they're away and living a life of their own, marrying, having kids.'

'Mandy isn't married,' said Mrs Higgins with a little laugh, realigning the photograph as he put it down. 'Not yet. She works for an international law firm, travels a lot. She hasn't had time to think about settling down.'

'She's a lawyer?' Tom hoped that he sounded impressed, not amazed.

'A paralegal. She's executive assistant to the senior partner. It's a demanding job. A lot of responsibility.'

There was the sound of a door.

'That's my husband. He said he'd be early.' She called out, 'Don, we're in here.'

The heavy-set, balding man Tom had seen in the photographs entered. He might have been a boxer or a football player in his youth, and still wasn't someone to tangle with. He looked at Tom with cold suspicion.

'This is Mr Shaughnessy,' Rosalie was saying. 'I finally had that accident I've been waiting to have for thirty years. I ran into poor Mr Shaughnessy when I was pulling out of the driveway.'

'Actually, I backed into your wife,' Tom said. 'I'm not disputing that. You can see what I've written here.' He passed over a form. 'The car's a rental. This is the insurance claim form I was given, and my driver's permit.'

Don Higgins took the proffered documents and sat down at a desk to examine them, shooting a glance of undiminished distrust in Tom's direction.

'Sounds like interesting work,' Tom said, turning back to Mrs Higgins. 'International law. Does she get back to visit much?'

'Whenever she can. She lives in Los Angeles, but she's away so much that her machine's almost always on when we call.'

'Is your husband a lawyer?' Tom asked, glancing over to where Mr Higgins sat engrossed in his reading, apparently paying no attention to their conversation.

'Don runs a haulage business,' she said. 'How about you? What do you do?'

Tom had prepared for this question in case it came up. 'I'm in the catering business,' he said. 'My company's thinking about opening a new steak-house in the area. Looks like a nice neighbourhood you've got here.'

145

'We like it,' said Mrs Higgins with sincerity. 'Good people. It's homey.'

Mr Higgins got up from his chair and removed the reading glasses that had been perched on his broad nose. 'This seems to be in order,' he said. 'I guess that's all we need do.' He handed Tom his permit back. Tom slipped it into his wallet.

'Again, I'm really sorry about this,' he said. 'I just wasn't paying attention.'

'No real harm done,' Mrs Higgins said. 'Won't you have another cup of coffee?'

'No, thank you. I've detained you long enough,' Tom said. 'It's been nice meeting you – even if under unfortunate circumstances.'

'I'll show you out.' Mr Higgins stepped toward the door as he spoke. Tom shook hands with Amanda's mother, and followed him out.

They walked through to the hall, then Mr Higgins led on down a short corridor. 'This way's quicker,' he said, opening a door into the gloom of an empty double garage. He shut the door as soon as Tom was through, and locked it.

Tom started to turn, but Higgins's hands were on him first, spinning him around and slamming him back against the wall hard enough to knock the breath out of him. He felt a set of broad, hard knuckles at his throat, exerting just enough pressure to let him know how much the other man could hurt him if he chose.

'What the fuck is this about? What do you want?'

Higgins's upper lip was drawn tight and curled back against his teeth. His eyes were black with hatred, and his voice thick with the anger he had been suppressing.

'I don't know what you mean. All I did was—'

He gagged as a pain shot through his throat and smothered the cry that tried to come from it.

'Cut the crap. I know who you are, you piece of shit. What did you say to my wife?'

'I didn't say anything,' Tom spluttered, barely able to get the words out. 'Just what you heard.'

The knuckles stayed where they where and the narrowed eyes

146

bored into Tom's. Then the pressure slackened and the man took a step back. But the threat behind the eyes didn't soften.

'I can take you apart. And I will if I have to,' said Higgins. 'Just give me the chance.'

Tom was no weakling and, after his first shock, was feeling anger and the instinct to fight back. But he held off, knowing that he could lose to this man, and that if he did he would lose badly.

Higgins, as though reading his thoughts, moved across the concrete floor and pulled open the drawer of a workbench. He took out a gun – a big revolver, a .357 by the look of it – and proceeded to load it with ammunition from a shelf behind him as he perched casually on the edge of the bench.

'What are you doing?' Tom asked, not quite able to keep the quaver out of his voice.

'What does it look like I'm doing?' said Higgins. 'I'm waiting for an answer to my question. Why are you here?'

'If you know who I am,' Tom hardened his voice to sound braver than he was and massaged his bruised throat, 'don't you know why?'

'I want you to tell me.' Higgins continued slipping bullets into the revolver's chambers.

'Because I want to know more about her,' Tom said. 'Who she is. How she grew up. What she's like.'

'You damn pervert,' said Higgins, his voice hardly more than a whisper. 'You damn pervert piece of shit.'

With a flick of his meaty hand he snapped the revolver shut and pointed it across the space between them at Tom's head.

'I could take you out right now, you know that? And make it stick.'

Tom began to sweat. 'I mean no harm to you or your wife or your daughter.'

'Oh no? You come prying around here into what's none of your business? No harm?'

'I . . . I've become . . . I'm very fond of your daughter . . .'

The older man slipped from the workbench with a lightness that belied his years and build. Balanced on the balls of his feet, he held the gun at eye-level.

147

'Get the fuck out of here. If you come back, or ever approach my wife again, you're a dead man. Understand?'

'I understand,' Tom said.

'You pervert piece of shit – what are you?'

Tom said nothing.

'Say it!'

Tom felt again the surge of anger that comes from physical humiliation.

'I'm an actor,' he said, realizing that he had reached the point where he would die for his dignity rather than grovel.

Higgins spat on the floor. The spittle splashed over Tom's shoes. He looked down, then up again at the older man. He could see a vein pulsing in the side of his neck.

'Get out of here,' Higgins said. He motioned with his gun towards the garage doors and reached for a switch on the wall. A motor hummed and one half of the doors began to pivot towards the ceiling.

Tom started walking towards the widening strip of light, aware every step of the rock-steady gun aimed at his head. When he got outside he gulped in the air with a sobbing sound that he hoped only he heard.

He didn't alter his pace as he walked down the sloping drive and off the property. When he reached his car and took out his keys he was shaking so hard that he had difficulty opening the door.

★

He took her for a walk along the beach and told her how he'd tracked her parents down and contrived a meeting. She reacted as he'd expected. If they had been in a restaurant she would have walked out. Here, out in the open, there was no easy escape.

'How dare you! How dare you pry into my life? You have no right!'

'Why did you lie to me?'

'I don't have to answer your questions.'

'Why lie if you don't have to?'

'Leave me alone!' She started to walk away, her feet sinking

148

into the sand with every step and pulling her back. He had no trouble keeping up with her. When she changed direction, he changed too.

'Amanda, listen to me.'

'Get away from me, you creep!'

'Answer me one thing. How did your father know who I was?'

'How would I know?'

'I think you know.'

She spun around to face him.

'My father knows what I do for a living. All right? Is that what you want to hear?'

'Did you tell him?'

'No. I told him I worked for a law firm. Then he saw one of my films.'

'He must have seen a few of those films to recognize me.'

'So – maybe he's a fan. Don't knock it. It pays your wages.'

'And your mother still thinks little Mandy works for the law firm?'

A strange look came over her face, a veiled smile of irony but not amusement.

'My mother knows what I do.'

'That's not the impression I got.'

Her smile pulled the edges of her mouth a little tighter. 'Then you got the wrong impression.'

'What I saw, your father was trying to protect her from finding out.'

She laughed openly, a hard sound, filled with scorn.

'This is pathetic,' she said, and started away again. He followed her.

'How does she know? From your father?'

'A friend showed her some pictures. She has nice friends.' She was a little breathless now with the effort of walking and slipping, walking and slipping.

'You mean they both know, but—

'They don't talk about it.' She finished the thought for him. 'Okay? Got it? Now stop following me, or so help me I'm going to start screaming rape till the cops arrive by helicopter.'

'D'you ever go back there?' he persisted, ignoring the threat.

'What do you think? Can you see us all sitting around making conversation? No thanks.'

'What did they do to you? Was it your father?'

'Just leave it. Okay?'

He had overtaken her now and was dancing backwards like a TV cameraman ambushing his subject. 'There's some reason why you do what you do,' he said. 'There has to be.'

Her eyes flashed with new rage. 'What is this – therapy?' She spat the word out in a way that made it sound dirty.

'Something happened to you.'

'Give me a break!'

'I want to know what it was.'

'Fuck you!'

'I want to know because I love you and I want to marry you.'

His words stopped her dead in her tracks. She stared at him as if he'd hit her. It took a while for her brain to devise a response, and longer for her mouth to convey it.

'You really are crazy,' she said at last. The way she spoke and looked at him suggested a woman just discovering that a harmless pet was capable of savage and dangerous behaviour. 'Stay away from me,' she said in a voice that was suddenly full of fear.

She turned and started off again across the sand. This time he didn't follow her. He stayed where he was, watching as her figure grew smaller in the distance. He had nothing left to say, and was surprised by the feeling of emptiness in the pit of his stomach.

★

When he got to his car there was no sign of her. She must have found a cab or a bus or hitched a ride. He drove back to his apartment and tried to call her. The machine answered. He didn't leave a message. Instead he drove to where she lived and rang from downstairs. She answered on the intercom, but refused to let him in. She said if he didn't go away she would call security from one of the production companies she knew. He didn't want that, so he got back into his car and drove around and tried to think, or not to think; he wasn't sure which.

A couple of calls were all it took to track down if she was working that week, and where. He sat outside her apartment in his car and waited for her to leave. Sometimes she drove herself, sometimes she took a cab. This time the production sent a car for her. He didn't follow it.

Next day he was due at some ranch out in the Valley to shoot a scene himself, not in the film she was making but in one of the dozens that were always shooting. He called in sick and said he'd be out of circulation for at least a week. He couldn't face the thought of work for the time being.

All he wanted was to see her and talk to her. He knew that if he could only do that he would, in time, win her trust. She would come to understand that he was serious, different from the rest: from any man she had ever known.

And yet she kept him at arm's length. There was no reply to her phone or to her doorbell. She had even disconnected her answering machine. He began to wonder if she'd moved out. Then one morning she picked up, sounding sleepy. It was six-thirty a.m.

'Amanda? It's me, Tom.'

'Oh, no.'

'Where've you been? I've been trying to get you for days.'

'Look, just forget it, will you? You'll be doing us both a favour. Please.'

'At least let me see you.'

'I'm going to hang up now. Please don't call again.'

The line buzzed in his ear. He hung up slowly, and made a decision.

She had apparently said nothing to anybody else about trying to avoid him, so it proved a simple matter to make a few inquiries and find out where she was working that day.

The studio was a converted warehouse somewhere off La Brea. No outsider would have got past the guards, but they knew Tom and greeted him as a friend.

'I didn't know you were called,' said one of them, running a ballpoint down his list.

'I'm not,' Tom said. 'I just want to see somebody.'

'Okay. Go on ahead.'

Dry ice rose up through a neon-lit torture chamber. A set-dresser and assistant fussed around checking axes and crossed swords on walls, the drape of a curtain by a staircase, and the positioning of an obscene coat of arms on a cardboard portcullis. The focus of the scene was an ingeniously revolving frame on which Amanda was spread-eagled, totally naked, shackled by her hands and feet. Two men stood on either side of her, also naked except for black masks on their faces. A fluff girl was on her knees ministering to one of them in readiness for the scene; the other was getting himself into the mood with rhythmic movements of his right hand, known among professionals as the Strasberg method. Amanda, her face composed and expressionless stared up into the darkness.

Tom hung back, unobserved except by a couple of techs who gave him a nod of greeting. His stomach churned with a nervousness he was unused to. He took several deep breaths and told himself that he would simply wait until the scene was over, then go to her dressing room and talk to her calmly and rationally. She would realize that she had nothing to fear from him, and they would resume their relationship where they had left off.

The assistant director called for silence, the camera operator called 'speed' a moment later, and the director said, 'Action!'

Tom watched, knowing that he didn't want to, telling himself that in a moment he would turn away, or go and wait outside till it was over.

But he didn't turn away, and he couldn't leave. He stayed where he was without the movement of a muscle or the flicker of an eyelid. If he had looked into himself he would have said that both his breathing and his heart had stopped.

But he was not looking into himself. He was looking at Amanda, and at what those two men were doing to her. And he snapped.

Nobody realized what was happening at first. A joke, perhaps. Some kind of a stunt. All at once there he was on the set, shouting incoherently, dragging the two actors off Amanda and wrenching her plastic chains from their flimsy mounting.

The actors, too shocked and vulnerable in their nakedness to react with force, backed off. One of them pulled off his mask. It was Hal.

'Jesus, what the fuck—?' was all he got out before Tom's fist hit him in the mouth and sent him staggering backwards, taking the dungeon wall with him. A clamour of shouting filled the air and half a dozen members of the crew plus three security guards stampeded to the rescue.

Amanda watched in horrified disbelief as Tom, his eyes never leaving hers and still shouting her name, was hauled struggling from the set. Then she realized that the wardrobe girl was wrapping a towelling robe around her, holding her, telling her that everything was all right.

The director, who was badly overweight, was also hyperventilating and looking far from well. He managed to declare a twenty-minute break, and was then helped out by his assistant.

It was really just bad luck that the producer happened to be present on that particular day. He had been in his office going through a budget when the commotion started. Tom was dragged before him, pushed into a chair, and ordered to explain himself.

The porno business, though widespread and with many separate companies and different producers, is ultimately controlled by a relatively small group of people – smaller than that which controls the legitimate film industry. Not since the days of the 'thirties and 'forties has a Louis B. Mayer, Harry Cohn or Jack Warner had the power to say to anybody, 'You will never work in this town again' and make it stick.

In the porno business, however, there is still that power. When the dread words were pronounced over Tom's head like a ceremony of excommunication, he knew this was the end. His career was prematurely and absolutely terminated.

Worse, much worse, were the dire warnings handed out as to what would happen if he ever showed his face around a set again, or attempted anywhere, at any time, to contact Amanda. The details of the injuries he might expect to sustain were not spelt out. They didn't need to be. He knew these guys weren't kidding.

He drove home in a daze. Not because he'd been physically beaten; the beating would come later, a first warning if he disobeyed the injunction to stay away from Amanda. He didn't relish it, but he knew he had to risk it. In fact he had to risk more than that.

Tom was a man with only one purpose in life: to marry Amanda Higgins. And if that failed, he was, he realized now, prepared to die.

★

He bought a wig and a false moustache and tried them on in front of his mirror. He looked like himself in a wig and a false moustache. He tried on spectacle frames with plain glass in place of lenses. They looked wrong.

This wasn't going to be as easy as getting in to see her parents. For one thing, her parents hadn't been guarded by professionals. Tom had cruised by Amanda's apartment three times now, always huddled down in the back of a cab. Each time he had spotted a parked car with different heavies watching the place. Obviously round-the-clock protection.

He had another cab make a tour of the area the building backed on to. What he saw was discouraging. Maybe a skilled burglar could have found a way through the high walls and locked gates, but an amateur would be a fool to try.

Of course, he told himself, they couldn't keep her under guard for ever. But as soon as the thought was formed, he realized that they wouldn't need to. The obvious thing would be for her to move house. Probably she was looking at places even now. Or they would have somebody find one for her. After that, in this city, he would never see her again.

He had to find a solution fast.

★

She peered at the ID pushed through her door. She looked again through the peep-hole and saw somebody in the maintenance company's uniform of peaked hat and blouse-type jacket. She couldn't see the face because a light seemed to have gone outside her door. She would call the manager to fix it. Meanwhile she unhooked the security chain to admit the man who'd come about the leak in her dishwasher. Tom was in with the door shut behind him before she realized who he was.

'I have to talk to you.'

154

She didn't show fear. She just looked right at him and turned her surprise into a warning.

'They're watching this place – you know what'll happen.'

'They don't know I'm here.'

She took a step back. He saw she was wearing a simple cotton dress, bare feet, her hair hanging loose on her shoulders.

'Don't be afraid. You don't think I'd harm you, do you?'

'You were pretty crazy the other day.'

'Can I come in? I won't stay long.'

She thought about it for a moment, then shrugged. 'Now you're here.'

He followed her into a room that was open and light, and seemed to him unfurnished at first. Then he looked around and saw that there was only what was needed for one person to live there. And the things in the room were good things. Something about them told him that the chest over there in beautiful old wood was a collector's item. And so was the modern chair in rich-looking leather with the clean, sweeping line. And the table with the glass top and the thin, angular lamp on it. There were a couple of paintings on the walls. Abstracts. No mirrors. It was cold, but it had something.

He looked back at her, standing with her back to the light, waiting for him to speak.

'I was wrong to go after your parents,' he said. Then added, simply, 'I couldn't help it. They're part of you, and I—'

'Tom, it's no use.'

Her eyes shone with a steady gaze out of the expressionless patch of shadow that was her face.

'All right. I'll just say what I came to say. I don't know what happened. That's the problem. I looked at you, and I knew. That first time. There was something in you that I wanted in my life. Needed. And all I hoped was that you might somehow want me in your life. But I knew it was impossible.'

'Until you found out who I was?'

His first impulse was to say that it made no difference. But he turned it into a question. 'What difference would that make?'

'Some.'

He didn't know what to say to this. Yes, it made a difference. And no, it didn't. Finally he said, 'Have I ever been anything but a gentleman to you?'

She shook her head with, he thought, the same slight sadness that he'd seen on that first night in the parking lot when she had refused to go home with him. 'No,' she said.

'Okay. Thank you for that.' He spoke like a man who had been given no more than his due. 'Look,' he continued, 'we're both old enough to know what we're doing. We have been for a while. I knew what I was doing when I asked you to marry me. I'm out of this business now. I always meant to get out of it. I dare say you do, too, one day.'

'Not necessarily.' She looked at him with a blankness behind her eyes that he hadn't seen before. It alarmed him.

'All right. If you say so.' He wasn't going to argue. 'Then I'm asking you to think about it. And to think about what I asked you at the beach. I've got a little money put by. Almost enough to try something that I've always wanted to try.'

He waited. She said nothing.

'Don't you want to know what it is?'

'What is it?' Her voice was flat, indifferent to his answer.

'Buy some land up in Napa Valley. Grow vines. Make wine.'

He didn't see anything, but he sensed something go through her, a kind of shock, or at least surprise. He felt her focus on him.

'Do you know anything about wine?'

'I was a waiter for a long time. I know enough to start. Of course, I don't have to do it. It's just an idea. If you had something else in mind, we could always . . .'

His words tailed off. He felt a sudden heaviness. He knew with an awful certainty that he was asking the impossible. But he didn't know why. 'Say something.' His words came out as a simple plea.

Her reply was almost a whisper. 'I can't.'

'Why not?'

She didn't seem to have an answer for this. After a moment she turned and began moving towards the window, swinging slowly and lightly from the ball of one bare foot to the other, across the

156

patterned rug and on to the plain, pale grey carpet beyond. When she spoke her voice had a clear, almost musical quality.

'At a time like this she would turn and walk to the window,' she said, describing her own movements, 'stop, and look out, deep in thought.'

'Who would?'

'The actress who plays me.' She continued looking out.

'I don't understand. "The actress who plays you?"'

'Try to understand.' She still didn't turn.

'I'm trying,' he said. 'It sounds like you're keeping a distance between yourself and what you do.'

'Maybe.'

'All right,' he said after a while. 'What would she say, this actress who plays you, after she turned back from the window deep in thought?'

'She would say,' she said, half turning, but not looking at him, 'that other people's illusions are not a good place to be.'

'But that's where she is, isn't she? She's an actress. Where else would she be?'

She looked at him.

'What about *you*?' he said. 'Not the actress who plays you.'

'I'm confused.'

The silence lengthened between them. Neither moved.

'It's going to take a long time,' he said finally, 'for us to know about each other. All I want you to do is to think about giving it a try. If you really decide the answer's no, then I'll leave you alone. I'm not crazy. I'm not a stalker. I'll get out of your life.'

He waited. She didn't say anything, didn't move.

'I'll leave now. I'm sorry to have bust in like this. I didn't know what else to do.'

He started for the door. She didn't do or say anything to stop him. He reached for the latch and turned back one last time.

'Think about it. That's all I ask.'

He opened the door, and stopped. The two heavies who'd been sitting in the car stood there, with the terrified maintenance man in his shirtsleeves between them.

'Fella here needs his uniform and ID back,' one of them said in a flat voice, surveying Tom with his head slightly back and on one side.

Tom made an effort to sound calmer than he felt. 'Sure,' he said, taking off the cap and the jacket. 'ID's in the pocket.'

The maintenance man took the garments with trembling hands and started away, not stopping to put them on.

'Hey,' said the man who had spoken before, holding something out. 'Take your money. It's his money,' nodding towards Tom. 'I don't want it.'

The maintenance man hesitated, then took three quick steps and snatched the hundred dollars that Tom had given him earlier. Then he ran for the emergency stairs and clattered down them two at a time.

'It's all right. He didn't do anything.' Amanda had come to the door and seen each of the two big men take one of Tom's arms. She looked worried.

'He got in, didn't he?' said the mouthpiece of the two.

Amanda looked from him to Tom and back. 'Don't hurt him,' she said.

'We know what we have to do.' They turned Tom around. 'Come on, you.'

She watched as they frog-marched him to the elevator. She was still standing there when the doors closed.

★

'Send her in,' said the man behind the desk. He was forty-ish, dapper in an impeccably cut dark suit, with black hair brushed straight back from a watchful, carefully tanned face. He wore a gold signet ring and heavy gold cuff-links.

An assistant in his twenties opened the door, admitting Amanda to the plush third-floor office overlooking the most expensive stretch of Wilshire Boulevard in Beverly Hills.

The man behind the desk did not get up, just looked her over with slightly hooded eyes. She wore the same simple cotton dress she had been wearing an hour earlier when she watched from her window as the car below drove off with Tom and the two men.

As it disappeared, she had reached for her phone and made a call to this office.

She sat obediently in the chair the man pointed to, and waited for him to speak.

'So – you have something on your mind. Tell me.'

She looked down at the small leather purse she was carrying, as much to have something to do with her hands as for any practical purpose.

'You said when I started working for you that I could quit any time I wanted.' Now she looked at him. 'You remember, I asked you? You said that was understood.'

The man was sitting back with his fingers steepled in front of his chin. He made a little open gesture.

'So?'

'I want to quit. Now.'

He looked at her a while before responding, a slight frown pinching his eyebrows towards the bridge of his perfectly straight nose.

'Have you thought about this seriously?'

'Yes, I have.'

'You're sure it's not because of some other problem I could maybe help you with?'

'Quite sure.'

Again he was silent a while. Then he made another open gesture with his hands, wider than last time.

'It's true, I made you a deal. And in this business a deal is a deal. We don't need contracts. You want to quit, you have that right. Provided . . .'

He leaned forward, one elbow on his desk and a warning finger in the air.

'Provided,' he said solemnly, 'that what you're talking about is permanent retirement. You don't go working for somebody else. That would be regarded as a breach of our understanding, and I would not want to reach that situation. You understand me?'

'I won't be working for anybody else.'

He nodded, satisfied, and sat back again. 'Naturally, if some day you change your mind and you want to come back, we can talk about that at such a time.'

159

She felt it incumbent upon her to acknowledge this generously left-open door. 'Thank you,' she said.

'I hope you've saved a little money. You're not walking away empty-handed.'

'No. I'm all right. Thank you.'

'That's good. I wish you the best.'

When she didn't get up to leave, he waited.

'There's something else?'

'Tom Shaughnessy,' she said.

'What about him? What d'you want me to do?'

'I don't want you to do anything. I want him left alone.'

The man tipped his head as though looking at a problem here.

'He did what he'd been warned against. He has to be made aware of this mistake.'

'Of course.' She knew there was no point arguing this. 'But after that, leave him alone. Please.'

The man looked at her for some time, not because he was trying to divine the reasons for her request; on the contrary, he found all human behaviour curiously predictable, and sometimes vaguely wondered why.

'If that's what you want,' he said eventually.

'It's what I want.'

'Very well.'

She got to her feet. The man remained seated.

'Thank you,' she said.

He nodded, but was no longer looking at her. She turned and started for the door. The assistant who had shown her in materialized as if from nowhere and opened it for her.

★

Tom winced in pain as the nurse eased him up on his pillows. He had three cracked ribs, a broken arm, and a face that had been remodelled in startling variations of purple, black, and a red-tinged blue.

'No,' he was saying to Amanda, 'the guys didn't do this. They worked me over, but they're professionals. This was later. I fell down the stairs in my apartment block.'

'How did it happen?'

He attempted something she deciphered as a look of total incomprehension.

'One minute I was going out to get another pint of bourbon, the next I was being lifted into an ambulance.'

'"Another" pint of bourbon?'

'Didn't I mention I was drunk?'

She didn't answer. 'I had a lot of trouble finding you,' she said.

'It's nice of you to come.' A pause, then, 'Do I take it you're rethinking my proposal?'

'Actually, no,' she said. 'But I think you should.'

'I don't have to.'

'All the same, I think you should. So I'm going to make you a counter-proposal.'

Somewhere beneath his blunted, inexpressive features a hopeful look replaced a downcast one. 'Go ahead. Shoot.'

'What I propose is that we meet in a year from now, and don't see each other during that time. If we both feel the same way then that we do now, we may get somewhere.'

He pondered the proposal for a moment, then asked, 'How d'you feel now?'

'I feel we may get somewhere – in a year's time.'

'*An Affair to Remember*,' he said. 'Doris Day and Cary Grant.'

'It was Deborah Kerr.'

'You're right. God, actors hate it when you do that.'

'They're right.'

'They agree to meet on top of the Empire State Building in a year's time if they feel the same way about each other. He gets there first, and she gets hit by a cab hurrying across the road to join him. He waits all day, and thinks she's changed her mind.'

He looked down at his immobile body, then at his broken arm, his right one, in its cast. 'I guess I get to play Deborah Kerr.'

When he turned to look at her again, he saw she was completely serious.

'All right,' he said. 'I'll meet your counter-proposal with a counter-counter-proposal.'

'What is it?'

161

'We'll make it six months, and only halfway up the Empire State.'

She thought this over. 'Six months, and the top.'

'Empire State's too corny. It's been done. Besides, what if it's windy and they close it?'

She thought some more. 'Malibu Pier.'

'Three months.'

She shook her head. 'Six.'

'Done,' he said, regretting that he couldn't offer her a handshake.

She got up to go. 'They tell me you'll be out of here in a couple of weeks, good as new.'

'Amanda . . . ?'

She stopped and turned on her way to the door.

'What'll you be doing between now and when we meet?'

'That's none of your business.'

'Are you going to . . . work?'

She hesitated before she replied, then said, 'Don't ask me that. And another thing . . .'

She turned to face him, preparing to issue a stern ultimatum. 'If you try to find me, or make any inquiries, or make contact with any members of my family or anybody in any way connected with me, then it's off. Is that clear?'

'Clear.'

'Good.'

She started out again. When she reached the door she stopped, looked back, and said with the trace of a smile, 'Watch out when you're crossing the street, Miss Kerr.'

The Ghost of Me Sings

Like the song says, be careful what you want, because you might get it.

Fame, wealth, beauty, youth – I had it all. In spades. I was the kid every kid in the world wanted to be. And now . . . ? You got a couple of minutes, let me tell you about it.

Me, I've got all the time in the world . . .

★

My dad dropped out of school and got a job in a steel mill in Cleveland, Ohio. He had this crazy notion that being grown up and earning money would mean freedom and independence. It took barely a year to knock that idea out of him; he learned that slavery didn't mean literally being kept in chains and locked up every night. He hit the road and started to work his way west, wondering if he'd wind up in California, or if he'd find what he was in search of before he got there. Not that he had much idea of what it was that he was looking for, but he figured he'd know it when he saw it.

He tried his hand at all the usual losers' jobs – worked in bars, amusement parks, pretty much any kind of casual labour he could get. Somewhere along the line he met my mom, got her pregnant and married her. I didn't meet her folks till years later. They were religious and kind of strait-laced, and made me very sad. It was no surprise that my mom, who was only a kid, had been keen to get away from home. My dad must have seemed like a White Knight on his charger, riding into town and whisking her off to a life of romance and adventure – which, as things turned out, wound up in a trailer park in Long Beach, California. That was the first home I ever knew.

Neither of my folks had any dreams for themselves about show business. Like everybody else, they'd go to the movies sometimes and think they could do whatever it was they were watching up there on the screen, but they knew damn well they'd never get the chance: people like them didn't get to be stars. My dad worked in valet parking now and then. One time he got sent out to a party at a house in Beverly Hills that belonged to some big producer. There were a lot of faces he knew from television and the movies there, plus a couple of real major stars. It was another world, he said. Just another world. Unfortunately he got fired for asking some television actress for her autograph, which was a dumb thing to do considering he'd been told up front that anything like that was a no-no. After that he got into pool maintenance, but his customers were just businessmen and lawyers and executives and stuff like that – nobody interesting.

Things didn't start to turn around until I was six years old. It was all really down to my dad, who was a country and western freak. I'd been brought up on that music, and when I saw the publicity all around the trailer park and down the road for a marathon amateur talent contest, I told him I wanted to enter for the under-ten category. My mom wasn't too keen on the idea; some hangover from her religious upbringing made her think that kids should lead ordinary lives and not get ideas about glamour and razzmatazz.

I won my category with no trouble, even getting a special commendation from the judges. It was the greatest day of my life. Despite all the incredible things that would come my way later, that moment has always remained special. It didn't just feel good: it felt right! When I stood up there, listening to the crowd cheer, I knew for the first time, and with absolute certainty, what I'd been born into this world to do.

A casting director was in the audience, which was how I got my first TV commercial. I played part of a family who loved their new car so much that they didn't want to get out of it and go back into their cute little suburban house. After that I did another one, playing a kid ostracized by his friends for not wearing the right brand of sneakers. Then I got my first sitcom. It was only a supporting role – the kid next door – but I started getting fan mail. When the show went into its second season they built up my part. Then I got my own show, with scripts tailored to what I could do best.

The trouble was I could do a whole lot of things. I could dance, I could sing, I could act; I was even learning magic tricks. I could play straight drama and I could play comedy. Timing came naturally to me. I only had to think of a look, a move, a vocal inflection, and I could do it with a precision that got exactly the response I wanted. So I sat down with my dad and we talked about which talents I should keep under wraps for the moment, and which ones I should exploit.

My dad was pretty smart in that way. In spite of what happened later, I still give him full credit for managing my career in those crucial early stages. He had an instinct for what was right for me and what wasn't; who I should be in business with, and who not. He and my mom had already split up at this point, and they divorced a year later. I have to say I wasn't entirely happy with the attitude he took over that, trying to shaft her financially the way he did by pretending his income was only a fraction of what it was. It's true that I was the one earning the money, not him; but that was a pretty phoney distinction, since in reality he had access to as much of the money as he wanted. I didn't mind that. Not once did I begrudge him his girlfriends, his dope, the cars that he bought, the house in Brentwood and the little place in Aspen. Sure, he was spending my money, but I knew I'd make it back tenfold and more. So did he, and no matter how much he partied he never lost sight of what mattered, never made a bad judgement call on my behalf.

All the same, I made him listen to me about Mom, and in the end we settled enough money on her so she wouldn't have to go out to work. Legally they had joint custody of me, but in reality I lived with my dad.

I starred in my first feature film at the age of ten, playing a kid abducted by aliens who were studying human nature in order to plan their takeover of Planet Earth. With comical resourcefulness my character saved the day and sent them packing in ninety-eight action-packed minutes. There were two sequels, each at a significantly increased fee. Between the second and third of these I made my first concert tour. Dad and I had had a talk and decided it was time to extend my repertoire. I'd been working up an act in secret – got myself a terrific choreographer and a great musical director, had a bunch of songs specially written for me. Wherever I played, kids lined up all night to buy tickets.

At fifteen I was on the cover of *Time* magazine when I made the year's top-grossing picture and became the biggest-drawing concert artist as well as the number one recording star. I worked hard, and yet I always had something in reserve. I made it look effortless, and yet somehow impossible. People said I had a God-given gift.

It was truer than they knew.

School had long since been a thing of the past. I had private tutors on tap for the requisite number of hours that the state said kids had to spend studying, but things were run strictly my way. I studied what I wanted to study and ignored what I didn't. Maybe it wasn't what you'd call structured, but I never lacked any knowledge that I needed. I could always find somebody to tell me all about anything that I wanted to know. I visited with sportsmen, politicians, scientists; in a short time I got to know just about everybody who was anybody.

The first time I got really mad with my dad was over a girl. I was sixteen years old and, as you can imagine, I had just about all I could handle in that department; and so had he pretty much. This particular one was a secretary I'd seen in the office of one of the studio heads.

How can you ever say what it is that makes a girl special? I won't even try to describe her, except that she had dark hair which she wore long, a kind of shy expression, a cute figure, and she wasn't very tall – which was perfect, because I wasn't all that tall myself. I got her phone number and address, and had a limo pick her up. I was living by then in my own house in Bel Air; my dad had kept his own place in Brentwood. I had a staff of four to look after the house and another three who took care of the grounds, which I'd turned into my own private theme park. There were waterfalls, a mystery train ride, an enchanted forest, a fabulous Aladdin's Cave (which was also the way into my underground nuclear shelter, the biggest and best in Hollywood), a couple of Shetland ponies, some baby deer, and a pair of monkeys called Fred and Ginger. I'm not exaggerating when I say it took people's breath away when I showed them around. I loved watching their faces; they didn't know what to say, and this girl was no exception.

We swam in my Blue Lagoon which, at the touch of a switch, was encircled by artificial rocks while remaining open to the sky and stars above. We made fantastic love right there in the water, then again on the body-contoured tropical minibeach I'd designed alongside. After that we had dinner by candlelight and listened to all her favourite tracks from my collected CDs; then we went to bed and I let her pick which of my movies we'd watch. She moved in with me, and I arranged for the studio to give her paid leave of absence. We were blissfully happy. Or so I thought.

It all came apart when my father brought a pile of scripts over about a week later. I was supposed to glance through the story synopses, then read any that seemed likely contenders for my next major project. I found a handwritten note folded between the pages of one of them. At first I assumed it must be a reader's report, though I'd never seen one before that wasn't printed. I am not in the habit of reading other people's personal mail, but once I'd started this it was impossible to stop. It was from her to my dad, and made graphically clear that there had been an affair going on between them for about six months before I met her. He'd spotted her at the studio the same way I had, and, apparently, when I started dating her he figured the best thing for him to do was back off. She had been reluctant about this, because she seemed genuinely fond of him – which I considered pretty obscene in view of their age difference. None the less, as she wrote in the letter, 'I guess I'm going to have to be careful if I want to go on working in this town. If I don't do exactly what he wants, that vindictive dwarf of a son of yours will have me banned from every studio, network, and major production company in the business. With any luck I won't have to put up with his spots and bad breath for long, since he has yet to develop the attention span of a flea, not to mention the sexual staying power of one. It's kind of pathetic, isn't it – a teenage carbuncle like that taking himself for a stallion?'

I had to go out into the garden and sit down for a while to absorb the shock. 'Vindictive dwarf.' I have already mentioned that I was not particularly tall, but I was certainly not a dwarf.

'Teenage carbuncle.' It was true that my acting was mostly in comedic roles, but that was because of my incredible gift of comic timing, and had nothing whatever to do with the fact that my face had a certain humorous roundness to it. Besides, kids fell in love and fornicated in their millions to my music – and tell me how many 'carbuncles' can say that!

As for 'spots and bad breath', even the finest skin suffers the occasional blemish, it's only natural. According to this defamatory filth, I appeared to be some grotesque, suppurating pustule on legs. That was a foul libel – not only against me but against my dermatologist, who was the best in Beverly Hills. My personal make-up artist had no problems whatever in preparing my face either for the camera or a public appearance. The bad breath was just a downright lie.

The bitch was right about one thing, though: she never did work in that town again.

As for my dad . . . Well, I was disappointed, but he was still my dad. I warned him never – ever! – to lie to me again. Then I left him mumbling apologies and looking like something you've just mopped the floor with.

What worried me about this whole episode, when I reflected on it over the next few days, wasn't the fact that I'd been made a fool of: more importantly, the fans had been made fools of. I'd let them down by being taken in like that. They looked up to me – millions of young people all over the world. I was an icon, a symbol of everything they aspired to, everything that was possible. I didn't drink, I didn't smoke, and I didn't do drugs. When I sang, I sang about how they felt inside. I was their voice. I realized then that I had no choice but to make manifest what I and they had always known, but which I had so far allowed to remain implicit.

The transformation began modestly: a little off the nose, a little on the chin. The implants in my cheek-bones, together with the work on my mouth and the widening of my bite, gave my face a whole different shape. After that, I decided on a little more work on the nose, which in turn required a further adjustment to the cheek implants and the shaving of some bone around the eyes.

It was a long, complex, often painful process, which took the best part of three years. Each time I appeared in public, whether for a concert, in a film, or just for a publicity layout, I looked slightly different. There was a certain amount of sniping from some quarters, but that was as unimportant as it was inevitable. There were also some uncalled-for criticisms voiced in public by certain members of the medical profession, especially when not only my face but also my body began to change its form, thanks to a judicious use of growth hormones and steroids. I was becoming tall and muscular, and my profile had the noble symmetry of a Renaissance statue.

The fans loved it, of course. They realized that I was growing up in my own image and not just according to the randomness of genes and body chemistry. It was everything they had expected and hoped for from me. My popularity leapt to new peaks. I had long been recognized as a phenomenon; now there was no word to describe adequately my unique stature in the world of entertainment.

I had at last parted company with my father. The fact that I was now a head taller than him had subtly altered our relationship; I no longer felt any lingering need of his approval or fear of his scorn. I was at last, in every sense, a bigger man than him.

The actual break came one afternoon when I was sitting with a group of architects and city planners, working on drawings for the public theme park which was to be built in Orange County along the lines of my own private park in Bel Air. In the first place, Dad had no particular reason to be at the meeting; I guess he didn't have much else to do. Secondly, he was drunk, which was probably what provoked him to make the obscene and offensive remark that finally cut the last remaining ties between us.

171

We were discussing the height of the tower which was to form the ornamental gate of the park. The tower was to be in the shape of my new, remodelled head, and visitors were to enter through its smiling open mouth. We were debating whether the mouth should be at ground level, which would mean losing the chin; or whether visitors should mount steps to reach the mouth. I favoured the latter approach, since a head without a chin – especially a perfect chin like mine – seemed unnatural.

For no reason whatsoever, and as though merely filling in a brief gap in the conversation, my father asked why we didn't turn the whole thing around and have them enter through a totally different and lower orifice of my body, since, according to him, that was how I generally preferred people to make their approach.

There was a shocked silence and several sharp intakes of breath. All eyes in the room turned fearfully in my direction. I got to my feet, drew myself up to my full height, and declared that my responsibility to the millions of decent young people around the world who looked to me for leadership made it impossible for me to tolerate such vulgarity in my presence. I announced that I would be leaving the room for a few minutes, and that when I returned I did not expect to find 'that man' still there.

And he wasn't. I have not heard of my father from that day to this.

By contrast, I felt that I had unjustly neglected my mother for some time, so I made arrangements to visit her. She had married a dentist and was living modestly in Tarzana. He was a religious man, and she too had returned some way to the piety of her childhood. When the seven black limousines which comprised my entourage pulled up in front of her house, I thought she would be excited and impressed. Instead she merely looked bewildered. 'Why so many people?' she asked.

I explained that I needed bodyguards wherever I went, plus assistants to keep me in touch at all times with the various aspects of my interests and activities. Also I had to have my own private chef and mobile kitchen to prepare the strict vegetarian diet to which I had been confined since the temporary lymphatic imbalance following my last course of hormonal treatment. And, of course, I never travelled anywhere without my own private physician, plus serums and blood transfusions should they become necessary.

When I had finished explaining all this, there were tears in my mother's eyes. I could not understand why, except for the fact that there had always been a strange quality of sadness in her. I did my best to comfort her, offering her holidays, a house in Florida, servants. But she did not want material things. She was only concerned, she said, that I was so unhappy.

Unhappy? Me?

At first I did not understand what she was trying to say, and then I began to see how deeply she had misconceived the true nature of the life to which she had given birth. I took her alone into her drawing room, where I sat her down and tried to reassure her. Far from being unhappy, I told her, I was undoubtedly the most completely fulfilled being ever to have lived on earth. I spoke of the different guises in which God came down to visit man, sometimes dying humbly on a cross, other times being venerated as a prophet, occasionally being mistaken for an alien spacecraft. Imagine, I said to her, that you are God, and that this time you want to experience the very best and highest happiness of which man is capable; would you not then come to earth as a superstar? As me?

I looked deep into her eyes to see if she had truly caught my meaning, but she seemed only to be on the verge of further violent weeping, so I let the matter drop. We parted company fondly, but with the sadness which is, I fear, her lot in life.

Four days later I collapsed on the stage of the Universal Amphitheater in Hollywood. You will all remember the headlines, I am sure. Journalists began playing with words they could barely spell, let alone understand. 'Hubris' is one that particularly stands out in my memory. Then there was 'vainglory', 'pride incarnate', and all the rest of it. Plus long articles by so-called medical experts on the 'recklessness' of what I'd done to myself.

The fans were desperate and camped for days outside the hospital, until the police finally had to clear them away with water-cannons and riot gear. The same thing happened in Bel Air when I returned to be nursed privately at home. I put out statements couched in carefully spiritual terms, telling them that all things were in God's hands and they should have no fear.

Certainly I had none. Even when the headaches started, and the strange distortions in my bones began twisting my body into the shape of a gnarled, wind-blasted tree, and turned my head, my classically beautiful and perfect head, into a malformed monstrosity, I still felt no fear. Although the fans continued begging to see me, I did not allow it. They would have found the pain too hard to bear. It was something to be played out between myself and the remains of the mortal form that I had always known I would ultimately discard.

My private physician had disappeared. The talk around town was that he had fled overseas to avoid the lawsuits, but he needn't have worried: I had no intention of going to law. I wished only to be left in peace.

Unfortunately that was not to be. After only a few weeks, and quite without warning, an army of grim-faced men forced their way into my house, waving police shields and search warrants in the faces of anyone who tried to stop them. I have to admit that my face stopped them, but only temporarily. As soon as they had recovered from the shock, they proceeded to begin searching the premises from top to bottom, after which they started on the grounds.

Let me tell you how this appalling intrusion came about and see if you do not share my sense of outrage. By far the most troubling aspect of the whole episode was the extraordinary lack of respect for any kind of individual privacy that it represented. I'm not talking about privacy for the famous, which is a much debated topic and for which I make no special case; in fact I tend to agree that well-known people, for whom publicity is part and parcel of their lives, have less cause than others to complain of media harassment. It is only natural that people want to see us, hear about us, read what we have said and done. They have every right: up to a point.

Beyond that point, however, we get into areas which are of no legitimate interest to anyone but ourselves and for which we should, surely, be afforded the protection expected by any ordinary citizen. If our innermost secrets are to be thrown open to everybody and his brother, then normal life becomes impossible.

I'm not just talking about prying – and sometimes lying – by the media; it's the whole question of constitutional rights and the protection, if any, that they offer us against the state: Big Brother! I mean, you probably don't think there's such a thing as Thought Police in this country, do you? Well, think again.

Are your thoughts your own? Do you own them? Are they truly your property? Are they *private*? If you still think so, then be prepared for a shock when you hear what happened to me.

I was feeling stronger. Specialists had been flown in from all over the world and I had been told that my condition was 'stabilized'. They didn't know how long it would last; there could be further deteriorations, but they hoped to find ways of minimizing them.

It was a reprieve of a kind, although my appearance remained as grotesque as ever and always would. Further plastic surgery had been ruled out of the question. I decided to make the most of my situation. I called a researcher, a kid I'd used before. Over the phone, I told him that I was working on an idea for a picture. I swore him to secrecy and promised a five-figure bonus if no word of this leaked out to the press. Within days he had faxed me a whole load of material: all the background I needed.

Over the next couple of weeks a series of deliveries was made to the house from all over the country. I had everything – the packages the sealed containers, the heavy boxes – carried out into Aladdin's Cave and down into my nuclear shelter.

From then on I spent most of my time down there. None of my staff were allowed in. I reprogrammed all the locks and neither wrote down nor told anybody else the codes. Is there any clearer statement of a wish for privacy than that? I was not writing a script, of course, but that was my business – a fact that didn't stop them bursting in the way I've described.

And all this came about because they'd probed my thoughts. They had somehow heard that I had been in touch with my researcher, then put him under the third degree until they found out what I'd wanted to know. After that they relentlessly made the rounds of every manufacturer and supplier I had done business with and demanded a list of everything that I had purchased from each of them. In that way they put together a picture of what was in my mind: they had stolen my thoughts. The only reason they burst into my house that day was because of what they had discovered I had been thinking.

Is that legal? Is that right? Is that American? Is that all the protection we have against the arrogance of government?

I'm proud to say that I gave them none of the codes to the locks on my shelter. They had to bring in equipment and burn through. My personal lawyer had arrived by then, but even he couldn't stop them.

And what did they find? They found exactly what they knew they would find: a fully operational life-support system as good as any in a hospital intensive care unit; enough supplies to drip-feed a comatose human being and keep him alive indefinitely; some electronic equipment for which it would have taken anybody less well prepared than they were some time to figure out a use; and a large tank filled with a viscous fluid in which a human body could be floated with ease.

The body in question, of course, was that of my doctor, who had not gone abroad at all.

It came as a surprise to me when, after lifting him out, they pronounced him dead. I thought I had taken every possible precaution. Certainly he had been alive the previous evening when I had put the last sequence of electric shocks through him; his screams had left no doubt about that. Something must have malfunctioned in the night. I should have taken extra care. It was annoying to think that, even without this brutish intrusion, I would have been denied my goal of making him suffer indefinitely, and without hope of any escape into an easy death, the full force of my outrage.

★

The first thing they wanted to know was how I'd got him there. I never went out, so they assumed I must have hired somebody to kidnap him. They wanted names. I didn't give them any, because there weren't any. Nor did I give them the truth, which was that he'd come voluntarily. Shortly after my return home from the hospital I had sent my car to pick him up. Once he was in the house, I immediately sent my driver off on some errand that would take him half the day, saying that the doctor would call a cab to return to his office. That was what everyone imagined must have happened. The rumour that he had gone abroad was none of my doing: merely a result of his widespread reputation for shiftiness. It was a natural assumption. Until, of course, the wretched Thought Police started asking questions.

It looked for about an hour as though they were going to arrest me for murder. But this was no ordinary case. There was too much at stake. I realized at once what was going on – the shuffling, the horse-trading, the uncertainty – and it made me smile (although, because of what has happened to my face, only I know now when I smile).

There were a lot of top-level phone calls between lawyers and prosecutors' offices, studios and record companies, publishers and networks, industry lobbyists and political allies. In the end, inevitably, deals were made – the way they always are when enough money is at stake. Millions were paid to that son-of-a-bitch doctor's family, but that was just loose change compared with the money that would have been lost if the whole story had come out into the open. People wouldn't have understood. Not even the fans. Not all of them.

My death was announced. Officially it was due to illness, but there was a rumour I'd committed suicide. You never know how these things get started, but once they do they're hard to kill. Let's just say that I was out of circulation. Period.

Everything I'd owned was put up for auction. Naturally it brought in a fortune. I heard later that my dad pocketed most of the proceeds. That hurt me.

My house was bought by some people in the retail garment business – kind of nouveau riche, though I don't want to sound like a snob. They say that sometimes at night my voice can still be heard, distant and faint, echoing through the silent rooms.

The ghost of me sings. Maybe so, I don't know.

I just want to know where I am.

Maybe you can help me.

What is this place? How long have I been here? How long will I have to stay?

Can you tell me?

Like I say, I've got all the time in the world . . .

Hollywood Royalty

She looked out of the limousine's darkened windows at the sidewalks of Beverly Hills. The way people dressed and the way they walked told you as much about them as you could ever need to know.

The thought amused her, because she knew that most of them were trying to be taken for something they were not. Tourists were trying to pass for jet-set sophisticates. Mid-level executives were trying to behave like the top brass. Agents, waiting for the walk sign to cross the street, made promises that were open lies. Minor actors, arriving at restaurants for lunch, adopted the insouciance of superstars. Overdressed has-beens strolled as though they owned the place. Almost everyone wore sunglasses – either to avoid being recognized, or to have an excuse if they weren't. That was the game.

Gail Prentice knew the game. She had played it just long enough, just well enough, to leave it behind. In one hour, she would be Mrs Gregory Conrad Jr, third generation Hollywood Royalty – and that in a community where two generations were described as a dynasty. Three were the stuff of legend. And so, she knew in her heart, was she.

A ripple of excitement ran through her body just as it had all her life in moments of excitement or tension. In a way it was a sexual thing, but it was also more than that. Nobody looking at her would have any idea it was happening. She wondered sometimes if her blood pressure surged, or her brainwaves shot off the graph, but had never tried to find out. That would have meant talking about it, and she would not have liked that.

This time, however, the thrill was followed by a darker

aftershock, as it had been each time for the past week. It scared her, but she told herself yet again that no one could come as far as she had and ever be totally secure in their good fortune. She wasn't the only person in the world who had spent the greater part of her life looking in through a window, envying what she saw; she was, however, one of the few to have been invited inside.

There would always be that lingering sense that she did not truly belong, the fear that somehow she would be found wanting, or simply found out. This was, she knew, something that people like her had to live with: some haunting insecurity that could be hidden, but never lost. She was prepared for that. It was a small price to pay for the future that glittered before her.

The limo bumped softly over the old railroad tracks between the top of Rodeo and Little Santa Monica, then headed for Bel Air. Her introspection broken, she looked over at the man who was to give her away in marriage – her agent, Ben Kanter.

'Feeling nervous?' he asked.

'A little,' she answered, giving him a smile that she knew had a disarming vulnerability. She saw its response in the crinkle of reassurance at the corners of his eyes. He was, she knew, genuinely fond of her.

In his late forties, Ben Kanter was as close a thing to a father as she had ever had. He was a handsome man, tall and in good physical shape from daily tennis and austere lunches, with thick, greying hair that was trimmed twice weekly to maintain its effect of perfect casualness. Unmarried, he had a reputation as a womanizer, but he had never come on to her. She had become his client two years earlier when she started to get noticed on television. He thought she had a future, and persuaded her to let him take charge of it. A good agent did not mix business with pleasure – not that kind of pleasure – and Ben was very good. None the less, her career had not taken off in the way they had both hoped it would. Several TV movies, then the lead in a mini-series, had led only to a couple of lacklustre features which had performed badly at the box office. The second of them, however, had been made by Crossover Films Inc., the production company of the Conrad family; and that was how she had met Greg.

With a little start of surprise, she realized that she was still staring at Ben. Unperturbed, with a smile that was both quizzical and reassuring, he reached out and squeezed her hand. It was the kind of thing, she told herself, that a father would have done – that hers would have done if she'd had one. Ben filled the role to perfection.

They passed the junction of Sunset and Beverly Glen, and a moment later turned right and entered the vast walled estate that was Bel Air. Within it were many separate walled estates, each one the last word in its own style of luxury. She felt the tightness in her stomach again. Within minutes she would be surrounded by some of the most famous faces in the world. Movie stars who had towered, unimaginably distant, over the bleak days of her childhood, would be taking her in their arms and wishing her luck. There would be royalty from Monaco and even from England. There would be a French baron whose château in Bordeaux produced wines by which all others were judged. Three of the most famous dress designers in the world would be there. Guests had flown in by private jet from New York, Paris, Rome – all to see Gregory Conrad, grandson of Gregory James Conrad, son of Clark Conrad, brother of John and Stephanie Conrad, marry Ellen Norma Traynor, professionally known as Gail Prentice.

The knot tightened in her stomach as the vast colonial-style mansion came into view over the crest of the drive. White-gloved hands opened the door, inviting her to step out beneath the columned portico. The rich, thick carpet beneath her feet had been chosen to blend with the colours she wore, as had the flowers in the ballroom and on the terrace, where the reception would be held.

She started to move forward on Ben's arm. The orchestra struck up 'The Wedding March' in the cool interior beyond the double doors. Then something caught her attention, something in one corner of her vision that she instinctively knew should not be there. She turned her head. A man stood between two pillars. He wore a cheap suit, a tie, heavy shoes. Thick hands were clasped in front of him, and there was a coldness in his eyes that cut through her.

A voice in her head began repeating, over and over: Surely not now, not this close, not now . . .

As though to confirm her worst fears, the music inside stopped abruptly in mid-chord. Two figures materialized out of the shadows. One was the police lieutenant who had questioned her a week ago; the other was Greg, resplendent in his wedding suit, his boyish face grey from shock.

Greg's father, Clark Conrad, appeared. There seemed to her to be a terrible finality in the way he closed the double doors behind him, silencing the murmured questions she could hear starting to come from the guests whom she would never now see. Clark Conrad's eyes burned into hers. She saw the same shock that she had seen in Greg's, but there was also a terrible anger. It was, she knew, the rage of power humiliated, betrayed by something trifling, less than dirt, something that should have been exterminated long since.

Ben Kanter, at a loss, looked from the Conrads to the two cops, to Gail, and back again. 'What's going on?' he asked, vaguely, of all of them.

Clark Conrad answered, his voice thick with the effort of self-control. 'Your client, Mr Kanter,' he said, addressing a man he had called 'Ben' for twenty years, 'is wanted on a charge of murder.'

He let the enormity of the situation hang in the air for several moments. An unreal silence enveloped them and seemed to grow like a nuclear cloud filmed from a great distance. Then he burst the bubble with a guttural and bathetic, 'How d'you like them apples!'

She knew that she was not going to faint. She was no longer truly there. She stood unflinching, staring, catatonic, as the younger of the two cops read Ellen Norma Traynor her rights.

★

'Ellie? Is that you?'

She had tried to close the door softly so that her mother wouldn't hear. She always tried, but her mother always heard.

'You're late. Bring up my juice – I'm dying of thirst.'

The little girl went into the kitchen. It was dark because the blind was still down even on a bright afternoon. She climbed on to a chair and released it, flinching as she always did at the way it snapped up, sending the wooden bead that hung beneath it dancing against the window-pane.

She pushed the chair back to the table in the centre of the room, then opened the fridge door. The only thing in there that had once been edible was a piece of cheese that had started growing a coat of fine green fur. Ellie knew she should throw it out, but she also knew that if she did her mother would fly into a rage and accuse her of stealing food, like the last time. She didn't want to go through that again. Avoiding the cheese, but fascinated by the way its fine spikes of fur had grown a fraction since the morning, she pulled forward one of the half-dozen bottles of thick, sweetened fruit juice that her mother was so fond of. It was heavy and she gripped it with both hands; another thing she didn't want a repetition of was the time she'd dropped a bottle.

Mae Traynor's bedroom was even darker than the kitchen. Ellie did not remember ever seeing daylight in this room. Her mother was asleep in the morning when she left for school, and watching game shows and demanding a fresh bottle of juice when she came home.

'Thanks, honey. Put it right here,' Mae said, pushing pills and a box of tissues to clear a space on her bedside table. 'I'm hungry. Go down to the deli and get me a nice tuna salad on rye.' She fished in her purse for money, counting it into Ellie's hand. 'Get something for yourself, too, if you want it. Go on now.'

Ellie went out, glancing back as she half-closed the door the way her mother liked it, and seeing the vodka bottle come out from its hiding place by the bed. Vodka and fruit juice, that was the stuff that got Mom on her feet and ready to go to work at night.

Mae was a waitress at Mac's Big Joint down by the station. The night shift paid better, and the tips from some of the truckers were double what you'd make during the day. Night and Mae Traynor had always been friends, right from the time she'd got her first job in a floorshow at Tahoe. Those had been good days.

She settled back, thinking about them, letting the vodka warm her veins.

The phone rang. It was Bob. She told him to speak up, because she couldn't hear him over the sound of *Bet Your Life* on television.

'I said I'll be home around ten. I'm getting into the car now, and I'll drive straight through.'

'Come down to Mac's and have something to eat.'

'Nah, I'll be beat. I'll hit the sack and see you in the morning.'

Bob was a salesman, away for days at a time, trying to sell office equipment across half the state. They were not married because both had had enough of marriage. Mae's first had been at eighteen. It lasted five years and they had a lot of fun, until her husband went to jail for his part in some financial scam which she never fully understood.

Ellie's father had been a more solid citizen, or so she thought. That was why she had finally decided to have a child. She was thirty years old and settling down with a man who owned his own dry-cleaning business. She knew she'd never drive through Paris in an open car with her hair blowing in the wind, but at least the bills would be paid.

Their marriage, like their daughter, was three years old when he went bankrupt. A month later he was shot in the head – everyone presumed by loan sharks he owed money to. Mae told herself she should have seen it coming. What was a man with a dry-cleaning business doing in Vegas, eyeing up a little cocktail waitress in a skimpy costume and playing blackjack like he hadn't heard that you could lose?

She examined her face in the mirror. She was forty-one, and could look a lot worse. A little puffiness here and there, but it was sexy. A fresh wrinkle? A nip of vodka made it go away. Miracle!

Stepping back, she examined herself in a longer perspective, and began to dress. She told herself, as she told herself every day, that the body was still good. Everything was right where it should be. Men still wanted her – she knew that as well as she ever had. This thing with Bob had been okay over the past twelve months, but had pretty much run its course. It was obvious they'd lost interest in one another, and sometimes she wondered why he

186

stuck around. She would give him the push if it went on too long. Time was no longer on her side, and she had her Big Plan to think about.

The Big Plan revolved around a little business of her own. She didn't know if it would be a bar, a restaurant, a florist's, or maybe even a gown shop. She knew she had a mind for business and could apply it in any direction that she chose. All she needed was the right man to give her a little financial backing, just to get over those first hurdles. Then she could make it on her own.

Ellie said goodbye to her mother at the door of their apartment. 'Keep the door locked, like I always tell you,' Mae said, slipping a finger down her neckline to adjust her bra. 'Bob will be in around midnight, and you'd better be asleep by then, or I'll hear about it.'

The child watched her mother down the stairs and out of sight. Even in those dingy surroundings, Ellie thought there was something glamorous, something dramatic, about her. She sometimes watched from the door as Mae painted her face, fixed her natural blonde hair, dressed herself up, perfumed herself with exotic odours, and finally stood up – like a star about to go out on stage.

That's the way it seemed to Ellie. She thought that Mae, for all her faults, was great to have for a mom. The way she talked sometimes, when there was just the two of them, about the people she'd met, the great times she'd had, the offers she'd been made – it was magic. She didn't know anybody else's mom who talked that way. The trouble was those times always ended with Mae drinking too much and getting into a bad mood. When Ellie saw that happening, she made herself scarce before the violence started. Once she'd stayed out of the house nearly all night, not going back until the sky started turning light.

It didn't matter. She loved her mother. That was why she had to keep so much to herself, things that her mother must never know.

It was just before midnight when Ellie heard the key in the lock. She was wide awake, curled up in bed, her heart beating. It was the sound she had been dreading, and at the same time there was something else, some other feeling – something that she didn't understand.

All she knew was that, if she was ever found out, she hoped

187

that someone, somewhere – God? – would forgive her. But she doubted it.

Bob called out, 'Mae?' No reply. He called again, checking. She heard the door of Mae's room open, then close when he saw that it was empty.

His footsteps started down the corridor, coming towards Ellie . . .

★

Ellie Traynor had already become Gail Prentice by the time she arrived in Hollywood eight years later. It was 1966, and the world was in party mood.

Mae had died six months earlier, having spent the last three years in and out of alcohol clinics. Two years before that, in the absence of better offers, she had changed her mind about marriage and told Bob to get out or get a licence. He caved in to the blackmail with a readiness that she wrongly attributed to her own voluptuous but increasingly blowzy charms. Eventually, as was inevitable, she came home unexpectedly one day and found her husband and daughter in bed. Ellie was two months short of fifteen.

Her mother had hysterics for a week, and was hospitalized. After that she never got back to any kind of a normal life.

For Ellie, Mae's tragedy was a surprisingly liberating experience. The blows and torrents of abuse that she endured had a strangely cleansing effect. Where she had felt soiled, she felt renewed. It was as though she had never been touched by him. When next she faced him, it was as a woman. She told him the relationship was over, adding a warning that if he ever tried to force himself on her again, she would kill him. He believed her.

She also reminded him that, with her mother institutionalized, he was for all practical purposes her guardian, and she had clear ideas of what this would entail. He was going to pay for three years in a school in Chicago she had read about. She would learn acting along with normal lessons. She wanted the money up front, now, or she would go to the police. There was no discussion.

Ellie was barely fourteen when she realized that she had learned

188

how to act. It was a strange feeling that took her some time to identify. It seemed both a connection with the world, and a way of staying hidden from it; a bridge, and at the same time an uncrossable divide which gave her a sense of security. She was sure that she could play any role she had seen in the movies, but she was smart enough to pay attention when she read about 'technique' in acting, and looked the word up in a dictionary.

The school taught her how to move, how to use her voice, how to understand a role and analyse a scene. They knew she was talented. Always, even in her most unfettered performances, there was a sense of something held back, some secret, something in reserve. It was a quality that could make her a star.

Her graduation performance in *Cat on a Hot Tin Roof* got her an agent, which meant she arrived in Hollywood way ahead of the game. She had chosen the name Prentice because of some obscure logical route between Traynor, Trainer and Apprentice – Prentice. Gail seemed to go with it, and anything was better than Ellie. Her middle name, Norma, would have worked, but she was nervous of comparisons with the legendary Norma Jean.

She was not showered with work. She had a good figure and an attractive face: high cheek-bones, a fine nose, expressive eyes and thick, dark hair. The trouble was that aristocratic good looks were going out just then, and the Julie Christie dream-girl-next-door look coming in.

Men showed interest in her, just as boys had earlier. She was friendly, but kept them at a distance. In school, she knew they called her the Virgin Queen behind her back. In Hollywood rejected men, no matter how graciously they had been turned down, speculated darkly about her preferences. Gail didn't care. Before getting involved with anybody, she was going to have to be sure that it was with the right person and for the right reasons. Sex, she felt, ought to mean something.

Meanwhile, with her career going nowhere, she did what every hopeful actress in Hollywood does at least once: she waited table. Which is how she met Lenore Holloway.

Lenore was a lunchtime regular at a particular corner table on the terrace. She invariably had two or three people with her, sometimes including actors whom Gail recognized but had not seen in any pictures for a while. Lenore herself was in her fifties and wore flowing caftans in dazzling colours to conceal her bulk, which, from the cheerfully unrestrained way she ate and drank, occasionally throwing back her head to give a gargantuan bellow of laughter, did not seem to bother her.

'Come over here, honey. You got five minutes? Come over and sit down.' Lenore's guests had gone, and she was lingering over an extra cup of coffee after getting the check. She gestured for Gail to join her.

Gail looked around. The place had nearly emptied, and nobody seemed to be needing her, so she accepted. Lenore gave a big smile from behind tinted glasses with long gold chains attached, and swiped the table with her fleshy, mottled hand as though about to make an announcement of importance.

'I've had my eye on you. You're an actress, aren't you?'

'How did you know that?' Gail asked.

'I know a lot of things. I can tell things by looking at people. And I can tell you're good. You're a beautiful girl, and you're talented. And I'm going to help you.'

Gail sat in silence, not knowing how seriously to take this, while Lenore forged on in a foghorn voice underscored by a repetitive emphasis. 'I'm a producer. I know a lot of people, and I'm going to introduce you to them. You're going places. I know it. I know these things. Trust me. What's your name?' Gail told her.

'What you have to understand, Gail, is this is a relationship business. You're as good as who you know. That's how it works. There's no other way. Anybody who tells you there's any other way doesn't understand this business.'

She stopped fixing Gail with a glare that challenged her to disagree. Gail said she was sure it was true, and felt Lenore's hand clasp over hers. The gesture held no intimacy; it was simply an affirmation of their agreement.

'I'm giving a party tomorrow. Just some good friends for drinks. Come around six. Here's my address.' She took a card from her purse and pressed it into Gail's hand. 'They're all very international, very influential people, the sort of people you ought to know. Good friends of mine.'

Next evening, at six precisely, Gail stepped from a cab outside a house at the lower and more fashionable end of Coldwater Canyon Drive. She had not brought her car because Lenore had asked what she had, and when she told her the make and model had given her ten dollars and said, 'Take a cab. Always take cabs. You take a lot of trouble to look great, so you don't want to muss yourself up driving. You want to make an entrance – you know what I'm saying? Besides, somebody may invite you out to dinner afterwards.'

The house on Coldwater Canyon Drive was a sprawling one-storey affair with a generous patio and pool at the back. It was furnished with the kind of anonymous, durable and neutral luxury that is found in rented properties everywhere. Lenore had added some floral displays, and set up photographs of herself with an assortment of semi-celebrities on top of a grand piano, but the place told you nothing about its occupant. Or perhaps, Gail reflected, it told you everything.

Lenore gave a bellow of welcome the moment Gail appeared, strode across the room, caftan flowing like the robes of Liberty, and hugged her. Then she took her arm and toured the room, making sure she was properly introduced.

Slightly more than half of Lenore's guests were women, ranging in age from around twenty to thirty-five maximum. All, without exception, were attractive, expensively dressed, glossily sophisticated. Their talk was of people they'd seen or were about to see, of places they had been or were about to go, of invitations they had received where they would undoubtedly – what fun! – run into each other again. They seemed to spend half their lives on planes, shuttling between LA, New York, Europe, Rio, and other exotic-sounding locations that Gail had barely heard of. Something steely in their smiles made Gail conscious of not being one of them, but she was a friend of Lenore's and therefore treated well.

About half of the men were Middle Eastern in origin, and were involved in oil or banking. They wore immaculate silk suits and a lot of jewellery. There were a couple of Texans, one in oil, and one in cattle who wore boots and a string tie. The rest of the men were all Hollywood, although there was only one face Gail recognized – a faded TV idol from the fifties whom Lenore had brought to lunch one time.

The man whom Lenore particularly wanted Gail to meet was forty-ish, with a rumpled, smiling face, and unruly curling hair. Gail recognized the name at once; Marty was a hyphenate, a producer-director who had created one of the most popular drama series currently on television. It was obvious that Lenore had already told him all about Gail, because he knew she had studied in Chicago and said how much he admired some of the actors turned out by the school. He invited her to have dinner with him, and as they left to get into his shiny black Porsche, Lenore squeezed Gail's hand and whispered, 'It's up to you now, honey. Go for it!'

They dined at a fashionable restaurant at the beach, where Marty was treated like royalty. He shook hands and waved to people all the way across the room until they reached their table. Gail thought it must be a very nice feeling.

During dinner she steered conversation away from herself, sketching a background of such dull, small-town conformity that Marty was easily persuaded to talk about himself. She wanted to hear about his life, about the people he knew, about Hollywood and how she could become part of it.

Halfway through dinner, Marty said that she should come by the office next week and read for a part in a new show he was preparing. Over dessert, he suggested coffee and a nightcap at his place, which was just up the coast in Malibu Colony. Gail accepted with a smile that she could see warmed his heart.

It was just as she had always told herself: sex ought to mean something.

★

Three years later, Gail had been to bed with only seven other men, and had been disappointed in the outcome only twice. On the first occasion a producer had simply lied about giving her a part that he knew had already gone to someone else; on the second, the executive was unexpectedly fired by the studio before he could be of any real use to her.

By now, however, she was an established television actress, and when Ben Kanter invited her to lunch and did not even hint that he wanted to sleep with her, she knew that her career was really taking off.

Ben's influence got her the first mini-series within a month. She invited Lenore to celebrate over lobster at The Palm on Santa Monica. The two of them had become friends; they understood each other. Right from the start it had been clear to Gail that Lenore was the kind of producer who produced little more than introductions between attractive girls and wealthy men. The moment she walked into the house on Coldwater, she had suspected that Lenore was some kind of high-class madam.

It was true, yet the reason it was still safe to be seen in Lenore's company was that it was only partly true. Lenore had actually been involved in a number of pictures. Her name had appeared on screen less than half a dozen times as associate producer – a vague description, often denoting only brief part-ownership of a script or even an idea, which had then been sold on to other, more effective producers before getting made. The films themselves were obscure, to say the least: low budget, independently financed, but respectable enough. They gave Lenore a modest, pivotal position between legitimacy and its opposite. Gail occupied the desirable end of this spectrum, and Lenore wanted nothing more from her than a connection with the world of her burgeoning success. Some of the other girls Gail had met in Lenore's company were unquestionably expensive, high-class call-girls. She never asked about the arrangements Lenore made with them, though she suspected that money changed hands and percentages were negotiated. Such matters were not discussed between Lenore and Gail. The older woman seemed genuinely happy that her protégé was doing so well, and never harped on the fact that she had introduced her to at least some of the men who had made it happen.

The failure of Gail's first feature film was a shock. She told herself over and over that it should have worked. It was a powerful story, the director had had a solid hit not long before, and the studio had spent money where it was needed. Even the reviews had been encouraging. But nobody had gone to see it. In her heart, Gail knew that it was her fault, her failure. Everybody else knew it, too. She couldn't carry a picture. Maybe she just wasn't a big-screen actress.

Next time out she was co-starred with Clark Conrad. He had been one of the biggest stars in the world, but his day was over – largely because he remained convinced at sixty-two that he could still play forty with years to spare. But, even if the big studios didn't call any more, his films got made. He was, after all, the son of one of the industry's pioneer directors, his daughter was Hollywood's biggest female star, and his son the producer of three consecutive mega-hits, none of them starring father.

Clark's latest was being made by his own production company and financed by foreign pre-sales. No star in her own right would have been willing to play second fiddle to Clark Conrad in what was essentially a vanity production, but it was the only serious offer Gail had received, and it meant a second chance at the big screen.

The picture did well enough in the Far East, where audiences still wanted Clark Conrad pictures, and surprisingly well in France and Italy, where it was hailed as some kind of high-camp cult picture – something far from anyone's intention. But a hit is a hit. It turned a substantial profit, and nobody was embarrassed.

In America, however, it sank without trace, confirming Gail Prentice as an also-ran in the Big Picture stakes. She could go back to television. Ben would get her work, but she was trailing failure and her lustre was diminished. She knew that soon she would find she was being represented by a junior member of the agency. On the whole, her best hope for the future lay in Gregory Conrad's obsessive passion for her.

Gregory was the younger of Clark Conrad's sons, by his third marriage. Stephanie, the star, was the only child of his first marriage; John, the big producer, was the child of his second. Greg was gentle, unambitious, and a little slow. But he was sweet-natured, had a great body, and was Hollywood Royalty. His father kept him busy as producer of the films that he, Clark, made through his own company, like the one in which Gail had appeared.

'I couldn't believe it was happening to me,' she had gushed to one of the gossip mags. 'Every day I worked on the picture, I could feel that something was growing between Greg and me. He was always on the set when I was shooting my scenes, and I could feel his support coming from behind the camera. Neither of us said anything for a long time. After all, we were both dedicated to doing our best for the picture, and that takes one hundred and ten per cent of your commitment.'

She had blathered on about how 'it was a great honour to be working with Clark Conrad', but the heavily ladled flattery cut no ice when the family contemplated her eligibility for inclusion in its ranks.

Greg had taken her down to his parents' Palm Springs house for the weekend. They thought she had gone shopping, but at the last minute she had decided to change what she was wearing, and she was still in the house when the argument started. The three of them were way down the far end in the family wing, but by opening a window and straining her ears she heard every word.

'For God's sake, have an affair with her,' Greg's mother was almost shouting. 'Her and any like her – there's no shortage! Just don't marry one of them!'

'Mom, I do not understand this family's attitude to Gail,' she heard Greg bluster weakly.

'Greg, we aren't snobs,' Clark's voice now, 'but your mother's right about this. You can't see it because, frankly, your head's up your ass. That girl's got her claws so far into you she's working you like a goddamn glove puppet.'

Gail slipped out of the house before they discovered her. She had heard enough; it had confirmed what she feared.

Driving to the shops, taking the long route through the quiet lanes between the walled-in, multi-million-dollar weekend compounds, she reviewed her situation. It was true that part of what she wanted from this marriage was a place in Hollywood – and in the world – that she could never get by her own efforts. She would give up acting and devote herself to being a wife for a while, and maybe a mother. After that, she planned to move into production. She was smart, she had ideas. With the Conrad name and money behind her, she knew she could do it. She just knew.

She racked her brains for evidence that she was being unfair to Greg in any way. She did things to him sexually that he'd never experienced before and couldn't get enough of. Aside from which, she positively coddled him, built up his self-esteem, and gave him the encouragement that he had never received from his parents. If that wasn't love, what was?

The four of them dined at Don the Beachcomber's that night. It was a glitzy crowd. Frank, Dean and Sammy got up and did some clowning and a set with the band – that kind of a night.

Going back in the car, Greg driving, they were quiet, but Gail didn't sense any open rancour. She worked hard the next couple of days to keep things that way. Above all, she didn't want a confrontation. She could only lose a confrontation. She did everything she knew to project an air of modesty and vulnerability, with even a little ditziness thrown in to dispel the myth that she was a calculating bitch.

A month later Greg's mother took her to lunch at Chasen's. She sensed a new, if cold, intimacy in their conversation. She was, she realized, accepted – reluctantly, but accepted.

Then Lenore re-entered the scene. From the moment she picked up the phone, Gail sensed that Lenore had money problems. The booming voice was still there, but sounded hollow. She had been in Europe for some months. 'setting up a big new international series,' she said, but didn't want to talk about it on the phone. Only when she persisted did Gail agree to go over for a drink.

Lenore had left the house in Coldwater and was living in a smaller place up on Mulholland. It belonged to her partner in the European venture, a producer who had given Gail an important TV movie some time back. She was glad to hear that he was still in London, because she had not much cared for some of the services she had been required to perform in that very house in order to secure the deal, and had no wish to run into him again.

196

They sat out on the deck sipping Chardonnay as the lights began to twinkle hazily in the city below. After a few civilities and some chat about the wedding in a couple of weeks – to which, Gail realized unhappily, she would have difficulty in not inviting her old friend – Lenore made her pitch.

'This series is going to be something totally new and original. Joe and I are very excited.' Joe was the owner of the house, the man Gail had no wish to see again, or indeed be in any way in business with. 'We're going to spend a lot of money – we've already got most of it in place – and we've got all the networks interested. *All* of them! If we don't get the right deal from the networks, we'll go straight to syndication – that's the coming thing. You're going to get more and more shows financed that way. Even without that, we can still finance this show on foreign sales. This show is going to happen, and it's going to be big.'

Standard stuff so far. Gail settled back and let it flow over her, enjoying the view. She wanted to let Lenore talk herself out before saying, firmly but politely, that she was no longer in the acting business.

'If you come in with me, I'm going to give you a piece of this show. I've talked it over with Joe, and he agrees. A big piece. I know you're getting married, but it does no harm to have a little money of your own. Makes them respect you more. They're tough, that family, I know them.'

A lie, Gail knew.

'They're tough, but they're as talented as hell,' Lenore went on. 'It's in the genes. Let me tell you about this show. It's about this retired American cop, former police chief, who goes to live in Paris. Or maybe London, we haven't decided yet. It depends on which of two real sweetheart deals we make – Joe's working on that now. Anyway, the cop's had this tragedy over here, his wife's died, his kids are married or away at college or whatever, and he wants to start his life over somewhere else. So he sets up as a private detective in Paris. Or London.'

Gail was listening without paying attention, waiting for the string of clichés which would describe the character she should play. She went on listening, but they didn't come. In fact, she realized after a while, there had been no mention of any female roles, except incidentally. It was all about this retired cop ... Suddenly Gail understood what she was being asked.

She was being asked to get Clark Conrad to do a television series for Lenore Holloway.

'I can see you love it. It's great, isn't it? I knew you'd see the potential in this.'

Gail must have sat forward. She hadn't been aware of the movement, but she had felt the colour drain from her face.

'This would be the best thing Clark's ever done.' Lenore was refilling Gail's glass. 'It'll put him in touch with a whole new generation. They've never seen him in a role like this. It'll be just great for him!'

Gail's mind raced to find the words to stamp on and extinguish this insane idea right there and then.

'Lenore, Clark is an old-style movie star. He isn't going to do television. Period. None of those people will do television.'

'All that's going to change. This is a business of change. Clark Conrad isn't where he was ten years ago.'

'He's still a big star.'

'We'll pay him anything he wants.'

'He's already richer than God.'

'He's an actor. No actor can turn down a great role. Any actor worth his salt would kill his mother to play a role this good. Read it – it's great. You'll see.'

Lenore pushed across the table a script that Gail had not consciously registered before. It had obviously been placed there in readiness for this conversation.

'I'll read it. Of course I'll read it, Lenore.' She didn't know what else to say as she picked up the dog-eared script, the corners of its pages curled and grubby.

'It's not the final draft,' Lenore went on. 'Things can be changed. We're open to ideas. You have to be. That's the only way to be creative. But it's a great character, that's the important thing. A great character.'

Gail looked at her watch, made excuses, and drove back to the place where she still lived in West Hollywood. Greg picked her up for dinner, and they spent the night at his place. She said nothing about her meeting with Lenore, nor did she intend to. The following afternoon she read the script, her heart sinking with every page she turned. It was even worse than she had feared. When she had finished it, she sat for a while, curled up on cushions by the window, figuring out the best way to handle things. Then she called Lenore and said she was coming over.

This time they stayed indoors because it was already dark. Lenore poured drinks and got right down to business.

'Did you talk to him?'

'Lenore, I've only just finished the script.'

'What did you think? It's great, isn't it? He'd kill his mother for this, right? That's the only test of a great actor, you know.' She gave one of her foghorn laughs. 'If an actor won't kill his mother for a great role, he's not worth hiring – that's what they say.' Bellowing with fabricated mirth, she slapped a massive thigh that became briefly outlined beneath her caftan.

Gail suddenly hated Lenore: the rank vulgarity of everything she did and said and wore; the endless artificial laughter honed to flatter others into thinking themselves witty; the apparent belief that size and noise and brute relentlessness somehow passed for talent. Above all she hated this woman's lumpen intrusion into a world in which Gail's own position was still precarious, but from which she did not intend to be dislodged by some half-forgotten, misplaced friendship.

'Lenore,' she began, choosing her words carefully, 'the script has a lot of promise.' She tried not to sound evasive, but knew that she did. 'It has a lot of good things in it, some very good things—'

'That's what I'm saying. The idea's great. There are things that need fixing, sure, but we'll take care of that. The idea's the important thing. The character.'

'I agree, and I truly hope you have a big success. I think you will. But I can't give this to Clark.'

'Why not? Come on, can't you just see him in this role? It's the best thing he's been offered in years.'

'Lenore, I'd like to help you, but I can't. Not with this. I really can't.'

There was a silence. Lenore sat with her head lowered, a

posture she normally avoided because of the prominence it gave to her multiple chins. She was thinking. Eventually she looked up, not at Gail but off across the room.

'I have to say, Gail, that I'm really disappointed by this attitude. I thought we were friends.'

'We are friends, Lenore. It's just that you're asking me to do something that is not within my power. It wouldn't work.'

'At least you could try. You could talk to him. Or fix for me to talk to him.'

'Nobody talks Clark into doing anything he doesn't want to do. I'd just make a fool of myself, and that would be no help to any of us.'

'Okay, okay!' Lenore held up two plump hands, palms out. 'Let me lay this out for you – okay? I'm going to tell you the truth now. I'm going to tell you the truth, and then you're going to help me, because I know you'll want to. Gail, if I don't get Clark Conrad for this role, I'm in deep shit. I talked to Joe on the phone again last night. Clark is the one name that the French will go for, he's top of the list for the Germans and the British, and he's our only chance of making a deal over here.'

'Lenore, nobody's ever your *only* chance,' Gail countered, wanting to end this before it became embarrassing. 'There are at least four, five other male stars who—'

'I don't have access!' Lenore cut in. 'I'd have to go through agents, managers, the whole damn circus, and it'd take for ever.'

'I don't know what to say, Lenore, truly I don't. Maybe I could get Ben to help out.'

Lenore ignored the offer and made one last effort to persuade Gail. 'If I could just tell them that Clark Conrad was reading it, they'd wait. They'd wait for him. At least that would buy me some time to talk to other people. Now I don't even have time. Help me, Gail. Do this thing for me. And for Joe. We've got a lot of money riding on this – our own money. Do this one thing.'

It was time to end this. Gail wanted to be out of that house and away from the atmosphere of phoniness and desperation that permeated it. 'Look, Lenore, you know that I'd do absolutely anything for you that I could. But I can't do the impossible. I just can't do this.' She had got to her feet as she spoke, ready to leave.

Lenore looked at her. She was shorter than Gail, but her upturned head with its lower lip thrust petulantly forward gave her a bulldog look, combative, ready to get down and fight dirty. 'I never thought I'd hear this from you, Gail. Not from somebody who's been as close to me as you have. This hurts me. I really find this hard to take.'

'I'm sorry, Lenore. I wish it were otherwise.' She started for the door. Lenore's voice followed her, louder, accusing.

'You've changed, Gail. You just think about yourself now, forgetting the friends who've done you favours.'

This was the one line Gail had hoped they wouldn't get started on. She had to get away now, fast.

'I'm leaving, Lenore. I think we should both avoid saying anything that we might regret – don't you?' She asked the question without turning, having already decided that she was going to leave the room without looking back.

Lenore's voice barked after her. 'I wouldn't leave yet if I were you. Not until you've seen this.'

Despite her resolution, Gail paused, and turned. Lenore was holding up a reel of 8mm film. 'What's that?' she asked.

'Let me put it this way. It ain't holiday snaps.'

Gail didn't need to see it. She knew. She didn't know when or where, who or how, but she knew. It was a fear that had always hovered at the back of her mind, but she thought she had escaped it, confident that she had vanished without trace from a past in which she had no choice but to use what she had to get what she wanted.

She didn't need to see it, but still she followed Lenore through to the den where a projector was set up and a screen already in place. She didn't say a word, just sat down and let Lenore get on with the process. It gave her time to think

The quality of the film was nowhere near professional pornography. There were no cuts or zooms, and the lighting was patchy. In fact, somebody could have watched the film without ever saying, 'Hey, that's Gail Prentice!' They might have been vaguely reminded of someone. They might even in time have realized who that someone was of whom they were reminded. But it wasn't obvious.

Yet it finished her. Proof was not essential; the rumour mill would do it. The others involved in those grainy, groping images could be traced and persuaded to tell what they knew. She couldn't remember their names, and suspected she had never known them. The only one she knew was Howard, the network executive who got her that first crucial above-the-title billing, and who sprang this 'party' on her without giving her time to think. It was at his house and the slimeball had a hidden camera. Howard had died two years ago. Lenore had told her that he had a coronary in bed with two seventeen-year-olds.

The clicking of the spool as the film came to an end brought her back to the present. She hadn't even registered the final half of what had passed on screen: not out of revulsion but because it simply wasn't relevant. The point had been made.

Neither woman looked at the other as Lenore rewound the spool. Eventually Gail asked, 'Is that the only copy?'

'That's for me to know,' Lenore answered flatly.

First mistake, Gail thought. If there were other copies, Lenore would sure as hell be crowing about it, making clear that there was no possibility of escape.

Next question: 'Does Joe know about this?'

'Joe knows I'm a very good friend of yours. What passes between us is none of his business.'

Fine. In fact, good. But double check. Think clearly now. Be careful.

'If I take the script to Clark, do I get the film?'

'That depends.'

'On what?'

'On whether he says yes.'

Pause

'Suppose I get him to say yes.'

'Then you get the film.'

'How do I know you won't come back at me with another print of the film when you want something else?'

'Don't worry about that.'

A longer pause. Good. Everything seemed clear: Joe didn't know about this, and there was no other print of the film. Lenore was probably too broke to have one made. Bad mistake. Lazy.

Gail got up and started slowly back to the main room. She was aware of Lenore's gaze following her, but didn't meet it. What she did note out of the corner of her eye was the shelf on which Lenore placed the spool of film as she switched off the projector.

When Lenore entered the main room, Gail was standing on the far side, the script in her hand, leafing through it. Sensing Lenore's presence, she turned, closing the script and holding it loosely in front of her. For the first time in a while their eyes met. There was the ghost of a smile on Gail's face.

'It's a shame it had to come to this, Lenore, but I guess you were right and I was wrong. I should have realized how much you needed help.'

'I'm glad you see it that way.' Lenore's tone was neutral, wary, but confident that things were going her way.

Gail started walking towards her, taking slow, casual steps, the script still dangling loosely from her hand. She wasn't looking at Lenore; her eyes were somewhere off to one side, wandering vaguely over various objects in the room, seeking out shadows and flat surfaces so as not to distract her mind from the words she was choosing with such care.

'It's not that I didn't want to help you, please believe that. And never, ever, think I'm not grateful for what you've done for me. Because I am, deeply, and always will be.'

She was standing in front of Lenore now, and finally brought her gaze around to meet hers. She went on: 'In spite of whatever happened tonight, you're still my friend, Lenore. And I'm yours.'

The twelve-inch paper-knife shot out from beneath the script and embedded itself deep in Lenore's abdomen. It was razor-sharp, and each new thrust cut with absurd ease through the increasingly confused mess of flesh and blood and fabric. Gail had noticed the knife earlier and merely thought what an elegant shape it had. When she came back into the room after watching the film, she had just had enough time to pick it up and test its sharpness with her finger before Lenore followed her.

At no point during the whole process, which was fairly brief, did Gail lose control. That was the thing about which, looking back, she was most proud. There had been a moment when she was surprised to hear a string of obscenities – cunt, bitch, fuck, shit – tumbling from her mouth in some kind of strange coordination with the rhythm of the knife-thrusts, but that came to an end as soon as she became aware of it. A moment later she was perfectly still, hearing only her own hard breathing and the beating of her heart.

The body slid slowly down the bookcase against which it had been driven and fell to the floor, like a great sack oozing brownish liquid through the livid greens and blues and yellows and reds of the multi-coloured caftan.

Gail checked off in her mind the things she had already decided she would have to do. She was covered in blood, as she had anticipated. The first essential was to get out of her clothes, shower, and put on something else – otherwise she ran the risk of leaving ineradicable bloodstains in her car.

She showered and dried off with a big white towel in the main bathroom, then went through to the bedroom, where she found a pair of trousers that were big enough for three of her but which she secured with a belt. Over that she pulled on a man's sweater, and finally a lightweight raincoat. She found a pair of tennis shoes which she stuffed with paper to make them fit.

The soiled clothes she wrapped in newspaper and then in two double-strength plastic garbage bags which she found in the kitchen. She debated whether to leave the murder weapon by the body or take it away. It was covered in blood, which would probably obscure her fingerprints, but she wasn't sufficiently sure that this would be the case. Finally she picked it up with tissues and added it to the things she had to take with her. If this murder was to be passed off as the act of an intruder whom Lenore had disturbed, it would probably be more credible that the intruder had used a weapon of his own rather than picked up the nearest thing to hand.

Next she made a search for money and valuables. She found a couple of hundred dollars and some jewellery, not much. She had worn gloves for the search, and she kept them on as she went back into the den to retrieve the film.

She took the two glasses from which she and Lenore had drunk earlier, washed them, and put them back with the set to which they belonged, taking care to leave no fingerprints. She knew that her fingerprints would be found somewhere in the place, but that wouldn't matter. She would make no secret of the fact that she had visited her friend yesterday. The important thing was to leave no trace of today's visit. She had arrived after dark and was sure no one had seen her. When she left, she would not switch on her headlights until she was clear of the drive. She would loop over towards Cahuenga, where there was some landfill going on for the freeway extension. That was the best place to lose the bags of bloody clothes and the knife. When she got back to her apartment, she would change into some clothes of her own and get rid of the ones she had taken from the house. The film she would burn in the big glazed sink in her kitchen. That seemed to be everything. She tried to think of anything she had forgotten.

The script! My God, the script! It was still on the floor, splattered with blood and covered in her fingerprints. She retrieved it and stuffed it into the garbage bags, which she then hauled out to her car.

It was three days before detectives called to see her. Gail was dreadfully upset, but gave them all the help she could. Yes, she had seen poor Lenore the day before she died: they'd had a glass of wine and a chat about old times and Gail's forthcoming wedding. Wasn't it terrible that things like this could happen? She prayed they would find the killer soon. It was her best performance.

She knew, as the days went by and she heard no more, that she had beaten them. The days became a week, and the week became two weeks.

And finally came her wedding day . . .

★

Joe had flown back from Europe when he got the news of Lenore's death. He told the police everything he knew, including the fact that Lenore's chief reason for being in California was to enlist Gail Prentice's help in getting their script to Clark Conrad. None of that led the police to charge her with murder. What did was something absurdly simple.

205

In the course of her efficient dispatch of Lenore and all incriminating evidence, Gail had made one tiny mistake for which she would pay for the rest of her life: she had picked up and burnt the wrong spool of film.

It had not occurred to her that there might be more than one. She had seen Lenore's hand go to a shelf, and had picked up the first spool of 8mm film she saw there. The one she wanted, however, was tucked behind an old-fashioned chiming clock; the one she picked up was of Joe's last skiing holiday in Aspen. The mistake came to light only hours before the wedding, when Joe was trying to persuade a girlfriend of what a good time she'd have if she came up there with him for the weekend. He called the police first thing in the morning.

The scandal was one of Hollywood's finest. The Conrad family machine went into overdrive to distance itself from the whole thing, and was surprisingly successful. Greg gave a couple of carefully stage-managed interviews to sympathetic journalists, and the family closed ranks to help him get over the heartbreak and the shock. The other royal families of Hollywood then closed ranks around the Conrads. Word went out to the whole community: Gail Prentice was henceforth a non-person. Even Ben washed his hands of her. No one who wanted to work in that town defied the edict of its massed aristocracy.

So it was an anticlimax when, only a month later, all charges against her were dropped. The problem for the District Attorney's Office was simply lack of evidence; no prosecutor could go into court with a case as circumstantial as that against Gail and hope to win.

When the police arrested her, they had been confident either of getting a confession, or of discovering further evidence of guilt. Gail, however, was not about to confess to anything. She refused to answer questions, and even the most stringent forensic tests failed to come up with so much as a fibre or speck of dried blood to connect her with the murder. The blood-soaked clothing and the murder weapon were by that time buried beneath thirty feet of concrete, and only Gail knew where. The cops used every known interrogation method short of torture, but she just smiled infuriatingly, as though pitying the inadequacy of their efforts. After a week she knew she had them beaten, but still she was surprised when they decided not to bring her to trial.

They had their revenge, however. Blind eyes were turned, and the spool of film – the putative exhibit A – was magically spirited over to a lab, where copies were made which would change hands in the Hollywood underground at two hundred dollars a time. No one who was anybody had failed to see it at least once by the end of that summer.

It was 1970, and the word was that Gail, who had disappeared from Hollywood the day after her release, was living in Italy under an assumed name. The world's press spent fortunes trying to track her down, but with no luck. Eventually, over a year later, she surfaced to make a couple of low-budget pictures, one in Italy, one in Germany. Despite her curiosity value, they did badly, and nobody else showed any interest in hiring her.

This time she sank effortlessly into obscurity; nobody was interested in her any more. It was 1973, and the world's eyes and ears were on Watergate and the Vietnam fallout. Lawyers for the Conrad family maintained a certain interest for a while, following rumours that Gail had had a child at some time during the twelve months between her disappearance from Hollywood and her abortive acting comeback in Europe. The possibility that it was Greg's child had to be considered, but, in the absence of any such suggestion from Gail herself (it being taken for granted that a person of her sort would miss no opportunity of getting her hands on such of the family's funds as she could), was soon dismissed. Nobody even seemed to know for sure what sex the child was, always supposing that there was one. In the end the family let the inquiry drop, only too happy to see the scandal recede and vanish in the mists of time.

The final footnote came in 1987. A woman known as Ellen Traynor failed to turn up one morning at the store on Lexington Avenue, New York, where she worked on the hosiery counter. After more than a week without any word, her employers, who had found her reliable during the four years she worked for them, began to make inquiries. They discovered that she had died of heart failure eight days earlier; a friend had found her stretched out on her bathroom floor. As there had been no family, the friend had arranged a cremation.

There the matter would have ended, except for the discovery in the woman's modest apartment of papers and old newspaper cuttings that identified her as Gail Prentice.

With hindsight, those who had known her at the store on Lexington, colleagues and customers alike, convinced themselves that they had always sensed there was something out of the ordinary about Ellen Traynor. Although she had changed much from the face that could still be found in yellowing fan magazines in specialist stores, the resemblance was nevertheless sufficiently pronounced to have been evident.

The story earned half a column and a photograph on the inside pages of some newspapers, but was little commented on in Hollywood, as though her excommunication, ordered from on high some seventeen years earlier, remained effective.

Greg Conrad felt a pang of something – he wasn't sure what – when he read the short obituary in *Variety*. Relief? Pity? Regret? Two years after the scandal he had married a well-born girl from a banking family in the east, a far more satisfactory match in his parents' view. He had two children, and was, he supposed, happy. He had formed a partnership with his brother, John, and together they had produced half-a-dozen major hits as well as a number of solid successes. Like everybody else in the family, he now had his own Oscar, and had become a force to be reckoned with in the industry. He had lived in the Bel Air mansion since his mother died nine years earlier. His father, still sprightly in his eighties, lived almost full time in the Palm Springs house. Sister Stephanie remained as big a star as ever, and had recently married a senator who was being seriously touted as a candidate for the White House.

Certainly, Greg had nothing to complain about; nor would he have dreamed of claiming that he had. He just wished that once, among all the women he had been to bed with in the casual way that wealth and fame allow in Hollywood, he had found one who fucked him the way Gail Prentice had. He could never quite get her out of his mind – especially when he was having sex.

208

For him, in that most intimate of all ways, she would always live on.

★

Robbie Carlyle caught sight of his own and Kay Taylor's reflection in the window of a Fifth Avenue store as they passed. They were, he had to admit, a good-looking couple.

Kay, although he didn't know it, glimpsed the same reflection. Less sure of herself than Robbie, she wondered what such a fabulous-looking young man was doing with an ordinary girl like her. He was tall, with thick blond hair and a smile that could light up the darkest of days. She had thought, since she first set eyes on him in acting class, that he exuded glamour. Robbie, she knew, was going to be a star.

As for herself, she believed she would make a competent actress. To hope for more, she thought, would be tempting fate. She did not think she was glamorous, although perhaps, if the part called for it, she could act it. Certainly, there were no insurmountable obstacles in her way. She was slender without being skinny, and in the right clothes could make an impact; but it was all a performance. Whenever she contemplated her face she found it anonymous, a blank space requiring the stamp of events to create in it some response that might pass for personality. But it was not an ugly face; it was for a young actress, she had to admit, a perfectly serviceable face.

So why did she feel always that she lived so far from the surface of herself as to have no contact with the world? She was not unhappy, nor even particularly lonely; it would have been self-indulgent to pretend she was. Nevertheless, she knew there was some barrier between herself and others, and knowing what it was did not help. It was a truth that she dared never tell.

Yet she would have to, some time, to somebody; for instance, to this beautiful young man at her side. He seemed so confident, so at ease with himself. How she envied that, and loved him for it. Of course he was older than her – by almost two years – but that was not the reason for the difference between them. It was something in him, just as the lack of it was something in her.

Was she going to go to bed with him this afternoon or not? She ached to do so, and yet she was afraid. Not just of all the obvious things: this was 1993, it was New York, and the AIDS thing wasn't getting any better.

But that was not what worried her. That was a measurable risk, and she could protect herself. What worried her was something inside herself, the 'Great Secret' which she had carried since she came to this city.

She would have to tell him soon. Should it be before or after they had made love? What difference would it make? Would it turn him off, or turn him on? Both possibilities were equally disturbing in different ways. She was so beset by worry on this score that she was totally and touchingly unaware of the heads that turned instinctively to get one more glimpse of this glorious young couple, so obviously in love and with all their lives before them, strolling arm in arm down Fifth Avenue on a warm, bright day in early summer. To all who saw them, they were a part of some archetypal notion of perfection.

The pretext he had used to get her to his apartment that afternoon was that he thought they should work together on some scenes they had been doing in their acting class. He professed to be enormously moved by her reading of Maggie in *Cat on a Hot Tin Roof*. He had told her several times now that he thought she was talented, but sensed that she was holding something back, which, if she would only relax, could take her through the stratosphere.

How to tell him? How?

His room was part of a divided loft where he lived with three other students. It was quite large, and tidier than most, not that she had seen the inside of many young men's rooms. She had had two affairs before coming to New York – if she could call them 'affairs': more accurately, unsatisfying, inexperienced sexual fumblings. She did not regret them, but had dismissed them from her memory; for all that they had taught her, they might as well never have happened.

They read a while, played with the scene, tried it some of the ways they had done it in class, then a couple of new ways of their own. She realized that not only was he beautiful and could act, but had the makings of a fine director.

210

Then, quite suddenly, his concentration went. He was looking at her, his face close to hers, and she saw the focus change in his eyes. He was no longer looking at the character she was playing, but at her. His hand went very gently to her face. She felt his long, slim fingers pushing back her hair.

'You're very beautiful,' he whispered, and kissed her.

She leaned towards him, knowing that she wanted it to happen. Then she stopped him.

'Wait. I have to tell you something.'

He looked at her, smiling. 'Wouldn't you like to tell me later?'

'Yes. No. I mean, I must tell you. I must tell you now.'

'All right.'

He did not take his hand away or move back. Instead, she moved away from him, not far, not willingly, but knowing that she must. She turned, awkwardly, searching for a way to begin. He waited patiently.

'My name,' she said eventually, 'isn't Kay Taylor. It's Kay Conrad. My father is Gregory Conrad. My grandfather is Clark Conrad, my great-grandfather was Gregory James Conrad. I guess you know who my aunt and uncle are. I guess everybody in this business knows. And just about everybody in this country, and the world, too.'

He looked at her for what she felt was an age. There was no expression on his face. Then, abruptly, he threw his head back and laughed. She looked stricken.

'I'm sorry,' he said, still laughing. 'It's just that you looked like it was such a terrible confession. I mean, like you'd murdered somebody or something.'

'Maybe I did in a way,' she said. 'Maybe I murdered me. It's so awful going around being one of this great clan of famous people, with everybody looking at you as though you're supposed to be special or something, just because of your name. I'm not special, I'm just ordinary. That's all I want to be. I just want to be me.'

'You're both,' he said. He placed a hand, arms outstretched, on both her shoulders and looked into her eyes. 'You're you, and you are special. And that won't change, whatever you call yourself.'

She bit her lip, suddenly afraid that she might cry, and her voice faltered as she spoke. 'But you do understand, don't you?' she

211

asked. 'You understand why I had to be somebody else. I just couldn't come to New York to study and call myself Kay Conrad. Can you imagine what that would have been like?'

'Of course I understand,' he said. 'And don't worry, I'll keep your secret. And I want to tell you something else. I know I laughed, and I shouldn't have, and I'm sorry . . . but I really respect you for what you did.' She watched him as he moved away from her slightly, speaking thoughtfully. 'A lot of people in your position – privilege, and connections, and all of that – wouldn't have had the nerve to go out and make it on their own. And you have. I mean made it. You're good, Kay Taylor. You're very talented, and everybody knows it.'

This time she really was on the edge of tears. He saw, and switched his mood to something lighter to tease her out of it. 'Hey, Miss Taylor – and that's a pretty famous name, too, come to think of it – can I ask you a question?'

She nodded, not trusting her voice.

'Would you like to make love?'

She flung her arms around him and held him tighter than she'd ever held anyone in her life.

Silly bitch, he thought to himself. She actually bought it. She fucking bought it. She actually thought I didn't know who she was.

★

They lay in bed together for a long time after they had made love. She fell into a deep sleep, and he, not wanting to wake her, didn't move but just gazed up at the ceiling and listened to the traffic sounds outside.

The sex had been good. Very good indeed, he thought, for her; and good for him. It never ceased to amaze him the way people lost themselves in sex; not just in orgasm, but in the blind, lunging, single-minded climb towards it.

With him it was different. With him, most things were different. Kay Conrad was just playing at being someone else; he *was* someone else, always. It didn't matter what he called himself or what he said, or what attitudes he had to strike. He could call up as many versions of himself as necessary, each one as convincing as the last, but none of them beginning to define who or what he really was. That was his secret. That was a *real* secret.

He smiled as a thought crossed his mind. The reason his secret was such a good secret was because it remained a secret even from him. Up to a point. He had had a fantasy, ever since he was a child, that his life was not his own. It was, when he thought about it, as though someone else was living his life, not himself. But he didn't entirely understand how.

If he thought back, he knew where it came from, this feeling. It came from those dreams. Those strange, disturbing dreams that had so frightened him – until his mother had explained that they were only dreams, and that he shouldn't be troubled by what happened in them, because it was normal. Everybody had those sort of dreams.

But then, if everybody had those dreams, why wasn't everybody like him? He knew they weren't. That was his strength.

'Listen to me – this is the truth, this is important,' his mom had said to him in those dreams. 'I love you. I truly love you. You are the only man I've ever loved and trusted, and the only one I ever will. You must believe that. It is important to me.' And then she had showed him, time and again, how much she loved him.

But that was in the dreams. Because always, when the dream was nearly over, she would take his head between her hands and tell him that when he woke up, he would remember this, but he would know it had not happened. It was a dream.

And as if to prove the point, whenever in the full light of day, when they might be having breakfast or going to the beach or she'd be dropping him off at school or whatever, when he asked her about the dreams, or said anything about what happened in them, she just looked at him blankly and said she didn't know what he was talking about.

After a while, when he'd persisted (he must have been about fourteen by then, thinking back), she'd sat him down and said they had to deal with this. She had given him a book by a psychologist, someone he had seen on television. It talked about dreams like the ones he had. It called them fantasies and said they came from a thing called the subconscious, and that everybody had them, like his mom had said. They were just part of being human, part of growing up. It didn't say that everybody had them as vividly as he did, but he guessed there was room for individual variations between people. What a dull world it would be if everybody was the same.

Anyway, it was reassuring to know that children had these weird relationships in their heads with their parents. It was amazing, the things that could happen in your head. After that he stopped worrying and just let the dreams happen as often as they might.

His mom was such a great person, though. Great looking, too. At least, she had been then. That was probably why it was all – this fantasy – so much more powerful in his case. She used to talk about her life, tell him things. He could listen for hours. She'd had a tragic life in many ways, but come through it like a star.

That's what she would have been – a star! – if it weren't for that Conrad family who'd thought she wasn't good enough for their son, and had faked up that phoney charge of murder to ruin her happiness. Boy, those fuckers really deserved whatever was coming to them! He didn't know what it was going to be. Mom knew, and she would tell him when the time was right.

Meanwhile, as soon as this Kay Conrad girl woke up and he could get her out of here, he would phone Mom and tell her all about his triumph.

No – *their* triumph. It had gone exactly as Mom said it would. She had planned every step, rehearsed him in everything he had to do and say. He could never have done it without her.

*

Robbie's earliest memory was of being swept high into the air and dandled over the head of a hideous one-eyed monster with half its brain bursting through a paper-thin skull. He was not to know at the time that he was in Rome's Cinecitta Studio, and his screams brought his mother running from the set of what she hoped would be her European comeback picture. He always remembered with a little frisson of awe how she had snatched him to safety and sent

214

the monster packing with a torrent of abuse ringing in its mutant ears.

Oddly enough he had no memories of the making of her next comeback film in Germany, although he was with her throughout the shooting. The next time he remembered clearly was when they were back in Rome and living in a large apartment over a busy, fashionable street. There was a maid who came in every day. Occasionally a man would be around: not always the same man, although one of them, older than the others, showed up fairly regularly, and sometimes even used to bring him toys and things to eat. One day there had been a lot of shouting between the older man and Robbie's mother, and the man had left, slamming the door, and never came back.

After that, Robbie remembered his mother spending a lot of time alone with him in the apartment, rarely going out. The maid stopped coming, and Robbie became aware that his mother was sometimes in strange moods, alternately laughing and crying, and sometimes lying still for hours on end, as though asleep, but with her eyes open.

They moved from the large apartment in the fashionable and busy street to a smaller apartment in a street that was merely busy. More men visited, but things always seemed to end in shouting between them and his mother. He had gone to a local school around the corner, and had begun to speak Italian fluently.

Then his mother announced that they were going to live in America. As he had never been there, the prospect meant nothing to him, but it seemed to cheer up his mother considerably. It was during the two weeks or so of preparation for the trip that she first told him about a rich and famous family called Conrad who had treated her so badly, and planted in his mind the idea of getting back from them what was rightly hers.

She also told him that they were going to have a new name – Traynor, not Prentice. She didn't want anyone to know that she had been an actress. She played a game with him, suddenly asking 'What's your name? What's my name?' until he could reply 'Robbie Traynor, Ellen Traynor' without thinking.

They invented a whole history of who they were and what their life had been. His father was a US army sergeant and was divorced from his mother. They never saw him any more. The truth would be known only to them. It bound them together.

It was around this time that Robbie began asking his mother who his real father was. She told him it was someone she had known when she first came to Italy, but who was dead now. Whenever he asked for more details, she either changed the subject or ignored him. Eventually he realized that the memory was painful for her, so he didn't bring it up again.

Before they flew to New York, his mother cut her hair and changed its colour. When he looked at old photographs of her, he could see how the years had altered her. She was still good-looking, but the face that had had so little character as a minor star now had a whole new determination etched into it. A couple of times he caught her old movies on television, and would have been hard-pressed to recognize her himself.

They hadn't known anyone in New York, which Robbie found a frightening place at first. Ellen had a succession of jobs, eventually winding up behind the hosiery counter in the store on Lexington. Robbie had gone to grade school and become a regular little American, although he always felt himself to be different from the rest of the kids. It wasn't just that he had no father; some of them didn't either. What the feeling really came from was the way that he and his mom had this secret life: they were not who people thought they were. They were special.

And then things changed again. Mom had made this friend, Madeleine Carlyle. He couldn't remember how they'd met: some chance encounter. Madeleine was only a year or two older than Mom, but seemed to come from a whole different generation. In truth, Robbie was a little spooked by her. She obviously had money – at least enough to live comfortably without working – but didn't seem to know anybody except him and Mom, and that was only because Mom went out of her way to develop the friendship, which was nice of her because Madeleine must have been lonely at times. Not only had she no friends, she had no family either, and she had never been married.

They had known Madeleine about a year when she died. He knew that because he had just had his sixteenth birthday, and he had just turned fifteen the first time Mom introduced him to Madeleine. The day she died, Mom had invited her over to their apartment. It was a Sunday, and he, because he found Madeleine a little hard to talk to and frankly pretty boring, had eagerly accepted the money Mom gave him and had gone out to catch a couple of movies.

When he got home he found Mom in a strange mood, clearing up the table where she and Madeleine had eaten supper. She had sat him down and said she had something very important to tell him. Madeleine had died, she said: a heart attack. Her body was in the next room, on his mom's bed.

She told him that Madeleine had left them all her money, but there was one rather unusual condition: Mom was going to have to live her life from now on as though she was Madeleine, and they were going to pretend that the woman who had died was Mom.

He thought that was pretty weird, but said if it was okay by Mom it was okay by him. Then something even more weird happened. He had picked up a bottle of fruit juice that was on the table – Madeleine never touched alcohol, and nor did Mom when she was with her – and started to pour himself a glass. Mom had snatched it away, and for a second he saw a look of blind panic in her face that he had never seen before. She pulled herself together quickly and told him the juice was off. Then she poured the rest of it down the sink and got him a fresh bottle from the fridge.

Next, she gave him the keys to Madeleine's apartment and told him to get over there – he knew it well enough, having been there maybe half a dozen times – and wait for her. He was not to answer the telephone if it rang, and not to speak to anybody. Mom said she would 'take care of things here', and join him tomorrow.

When she arrived, he was shocked by her appearance. She was wearing the clothes that Madeleine had been wearing when she died. And she had done something with her hair and used make-up to give her face a hollowness under the eyes that Madeleine had. She was playing a role.

'We'll have enough money now,' she told him. 'Not a lot, but enough. It was what Madeleine wanted.'

They had moved to San Francisco almost at once. Mom paid for some legal work that in effect made him the ward of 'Madeleine Carlyle', even to the extent of taking her name.

She also paid for him to have acting lessons with a fine acting coach. It was the career they both wanted for him.

Over the next couple of years, his mom's obsession with the Conrads became, if anything, more intense. She followed their every move through newspapers and joined every available fan club.

How she got the information that Kay Conrad had enrolled at an acting school in New York under the name of Kay Taylor he never knew, but as usual it was accurate. Mom didn't make mistakes when she wanted something.

★

'I hate that term!'

'What term?' asked Robbie.

'Hollywood Royalty,' said Kay.

They were sitting by the vast rectangular pool at her father's place in Bel Air. Robbie laughed, and tossed aside the newspaper where he had been reading something about Stephanie and John in a gossip column.

'If that's what you are,' he said, 'that's what you are. Why d'you hate it?'

'Royalty means titles, bloodlines, centuries of stupid traditions. It's kind of a sick idea. What it comes down to is incest, insanity and murder.'

'Sounds like the Hollywood I've always heard about,' he said, ducking to avoid the towel she threw at him. Then he pulled her, laughing, into the water. They swam for a while, then went into the house and made love for the rest of the afternoon in her room. They were still there when they heard her mother get back from whatever charity committee she had been sitting on with other wives of the famous. They didn't stir because they had nothing to hide. Although Robbie had been given his own room – in fact a suite of rooms – for the weekend, everybody knew that they were lovers and there was no awkwardness about the fact.

When Kay's father returned he found the two of them sitting with a bottle of wine on the hibiscus-shaded terrace at the back of the house. He gave his daughter a kiss, and Robbie a friendly slap on the shoulder. Greg liked this young man. He liked his openness, sensed his intelligence, and also felt (though he hadn't seen him act, and had only his daughter's assurances to go on) that he had some real talent. He was also amazingly good-looking, but not in the bland, empty way of most of the young hopefuls who hang around the movie business. Something about him suggested hidden depths. The boy was interesting – a thesis which Greg had plans to put to the test.

'I wonder if I could ask you a favour, Robbie,' he said, sitting down with them as one of the maids brought him a glass to share their bottle of wine.

'Glad to be of any help I can, sir,' came the immediate reply. That was another of the attractive things about Robbie: his manners were impeccable.

'My brother and I are putting together a picture. It's not a big budget, it's aimed at the youth market . . . We're a long way from ready. The script's in its tenth rewrite . . .' He paused to sip his wine. There wasn't a sound or a movement around the table. He wasn't even sure if Robbie was still breathing; such was the power of even the hint of an opportunity in Hollywood.

'Now, I'm not offering you a deal or anything, I want to make that clear,' he went on.

'No, absolutely, I understand,' Robbie quickly assured him.

'What we feel we need is to hear a read-through of the script in its present form. I think that'll help the writer a lot. We also have a director on board, Jack Manchester—'

'Wow, he's really good. I really liked his last picture.'

'Jack's made three pictures with us. We have a good relationship . . .'

219

'Look, sir, I'd be really happy just to help out in any way I can, whether you want me to read, or make the coffee, or set out the chairs . . .'

'I'd like you both to read,' Greg said, including his daughter in the conversation with an affectionate smile. 'That is, if you're willing, and can both stay over an extra couple of days before going back to New York. Can you do that?'

★

On Sunday Robbie flew down to Palm Springs in a private jet with Kay, her older brother Tom (an amiable football player home from Yale) and their parents to spend the day with Clark. He knew the old man's films mainly from television; you couldn't get through a week anywhere in the world without finding at least a couple in the listings. Robbie was excited to meet him. He had been one of the world's great stars, as much a legend as John Wayne or Humphrey Bogart.

He was also the man who had humiliated his mother, telling Greg that she wasn't good enough to marry him. What would be the punishment for that, Robbie wondered? Surely there should be some, if there was any law in Heaven.

After lunch, Kay's mother found an opportunity to sit down alone with Robbie over coffee. It seemed casual, almost an accident, but Robbie was well aware that nothing accidental happened around Hollywood matrons like Olivia Conrad. They made polite conversation, during which she elicited all the information which Robbie, with his mother's help, had carefully prepared for just such an occasion. He told her that his mother, Madeleine Carlyle, had been widowed while pregnant, so that he had never known his father, who had been in real estate. Heartbroken, she had never remarried, and lived now in San Francisco. Olivia recognized the neighbourhood mentioned as being 'on the right side of the tracks', though she would never have used such an expression. Robbie felt confident that he had passed muster when Olivia said how much she looked forward to meeting his mother.

The read-through of the script was on Tuesday morning. Greg, because he was so fond of his daughter, had been unable to conceal from her the fact that the whole thing was merely a ruse to audition Robbie for the lead. Naturally, he could have gone straight to his brother and Jack Manchester and said he wanted the kid tested for the part; but that, he felt, would have worked against Robbie. Far better to let them discover for themselves that he was good.

Kay, despite sworn promises to the contrary, confided to Robbie what was afoot. They were in bed at the time, and he was strangely silent when she finished talking.

'Is anything wrong?' she asked.

He looked at her, his gaze troubled. 'That's what I should be asking you,' he said.

'I don't understand.'

'Kay, it's against everything you believe in and everything you've done. You changed your name and went to New York without anybody knowing who you were – because you hated the idea of exploiting your family's name and influence. Now here am I, just by virtue of being close to you, getting a break that I wouldn't otherwise have got in a thousand years. Doesn't that seem wrong to you?'

She looked into his eyes in the semi-darkness for some moments, stroking his hair and loving him for what he had just said. 'Listen,' she murmured, 'let me explain something to you. Me being a Conrad is not the same thing as you knowing one. Don't you see there's a difference?'

'There is?' He sounded unconvinced, but touchingly hopeful.

'A big difference. You're not getting anything because of who you are, because of who your father is, or your grandfather. You're getting it because of who *you* are.'

He thought about this for a while, then said, 'I'm still not sure I see the difference.'

'It doesn't matter,' she said. 'Trust me.'

I'm her excuse, he thought. Her excuse to go on being rich and to feel good about it. She's superstitious: she thinks that if she shares her good luck, she'll get to keep it; and if she doesn't, she won't.

Without another word, he took her in his arms and they made love again.

★

Robbie frowned as he compared the dates one more time. The overlap was inescapable. His birth certificate and the dates in the newspaper files that he was going through meant that he was born eight months after his mother's aborted marriage to Greg Conrad. If he wasn't Greg Conrad's son, then whose the hell was he?

He walked out to the convertible that the Conrad family had lent him for the duration of his stay. The newspaper offices were downtown, where a handful of skyscrapers had gone up like percentage columns on a graph. From further away it looked like a fortress in the vast grey plane of Greater Los Angeles. He was happy to be offered its protection while he leaned against the hood of his car, and tried to come to terms with the knowledge that his mother had lied to him. He could not possibly be the son of a man she had met in Italy.

But had she not realized that one day he might make just this calculation and . . . what? Not care?

Or was there another possibility? Perhaps he was the son of an Italian she had met in Los Angeles? Why an Italian necessarily? Just somebody she had had an affair with a month before her marriage. Anybody! Anybody except Greg Conrad! He would ask her. He would make her tell him.

He got into his car and drove to the Conrad production offices on Wilshire, where he had a meeting with their head of publicity. After the read-through, there had been no question of his not getting the part. Both John Conrad and Jack Manchester thought he was absolutely right for the lead. They congratulated Greg on his smartness, then discussed several famous names for supporting roles. It would be far easier to get 'names' now that the lead was going to an unknown, and not to someone with whom they were already in competition.

Both Greg and John looked in to say hello to Robbie, tacitly letting the publicist know that she had better do a first-class job on their new star. Over Perrier and salad at The Grill, she began discussing a key part of her strategy. They must at all costs avoid

222

giving the impression that the role had gone to Kay Conrad's boyfriend. There was no reason at all, however, why a relationship should not have begun as a result of his getting the role and meeting Kay through her father. That was the way they would play it. Some people who had known them both in New York may see a photograph of them together and guess the truth, but the publicist thought they could make that work for them. It was intriguing and could be used to keep interest going. In the end it would be lost in wider publicity about the picture and would no longer be important.

That evening Robbie and Kay dined together at an Italian restaurant that had just opened to rave reviews on Cienega. People waited eight deep at the bar for tables, but Robbie and Kay were taken straight to one of the best.

Kay was concerned that he seemed subdued. He gave a warm, faintly tired smile, and reached for her hand. 'I'm all right. It's just a lot happening all at once. I love you.'

He had talked on the phone to his mother earlier and pressed her on the matter of dates. At first she had refused to discuss the matter, and they had the nearest thing to an argument that he could remember. It was only because neither could bring themselves to hang up in anger that they had continued. She had softened her attitude and he had apologized, but he still wanted an answer. So she gave him a name.

Ben Kanter. She told him she had had an affair with her agent, Ben Kanter, a month before the marriage. It was a brief, stupid fling with a notorious womanizer. She had reproached herself ever since. Could he forgive her for the lie?

He told her that he could and did. 'It was just that I had to know, Mom. You understand? I had to know.'

That evening, before dinner, he had had a drink with Greg at the house. Greg said he understood that the meeting with the head of publicity had gone well, and the conversation drifted to other things, including agents. Robbie would need one, and several were discussed. He brought up the name of Ben Kanter himself.

'He's just a name I've always heard. I guess he must be pretty old now, but he's kind of a legend. Does he still work?'

'Ben's a good friend of mine,' said Greg. 'He's one of the best agents in this town. If there's anything Ben doesn't know about this business it's not worth knowing.'

'So what d'you think? Is he a possible?'

Greg thought for a moment, a funny kind of smile on his face. 'Why not?' he said eventually. 'You're right, Ben's getting on a little now, and none of them play around like they used to. Besides, you have a girlfriend.'

Robbie looked at him in genuine incomprehension. Greg's smile grew broader.

'I'm sorry. It's not something to be making jokes about. Ben's gay.'

'Gay!' Robbie's mouth hung open.

'Don't look so shocked. This is show business, you know. We are a traditionally liberal profession. Or do you have some religious views?'

'It's not . . . It's not that. It's . . .' Robbie stuttered. 'I just thought he . . . Well, he always . . . I mean, he had a reputation as a womanizer.'

'Used to have. Ben's always been gay, but very few people knew it. That was back in the days when it wasn't always very good for business.' Greg shrugged. 'Some chose to stay in the closet, some didn't. Ben did, always showing up with a beautiful girl on his arm, always letting the columnists hint at some new romance – you know, "newsome twosome" stuff. Then when the AIDS thing hit – he told me this himself – he began to feel like a hypocrite. Couldn't take it any longer. So he came out, joined a Gay Rights movement. It took guts at the time, earned him a lot of admiration. And, as a matter of fact, quite a few new clients.'

Robbie was reassured to hear that doing the right thing could pay dividends in the Hollywood community, and made up his mind to live his life by that code.

Tomorrow he would work out what that would entail.

★

He stopped the cab a few blocks from his mother's house because he suddenly felt wretchedly nauseous, but a few minutes' stroll in the clear night air calmed his nerves and gave him time to think.

When he reached her street, he paused briefly on the opposite side and some distance along, looking up at the lighted bay window of her second-floor living room. She would be sitting there alone, he thought, probably reading some religious tract. She rarely went out and never had visitors, so although he had not called to say that he was coming, he knew he could be sure of finding her at home and they would be able to talk without interruption.

Not wanting to alarm her, he did not use his key but rang the bell instead. Her voice came over the entryphone. 'Who is it?'

'It's me.'

She did not reply, but moments later he heard the sound of a key turning in its lock.

'Why didn't you tell me you were coming?'

He looked at her in the dimly lit hallway and bent forward to kiss her on the cheek. She stiffened as she always did now when there was any physical contact between them. In these last few years, since she had assumed the identity of Madeleine Carlyle, she had changed remarkably. Her hair was straight and cut short, the way Madeleine's used to be. Her clothes were uniformly brown or grey, and from her high collars to her flat-heeled, laced-up shoes, she reminded him of nothing more than a small-town schoolteacher out of some age long past. Or maybe it was Bette Davis in the first part of *Now Voyager*. Reality or myth? What was the difference?

'Is anything wrong?'

'No, Mom. I just need to talk to you.'

He followed her up the narrow stairs, lined with pictures of religious subjects. They always made him feel uncomfortable, because he found such an extreme level of piety somehow unbalanced. That was his main worry: his mother had become, to a worrying degree, unbalanced.

She turned to face him in the modest living room, painted white with furniture in tones of pastel green and brown. Everything was good but functional, except for the images and icons of religious fervour everywhere, which were neither. He hated this house. It cramped his soul.

225

'I can't help thinking it must be something important to bring you here like this without calling first.' Her hands were crossed in front of her, the fingers of one holding the wrist of the other. It was both a challenge and a monarch's confidence. He began to remove his street clothes.

'I've never seen you wear a hat before,' she added, as though reading some untrustworthy intent into its possession.

He shrugged. 'They're coming back into fashion.'

She made no further comment. Fashion was something of which she knew – indeed, made it her business to know – nothing. Instead she sat down in her straight-backed armchair by a bookcase, which was his signal to sit on the sofa opposite. Both were covered in some faded, still faintly glossy green material with red dots which, if you looked closely enough, you could see were roses. This odd choice of perspective seemed to him still further evidence of eccentricity: the loss of any definable focus, any sense of what was and what was not. If he did not get the truth out of her soon, it would be too late.

'I'll come straight to the point, Mom,' he said, after a couple of vague, opening sentences which he didn't finish. 'I don't believe that Ben Kanter is my father.'

There was a silence. 'And may I ask why not?' she asked, eventually, as though fighting to contain her indignation at the suggestion.

He told her why not. Again she was silent. Then she spoke softly, fingers clasped in her lap, looking down at them. 'Stranger things do happen, you know.'

He didn't try to argue. 'Look, Mom,' he said, 'you've got to tell me the truth. Is Greg Conrad my father?'

She continued to look down at her clasped hands. 'I don't want to discuss this.'

'Mom, I have to know,' he persisted.

Again it was a while before she replied. Then she spoke in a strangely matter-of-fact, almost fatalistic and defeated voice that he was not used to from her. 'What difference would it make, anyway?'

He sat back like a man reacting to a blow in slow motion.

'What difference? What difference?!' he echoed. 'That would make me Kay's half-brother. It would be . . . incestuous.'

She brushed a speck of dust from the skirt stretched over her knees, and said, 'You have an obsession with that word.'

'I don't know what you mean. What d'you mean by that?'

'Don't be so naive,' she said. 'You're old enough to talk about it now. Those fantasies you used to have. Until I convinced you there was nothing to them.'

He wondered how deeply to get involved in this, finally deciding that it was irrelevant to the real issue. 'Mom,' he said, 'why don't you just accept that I know the truth?'

She looked at him, her head partly turned away, but her eyes flickering towards him. 'I did everything in my power to make you go out and live your own life,' she said. 'I was never a possessive mother. I wanted you to meet people your own age, young women. It was because of me that you met Kay.'

'Because you wanted me to meet her,' he replied, a note of whining self-justification creeping into his voice. He heard it and suppressed it at once. 'It was what *you* wanted.'

'I only wanted what was best for you. I wanted you to have what I had been denied. Is that so wrong?'

He was sitting slumped now, his spine curved forward against the uncomfortable back of the sofa. There was some truth in what she said, and no, it wasn't so wrong. She had always wanted certain things for him, and he had always gone along with that. It was a little late to start complaining now.

'Okay, Mom,' he said, 'let's just be practical. Can we, for a second?' The idea met with no objection – she was staring at her hands again – so he went on. 'They're going to want to meet you, Mom. What happens then? They'll find out who I am!'

'That's always supposing they know who *I* am,' she replied, with something twitching the corners of her mouth into the hint of a smile. 'Aren't you forgetting that?'

'Mom, they'll know who you are, believe me. Greg will. And Clark. Ben Kanter will.' It hurt him to say this. He knew that the one thing you could never say to any actor, whether retired or still working, was that they could not and never had been able to act.

It was true, she had fooled people in ordinary life for years now; but when it came to real scrutiny, in close-up, she just didn't have it. He had seen her old movies and a couple of the things she'd done on television, and it had to be faced: she couldn't act.

Whereas he, Robbie, had talent. But he knew now where it came from: the Conrad family, not from her.

There was, of course, another possibility, and this one even worse than her ill-founded belief that she could carry off such a sustained deception. It was that she knew she couldn't, but didn't care. She wanted only their humiliation, the shocked recognition of her vengeance. And if that brought everything down – her carefully reconstructed life, his future – then so be it. Such recklessness was hard to believe of her. But then, if she was no longer sane . . .

He shivered, she noticed. 'You're cold,' she said. 'Let me get you a warm drink.'

'No, thanks,' he said, getting up to anticipate her move. 'I'm thirsty, I'll get some juice. Can I get anything for you?'

'I'll have some, too,' she said. 'Some orange juice.'

He went into the kitchen, turning their conversation over in his mind. Was he being fair? All right, so he had always gone along with her, wanting for himself what she wanted for him. The reason was that he had always liked the sound of it, that life. And now that he was so close to it, he didn't intend to let it slip through his fingers as it had through hers.

Looking back, he realized it was absurd to complain that he had been manipulated by his mother. Beyond a certain point that had been passed long since, her obsession had become his. Latterly, it had been entirely his. He had, if the truth were told, been in control of his own destiny for many years. She had become an outsider, a spectator on the fringes of his life, not its centre.

And now here he was, being offered this fantastic double opportunity – marriage into Hollywood royalty, and with it the film role of a lifetime. It was a role that would make his career. That alone was something any actor worth his salt would kill for. He remembered his mother using that expression years ago, when he was small. 'A role that any actor worth his salt would kill his mother for,' she used to say.

He finished what he was doing, what he had come prepared to do if there was no other way. He poured the fine powder into one glass of juice, then carefully put the paper in which it had been wrapped back into his pocket. He carried the two glasses into the other room, and watched as she drank from hers.

'Listen, Mom,' he said, putting his own drink on the table, 'it's not the fact of the incest – me and Kay, I mean. That's not a problem. I've read some stuff about it. There isn't any big danger from in-breeding. As a matter of fact, in the short term it can even be beneficial – like, you know, racehorses. The trouble is, it's a *social* taboo. That comes from way back, where it became danger-ous to the herd to have the males fighting over the same females. See what I mean? Sex was less important than the social structure.'

He watched her as she took another sip of her drink.

'It's a taboo subject, Mom,' he went on in a soft voice, like someone counselling the bereaved or explaining a bitter truth that had to be faced. 'People can't handle it yet. Right now, only you and I know the truth – and that's the way it's got to stay.'

'Are you telling me,' she said, rotating the now half-empty glass in her fingers, 'are you telling me that I may not share in my own son's triumphs? Not even come to his wedding, if there is to be one?'

He went down on his knees by her chair, reaching out to stroke her wrist, where the pale skin was soft and slightly loose. She did not draw away from him this time.

'I'm telling you, Mom, that I love you,' he said. 'I'm going to have everything you wanted, and I'm going to have it for you. I'm going to be a big, big star. But everything I do, Mom, I'll be doing it for you.'

She felt a wave of something come over her. She supposed it was emotion, but then she realized it was a physical thing, a deadness in her limbs. She did not try to move, because she suspected she could not. She managed to turn her head a little and focus her eyes.

His glass of juice stood on the table, untouched, like the one she had poured for herself on that day that Madeleine Carlyle had come to supper, and died.

Slowly, very slowly, feeling the effort take her towards the very limits of physical exhaustion, her gaze travelled back across the room, and down towards her lap, where she saw, distantly, the empty glass that Robbie was carefully removing from her hands.